Writ Reveal

Praise for *Messianic Reveal* and Advance Praise for *Writ Reveal*

Messianic Reveal is a Clayton Haley action-packed political adventure that should be high on the reading lists of anyone who would absorb the history, culture, and politics of the clashes between Shiite and Sunni forces in the Arab world. Because these encounters are key to understanding much of what drives and challenges Middle East history and modern encounters today, this novel's backdrop and easy way of absorbing the personal impact of these conflicts is especially important. *Messianic Reveal* is a powerfully-written, fact-backed suspense story that reviews the challenges of American diplomacy and perceptions, the realities of life in the Middle East, and the special assignments and conundrums of one man who finds himself caught in the middle of it all, acting as a pivot point in a series of extraordinary encounters.

—**D. Donovan,** senior reviewer, Midwest Book Review

It can happen to you! Ethan Burrough's *Messianic Reveal* presents a young foreign service officer of the United States State Department going about his normal business on an ordinary day, when his curiosity thrusts him into a compelling journey. This journey takes him right into an unfamiliar but exciting roller coaster, a thought provoking, intellectual and emotional ride, swinging through the areas of law, politics, history, the spiritual and international relations of the United States and the current Middle East. Clayton Haley is his name, and Burroughs keeps the reader riding alongside Clayton. When you have time to breathe, you find so many of your presuppositions exposed as "not true." *Messianic Reveal* is a must read to set the stage for the 'what next.' There is more to come. Can't wait for the sequel!

—**Lauren Rohini Roberts,** retired attorney,
UN International Relations

***

Writ Reveal plunges readers into a jaw-dropping story spanning 1500 years. Connecting dots through the 1979 Iranian revolution to Operation Desert Storm to today's headlines. Ethan Burroughs brings an astonishing grasp of Islamic culture and history in this first-rate story of intrigue, action, and the United States' involvement in the Middle East.

—**Peter Rosenberger,** nationally-syndicated radio host

In *Writ Reveal,* Ethan Burroughs weaves a web of real history and smart fiction, with captivating action, and a professional's eye of how governments and societies work in the Middle East. He reminds me a bit of Tom Clancy and Joel Rosenberg, but has a style all his own.

—**Clifford Smith,** Washington project director,
Middle East Forum

Joining Clayton for the second tale in his journey was like existing in the possibility of 'new' and 'old' world simultaneously. *Writ Reveal* opens up the fracture lines of ancestral histories that shape our worlds but are often taken for granted as we go about the daily business of living. Whether Haley is trying to keep pace with the effervescent Khalil or exploring Abrahamic histories in Kuwait, Burroughs brings a respectful curiosity married with intimate observations alongside an ease of conviction that is refreshingly open to contrarian views. In doing so, Burroughs' Clayton reminds us of strength to overcome the hierarchies of power so we might celebrate commonalities and divergences. I can't wait to see where we follow Clayton to next.

—**KP,** South Asia foreign policy expert

Writ Reveal is a political treasure hunt across the Middle East. Protagonist Clayton Haley can't seem to get away from the troubles that began in prequel *Messianic Reveal*. Burroughs takes the reader on another fantastic adventure crossing political and religious borders in a hunt to prevent chaos from ensuing across the region, all the while dodging bullets and fishhooks. Burroughs' unique background gives the reader a behind the scenes look at Arab world politics and little known history to Westerners, and he presents it in an easy to read thriller. Burroughs does what he does best in offering a head scratcher to the reader who will try to decipher what is true and what is fiction. Each character brings unique traits to the story and quickly makes you laugh, cry, and want to know them more.

—**Henry Ashmore,** global business executive

WRIT
REVEAL

A Clayton Haley Novel

Ethan T. Burroughs

NEW YORK

LONDON • NASHVILLE • MELBOURNE • VANCOUVER

Writ Reveal

A Clayton Haley Novel

Publisher's Note: This novel is a work of fiction. Names, characters, places, and incidents are either products of the author's imagination or used fictitiously. All characters are fictional, and any similarity to people living or dead is purely coincidental.

Published in New York, New York, by Morgan James Publishing. Morgan James is a trademark of Morgan James, LLC. www.MorganJamesPublishing.com

ISBN 9781631956799 paperback
ISBN 9781631956805 eBook
Library of Congress Control Number: 2021940453

Cover Design by:
Saltdesign

Interior Design by:
Chris Treccani
www.3dogcreative.net

Morgan James is a proud partner of Habitat for Humanity Peninsula and Greater Williamsburg. Partners in building since 2006.

Get involved today! Visit
MorganJamesPublishing.com/giving-back

To my parents,
who exemplify unconditional love for each other,
for others, and for life.

Acknowledgments

Raised eyebrows. Puzzled looks. Incredulous questions. Fact checks. I received these and many more gratifying responses from the readership of my first novel, Messianic Reveal. My twenty plus years in the Middle East, including in interviews, coffees—Americano, of course, dinners, *majleses,* palaces, and Bedouin tents inspired the account, as did my many visits to refugee camps, historical sites, and business offices. And, now, I'm so pleased to bring Clayton Haley back to life to guide us further into the ancient past, political present, and uncertain future of the Arab world in Writ Reveal.

Haley's story continues to deeply explore the politics and belief systems, both God-inspired and man-distorted, in the Middle East. It's my hope Haley's adventures unveil some of the mysteries in the region, but more importantly, the goodness of the people there. As you'll undoubtedly fact check me on the people, places, events, and beyond imagination notions covered in the book, you'll realize the Middle East writ large can hardly be truly discovered. The land that gave us our faith, science, math, engineering, and so much more, also somehow created ISIS and its *Ikhwan* precursors. This contradiction is the Middle East in its essence. I therefore acknowledge the countless people who have shared with me their insights, homes, lives, meals, and love.

I must especially acknowledge the dedicated patriots in the Department of State who serve loyally and tirelessly to advance our values across the world, including in trying and dangerous circumstances. It's my hope that Messianic Reveal and Writ Reveal help readers appreciate the vital work carried out across the globe in our embassies and consulates.

Similarly, I offer my warmest acknowledgments to Green Berets. They will never seek fame, reward, or recognition for themselves. They are true war fighters and battlefield diplomats, deserving of our admiration and gratitude. And, they're only just a little insane. I'm proud to be considered by extension part of the Green Beret family.

I must also acknowledge KP, a colleague and friend I sincerely respect and admire. A South Asian immigrant to the United States and an accomplished American public servant, she read through both Messianic Reveal and Writ Reveal with a scrutinizing eye. Let's be honest. Some of the material in these books, if taken out of context, would be highly inflammatory, and potentially warranting of *fatwas*. She affirmed I conveyed in both books my deepest respect and affection for her Muslim co-religionists while pointing out the hypocrisy and exploitation of their faith by the power elite or faux pious.

Peter O'Donohue also deserves acknowledgment. A friend and mentor, he once challenged me to memorialize the work I did in the Middle East, and I'm grateful for his kind encouragement, which largely sparked Writ Reveal.

And, of course, Morgan James Publishing (MJP). I am so glad my inspiring coach and editor, Cortney Donelson, dynamic MJP CEO David Hancock, and my lifeline to MJP, Emily Madison, believed in and sought to help Mr. Haley continue his story. They love getting the printed word to the world, and I'm proud to be part of the MJP gang. I also salute the creative vision of Saltdesign for the incredible cover concepts and designs for both *Messianic Reveal* and *Writ Reveal*. Please judge my books by their covers!

Lastly, I am grateful to a support base that encouraged me to write, my wife, of course, and children, who have had to hear me talk about these books incessantly! I also appreciate my saintly parents, who taught me to love folks no matter what, and a kind mother-in-law who sent me the best books to read as a sign she believed in me. And, amazingly, all of my brothers read *Messianic Reveal*, including the ones I presumed illiterate, and urged me to keep pulling at threads of intrigue and mystery.

Author's Note

Names, characters, businesses, places, events, locales, and incidents mentioned in *Writ Reveal* are either products of the author's imagination or used in a fictitious manner. Aside from historical facts in the prologue and reflections from reports and research, any resemblance to actual persons, living or dead, or events is purely coincidental, unless intentional to pay homage to some wonderful people to whom the author has been connected. Furthermore, the author intends only the highest respect and affection for the people of the various faiths listed in this book and provides his personal opinion in this narrative that distortions in these faiths have proved motivating factors in contributing to the furtherance of Middle East unrest, surely an outcome undeserving for many who have needlessly suffered.

Haley continues to pull on threads of conspiracy and suspense in *Babylon Reveal*, coming soon.

Introduction

Messianic Reveal, the first in the Clayton Haley Reveal Series, ends with the death of the would be Islamic *Mehdi [Messiah]*, Mohammed Abdullah al-Qahtani. Al-Qahtani had purported to be the *Mehdi* during the 1979 siege of Mecca, a violent takeover of the holiest site of Islam. He and his cult had received popular support from Arabian peninsula tribesmen largely disenfranchised from the political, financial, and religious power of last century's usurpers, the House of Saud, from which the Kingdom of Saudi Arabia derives its name.

Al-Qahtani, who had remained in *ghaibeh*, a spiritual "absence" for forty years, received funding for his re-emergence from Muhsin Bin Laden, a construction empire scion who had been part of the cult in its early years. The shadowy Bin Laden drew from his enormous wealth to activate plots to rid the Arab world of perceived vestiges of old and new world colonialism. These plots include the theft of and an attempt to clone the mortal remains of the Islamic Prophet Mohammed and to consolidate religious support of the tribes to upend seats of power in Riyadh and other capitals friendly to the American government.

United States foreign service officer Clayton Haley found himself interfering in these plots, first at a visa window in France and then in the course of his political work in Iraq. He endured the loss of two friends and mentors and his own kidnapping, torture, and near execution, only prevented by a last minute rescue by a rambunctious team of Green Beret soldiers.

WRIT REVEAL

The death of al-Qahtani proved only a temporary setback for Bin Laden's designs, which now pursue Haley to his diplomatic assignment at U.S. Embassy Kuwait City.

Writ Reveal follows.

Cast of Characters:

Clayton Haley: Protagonist, United States foreign service officer assigned to Embassy Kuwait and key to thwarting the rise to power of a faux Islamic Messiah in *Messianic Reveal*.

Nate Philson: U.S. Army Captain and commander of Operational Detachment Alpha team of "18 series" Green Berets. Haley, as an enlisted soldier, served with Philson during previous tours in Iraq.

Wilson Edger: Intelligence officer, known to Haley from their shared service at U.S. Embassy Paris.

Jordan Cooper: Second tour foreign service officer assigned to Embassy Kuwait.

Nasser Khalil: Locally hired political expert at U.S. Embassy Kuwait.

Dr. Hamad al-Marri: Kuwaiti National Archives Director.

Dr. Khalid Bargouthi: Palestinian-Kuwaiti political science professor at Kuwait University.

Mohammed Abdullah al-Qahtani: Yemeni/Saudi exile and self-proclaimed messiah implicated in the 1979 siege of Mecca.

Ali al-Sadr: Iraqi Shia connected to events surrounding the 1979 siege of Mecca.

Dr. Abdulaziz al-Onezi: Iraqi *in vitro* specialist recruited by Ali al-Sadr, father to young Mohammed.

Abdullah Mohammed al-Otaybi and Ali Mehdi al-Qahtani: Young cousins and relatives of Mohammed Abdullah al-Qahtani.

Muhsin Bin Laden: Half-brother of Osama Bin Laden and construction empire scion.

Prologue

The Fall and Rise of Baghdad

In the year 1251, Möngke Khan, grandson of Genghis Khan and heir to the expansive Mongol empire, dispatched his brother Hulagu to subdue lands to the west toward the Mediterranean Sea which had not yet been conquered by their forebear. Hulagu Khan viciously plundered all that lay in his path, including modern day Iran, Iraq, and Syria. Key in his sights was the wealthy city of Baghdad, the seat of power of the Abbasid Caliphate, the third dynasty in succession of Islamic empires. It endured from 750–1258 AD. Until its abrupt fall, Baghdad was the symbol of Islam's Golden Era and a worthy heir to King Nebuchadnezzar's trophy city of old, Babylon, roughly one hundred kilometers to the south. The acclaimed city was revered as a world center of philosophy, invention, science, math, and culture. Once perceived as the greatest city on the planet, it nearly ceased to exist, courtesy of havoc wreaked by Khan and his allies seven years later.

Baghdad represented for the world, at that time, a beacon of temporal power and spiritual illumination. In only a few weeks, Khan nearly extinguished the light of the preceding six hundred years of Islamic rule. The world suffered a great loss at the hands of Khan's barbarians. In addition to their murderous rampaging, they looted and destroyed places of worship, palaces, public libraries, and hospitals. They ripped apart priceless ancient books and historical documents. Accounts exist that indicate the Tigris ran black with ink from the thousands of books thrown into the river, blended with the red from the blood of their authors and other scholars, also dispatched into the water. Given little defensive preparations ahead of the siege, and the thoroughness of the marauding forces, it is likely that very few of these treasured manuscripts survived the Mongol devastation.

The last Caliph of Baghdad, al-Musta'sim Billah, either underestimated his foe or overestimated the allegiance of surrounding allies in losing the treasured city. The invading Mongols allied with Armenian and European Crusader Christians, and according to some reports, the Persians next door in modern day Iran in an effort to destroy the capital of Sunni Islam and perhaps the faith itself. The sacking of Baghdad was brutal, with estimates of more than a million killed in a battle that lasted less than a fortnight and more than a hundred thousand residents murdered after the city's surrender. The superstitious Mongols believed the spilling of royal blood a bad omen, so per some accounts, wrapped Billah in a carpet, and then beat him with clubs and trampled him to death with their renowned war horses.

It took centuries for Baghdad to recover, and the city never reclaimed its full former glory. By the early twentieth century, however, it regained a portion of its rightful place as a leader among the Arab capitals, with advances in civil engineering, arts, education, culture, diplomacy, science, and medicine. It also emerged from 400 years of Ottoman rule seated in modern day Turkey followed by British vassalage under a mandated kingship. Efforts at self-determination gave rise to Saddam Hussein in 1979, bolstered by his leadership of the Ba'ath Party political movement. Much like his Abbasid forebears, Saddam Hussein sought to blend secular and religious rule to govern Iraq's diverse ethnic and religious demographic. And, who is to say, but in launching a senseless 1980–1988 war against Iran, perhaps he sought revenge for perceived

Persian complicity in the 1258 fall of Baghdad and the Abbasid Caliphate which he desired to restore?

Regardless, just as Mongol hordes looted the treasuries of Baghdad in 1258, Saddam's troops and civilian pillagers ransacked neighboring Kuwait in 1990, ostensibly to steal from the small emirate's oil wealth to pay for the damages incurred during the war with Iran. And like Mongol predecessors, unruly mobs targeted treasuries and seats of knowledge, destroying what they could not steal. Thousands of items and documents were destroyed or stolen, ranging from priceless artifacts such as jewelry and gems to pottery, arrowheads, and original print Qurans, held in reverence in the Kuwaiti National Museum. Hundreds of these precious treasures have not yet been recovered.

PART I

Chapter 1

The barber gestured brusquely with his chin at the nearest unoccupied chair. Clayton Haley moved uncertainly toward it, eyeing a counter replete with sharp items—scissors, electric clippers, and the more ominous straight razors lying about or soaking in an opaque alcohol solution. Given that he had recently been the recipient of excessively violent treatment, Haley did not relish submitting himself to the care of a swarthy stranger with a sundry of sharp torture devices. He just needed a haircut.

He settled into the chair, which looked strikingly similar to that in his favorite barbershop in Walhalla, South Carolina. Instead of posters of the obnoxiously orange Clemson Tigers football team, this barbershop was decorated with gaudily golden Islamic iconography, shelves of gels, and what must be henna or pomade, and oddly, a TV in the background playing a grainy movie with Arabic subtitles.

Haley had arrived in Kuwait only a day prior and was just settling into his new home in the Adan suburb of Kuwait City, just beyond the fifth ring. Kuwait, as he had learned from his U.S. Embassy sponsor, was roughly arranged according to a series of concentric circles, going from the first ring in the city center to the outlying regions around the small country. His colleague had also informed him that Kuwait's inner circles were roughly demarcated along the traditional city walls in which the *hadhar*, or *civilized* tradesmen who established the country, lived. The tribal Bedouin and *Bidoon [without (residency)]* stateless people, who still remained somewhat unassimilated as he understood, lived on the outskirts of the city, including in Adan and nearby Messilah, which was just across the highway from Haley's new home.

"Dees your *cownt-diree?*" said the barber, shaking Haley out of his reverie and somehow stretching the word 'country' into three syllables.

"I'm sorry?" Haley replied, not understanding the question.

"Your *cowntdiree?*" the barber repeated, this time with a wobble of his head that wasn't quite a nod or a shake.

"I'm not from Kuwait." Haley assumed this would answer the odd question.

"No, dis your *cowntdiree?*" the barber insisted, this time pointing, again with his chin, at the television, mounted from the ceiling in the corner.

Haley laughed as he noticed that the movie on the screen was actually Mel Gibson's award-winning flick, *Braveheart*. Given the poor satellite signal, the video wasn't clear, and though he had seen the movie several times, Haley couldn't quite make out which scene he was viewing. "No, this is not my country. My country is also green with mountains and lakes, but this isn't my country," he repeated, not sure where the conversation was going.

"This Amedika? You from Amedika?" the barber inquired.

"Yes, I'm from America, but no, this movie takes place in Scotland," Haley replied, realizing that he had only confused the barber more. It probably would have been better to simply imply that yes, *Braveheart* is all about America.

"Okay. I go Amedika. How I go Amedika?"

"I think you would like America, and I encourage you to apply for a visa," he hastily concocted, knowing that this guy's low salary and lack of economic and social ties to Kuwait would preclude his ever receiving a visa. He didn't know what else to say though.

"Okay. You *gib bisa?*"

4

"I am sorry, but I don't issue visas. You're welcome to apply for a visa at the U.S. Embassy. But for today, however, maybe I can get a haircut?"

"Yeah, yeah, yeah. I gib you *hairdcut*, you gib *bisa*."

"No. You give haircut, I give dinar. How much for a haircut?" Haley asked.

"As you like." Another head wobble.

"No. How much for the haircut?" Haley persisted.

"It's okay. I gib good *hairdcut*."

Haley pondered his next move but then noticed that just right of the now blue-faced William Wallace, there was a chart in Arabic listing charges for services, which ranged from beard dying to mustache trims. His haircut was priced, with exchange rate, at about $2. If Haley survived this ordeal, he might throw in an extra buck. "Just a trim, please, with scissors, no electric razor."

"Yeah, yeah, yeah. It's okay." The barber, perhaps from India or Bangladesh, began issuing his colleague instructions in what might have been Urdu, Hindi, or another language Haley couldn't detect. The barber's colleague suddenly offered up a warm towel, a squirt bottle, and some scissors.

Despite earlier misgivings regarding the sharp objects and an occasional thought toward how this guy might respond to some of the more unpopular U.S. policies in the region, jet lag got the better of Haley, and he began nodding off. He awoke to a vigorous massage. The barber dug deep into his neck and back muscles, and then stretched out his arms and began popping his joints, down to each knuckle. Inexplicably, the barber moved the massage to Haley's forehead, and then to his eyeballs, digging deep into his sockets. Not realizing that eyes had muscles needing massaging, Haley found this quite uncomfortable and hoped it would end soon. As a typical, inhibited southerner from rural South Carolina, he just didn't enjoy the touch of a stranger, especially digging in his eyes with fingers that smelled strongly of curry and cigarettes.

He wondered what else Kuwait held in store for him.

Chapter 2

Clayton finished his haircut without incident, however, and before the drawing and quartering of one of America's finest Australian actors playing a Scotsman, he swung by a small *dukkan*, or convenience store, to pick up some staples. Having been in the Middle East before, he had an idea of what to expect in the little shop and knew though he wouldn't find peanut butter or familiar U.S. brands, he would be able to purchase eggs, milk, rice, bread, and some of his favorite snacks called "digestive biscuits;" he had long presumed truth in advertising with this product. He took issue with the characterization of these cookies as biscuits, however, but forgave the linguistic confusion, knowing that folks in this part of the world would never have the delectable experience of eating *real biscuits*, made from buttermilk and lots of love, served with spicy pork sausage, a dab of mustard, a slice of cheese, and fresh cut tomatoes.

"Groan," he thought. He had been out of South Carolina only a week and was starting to reminisce over home cooking. Ironically, there was a Hardee's on the way to the Embassy, so he promised himself he would stop by to see if southern biscuits made the import list to Kuwait; he knew there was zero chance that pork sausage would be on the menu.

The little store was dusty, and the layout appeared to have been designed with no apparent methodology, but the goods on the shelves seemed fine. And as a bonus, the shop had a nice, albeit small, produce section with fruits and vegetables—likely imported from not too far away in India. In particular, he knew he would be able to find nice mangoes, passion fruit, and even some plums. Odd, he thought, but southern fares of spinach and okra, called *bamia* in Arabic were readily abundant as well. He grew up on okra in the south, either fried or stewed with tomatoes, but never imagined that this "comfort" or "poor folk" food originally hailed from and was common in North Africa and the Middle East.

He made his purchases and winced a little as he grabbed two grocery bags with his left arm. A pain shot through his arm as a reminder of an injury he suffered in a car bombing in Iraq, which had cost the lives of two colleagues. It also flooded his memory with the subsequent beating and torture at the hands of a brute named Abdullah. Also present, and whose honey-tinged eyes were still seared in his mind, was the would-be Islamic Messiah Mohammed Abdullah al-Qahtani[1]. With some satisfaction, Haley consoled himself over the loss of his colleagues with the knowledge that both Abdullah and al-Qahtani were dead, and if somehow still sentient in the afterlife, they were surely and painfully cognizant of the errors in their violent beliefs. Good riddance.

Haley lumbered toward his new apartment, hoping he could remember the correct building to which he had been assigned housing. The air was thick and humid, making it difficult to breathe. Though late in the day, the sun reflected blindingly on the local structures, all painted monotonously white and covered in dust. Haley did not enjoy the oppressive climate but did enjoy a bit of the freedom he was not afforded when in other Arab countries.

He had spent two tours in Iraq as an enlisted military intelligence linguist. During his time, of course, he never had the freedom to explore the country and get to know the people there. Correction: He did quite a bit of exploring, but such ventures were usually done late at night in heavily armored High Mobility Multipurpose Wheeled Vehicles, referred to in shorthand as Humvees. This means of transportation typically

---

1   Haley's role in revealing the Messianic ambitions of al-Qahtani is spelled out in the prequel to this story, *Messianic Reveal.*

precluded warm and personal engagement with the locals. And, given his injuries suffered in the line of duty and months of convalescence and therapy, his time in Iraq was cut short.

As a result, Haley perceived his time in Iraq as an opportunity lost. He went back there as a foreign service officer in the State Department's diplomatic corps and enjoyed meeting with a number of Iraqis, improving his linguistic skills, and experiencing a bit of the culture. But again, his time was tragically cut short, and given the security profile for diplomats in the country, he never enjoyed the freedom to roam about.

Kuwait, however, offered a chance to get back to the region he found so intriguing and was just safe enough that Haley believed he could stay out of trouble.

Chapter 3

U.S. Embassy Kuwait.

"You are most welcome, Mr. Haley. *Ahlan wa sahlan [Welcome. It's good to see you].*" Welcome to Kuwait. My name is Nasser, and we will work together," said Nasser Khalil, a gentleman in his early sixties with a bit of a paunch and thinning white hair. He studied Haley intently and appeared unimpressed. "You need to come with me to the al-Ajmi *diwaniya* tonight. Please clear your schedule. I need your green eyes."

Haley was a bit taken aback by the rather forward leaning approach of the locally employed staff member with whom he would be paired. Haley, technically on his third tour in the State Department—though he was curtailed in both of his previous assignments—still marveled at the different command structures between the Departments of Defense and State. He equated his working with Khalil to that of a young lieutenant or captain looking to a first sergeant or even a sergeant major for guidance. He appreciated the military system enough to know that he should trust Khalil and do what he was told. Mostly.

"Sure thing, Nasser, and it's nice to meet you. I look forward to—"

"Yeah, yeah," Khalil interrupted. "We'll meet my friend, Ali al-Ajmi. He knows me very well, he is my brother, and then tomorrow, we'll visit the al-Awazem diwaniya, and then the al-Dowasir, and then al-Mutair. I'll set it up. Be ready to leave at eight o'clock tonight."

Haley wondered when he might recover from jet lag. "Sure thing, but what is a diwaniya?" He had a familiarity with Arabic, but not this term.

"Diwaniya is majlis, or parlor. It's where all the decisions are made. All the big families have one. They are open to the public and are announced in the paper. I'll set it up. They love me there. They know me. They'll like your green eyes, too. You do what I tell you," Khalil said hastily, imparting to Haley a small sense of foreboding that this might be a difficult relationship.

Haley wondered how he would be the boss in the situation if it's Khalil who was giving out instructions. *"Ana souf akun musta'd qabl saa'a themaniya [I shall be ready before eight o'clock]."* Haley responded in his best and most proper Arabic.

Khalil exhaled while rolling his eyes.

***

After meeting Khalil, Haley moved upstairs to his office to introduce himself to his supervisor, the head of the political section.

"So, you met Nasser already?" smiled Don Glennon after shaking hands with Haley. Glennon was in his mid-thirties, a bit overweight, and his dark hair was graying at his temples. He sniffed and cleared his throat rather loudly.

"Yes. I'm not quite sure how to take him," replied Haley, speaking to Glennon but allowing his gaze to wander around his new office digs.

"With a grain of salt. I've been trying to fire him for two years. He's good in terms of networking and knowing what's going on here in Kuwait. He's really sharp on political dynamics of the parliament and among the tribes, but he's crotchety and ornery, and simply put, full of himself. I have to remind him that he works for the U.S. government from time to time, instead of for himself. He sometimes thinks he's only in this business to charm the Kuwaitis into giving him and his family nationality. He knows all the players in town, otherwise I'd fire him tomorrow," soliloquized Glennon, again clearing his throat. "You'll be supervising him. Please keep him in line, so I don't have to weigh in."

"Wow. Okay. Should I go with him to these diwaniyas?" asked Haley.

"Sure. It's a great way to network and get to know folks. It's up to you, if you want to or not, though. It makes for very late hours," Glennon replied.

"And a word to the wise: Khalil's burned his bridges with the other local hires in the embassy. They all refer to him sarcastically as the Palestinian ambassador to Kuwait. He has Jordanian travel docs but hails from the Palestinian Territories. He has no connection and can't go to his ancestral home in the West Bank. He's pretty embittered that he essentially has no home to call his own. He almost got kicked out of Kuwait after the Iraqi invasion," Glennon added.

"Thanks for the heads up, Don. I'll take all this to heart and tread lightly," responded Haley.

"That's smart. And speaking of treading lightly, I'm just flagging for you that your reputation precedes you. The ambassador was not keen on 'accepting you' here, but we had no other bidders for your job. Let's please keep a low profile and not rock any boats? We're all glad you're okay, and at some point, some of us would like to hear about your little adventures, but to be blunt, we don't want any escapades here. That's straight from the ambassador. We have your initial call with her later today. I recommend you keep your head down, okay?" admonished Glennon.

Glennon's words were painful for Haley to hear, but not unexpected. He had been accused of being a glory hound by his former ambassador in Baghdad. To be clear, he never sought adventures during his time in France, nor later in Iraq. He had simply pulled on threads of conspiracies, which had pointed to the potential advent of a new Islamic revolution among the Sunni Arab world that could have rivaled that of the rise to power of the turbaned Shia theocrats of Iran in 1979. Yes, Haley's actions contributed to thwarting the violent upheaval and the rise to power of a faux Messiah, but it cost him dearly in terms of personal injuries and in the lives of people he cared about. And the episode was swept under the carpet by the Saudis as if it never existed. He resented Glennon's assertion of him having "little adventures," and determined to yes, keep his head down, but he would also continue to use his best judgment in all aspects of his job.

***

His meeting with the ambassador and deputy chief of mission (DCM) was unexpectedly cordial, both extending him a warm welcome and laying out their priorities for his work, which would be to cover parliamentary elections, tribalism as a motivating political factor, succession, and other internal concerns and some external issues, namely Kuwait's relations with Iraq. In fact, they didn't mention their suspicions at all, leaving Haley to believe they had conscripted Glennon to play bad cop. This allowed them a more magnanimous role in greeting the new kid, notwithstanding his reputation in Foggy Bottom, or the State Department's headquarters as it's known in shorthand, as damaged goods.

Ominously, though, the ambassador in concluding the meeting said, "Please keep Don, the DCM, and me copied on any extracurricular activities you might wish to engage in, okay?"

Chapter 4

Adan District of Kuwait. 7:40 p.m.

A very conspicuous GMC Suburban parked just outside Haley's apartment in Adan. He approached it slowly, uncertainly, and then recognized the man in the shotgun seat, an already exasperated looking Khalil. Haley entered the vehicle.

Haley tried to greet Khalil. "Good evening, Nasser. It's good to—"

"Yeah, yeah. We'll be late. We need to go. We need to go across town, *Yalla, mashi. Mashi.* Let's go!"

Haley was uncertain if Khalil was talking to him or to the driver. Then, Khalil immediately turned to his phone and began talking into it, or perhaps at it, giving Haley the opportunity for a quick introduction with the driver. He learned his new colleague was a Filipino gentleman named Herman, pronounced Her-MANN, with a rolled *r*.

"*Kamustaka? [How are you?]*" Haley directed at Herman, eliciting an immediate, "*Mabuti, sir, mabuti [very well].*"

"How long have you worked at the embassy, Herman?" Haley queried.

"Pipe years, sir. Pipe years." Haley had worked with Filipinos before and found them universally polite, professional, and all somehow unable to pronounce *f*s and *v*s. Otherwise, their English was quite good. He found it charming and endearing, especially how they tended to repeat themselves.

Khalil did not. "*'Er-man, brom bi-li-bines, sir, bi-li-bines*," he interjected, mocking Herman's accent. "You should drive faster. You're going too slow."

Herman dutifully ignored Khalil, instead gesturing for all passengers to buckle their seatbelts. Khalil seemed to notice this act of defiance, evident by his eye roll, but he acquiesced. Herman's lips stretched into just the hint of a smile. The scene all played out from Haley's vantage point in the rear seat looking from Khalil to Herman in the rearview mirror. Meanwhile, Haley found it amusing that an Arab was mocking a Filipino for the English pronunciation of the letter *f*, when Arabs struggled with the *p* sound, as noted when ordering *Bebsi* at *Bizza Hut*.

"So, Nasser, can you tell me a little about tonight's event and what will be expected of me?" inquired Haley, who recalled nervously that in the past he either went into someone's home in full "battle rattle"— meaning geared up with weapons and standard military accoutrement— during his military days or when kidnapped, tortured, and awaiting execution. So far, he had not enjoyed what was celebrated as Arab hospitality. He was apprehensive.

"Nothing, Carlton. Nothing. Just show up with your green eyes and look like an American."

"It's Clayton," he replied, holding in a number of quips and comebacks to Khalil's inane suggestion.

"I'm sure it is. That's fine. Don't worry. All is well. They love me too much at this diwaniya. I know the host, and I know his father and his uncle. They all know me too much. They love me," exclaimed Khalil.

"I'm sure that's the case, but how does this advance our mission and that of the U.S. government?" shot back Haley. "And you know the difference between the words very and too in English?"

"Just bring your green eyes," Khalil said unhelpfully.

Haley noticed Herman's eyes staring unfazed at the road and traffic ahead.

Khalil was going to be a handful.

Chapter 5

Al-Ajmi Diwaniya, Salmiya District.

"You are most welcome, Mr. Henley," greeted the patriarch of a branch of the al-Ajmi family. Sheikh al-Ajmi was a gentleman in his late sixties or early seventies, attired in a traditional *Khaleeji* [Gulf] white robe called *dishdasha*, or *thobe*, and headcover, called *ghutra*. He had a wispy unkempt beard and a welcoming smile.

"It's pronounced, Ha-il-ee," interrupted Khalil, exaggerating the diphthong in the first syllable. "Just like Is-ra-il-ee," he smugly proclaimed.

"Actually, it's not. It's a simple Hay-lee sound," Haley said, sending Khalil a sideways glance.

"No worries, Mr. Hurley. We will simply call you by your first name, Cla-ya-toon," the tribal sheikh announced.

"Close enough," resigned Haley, quickly desiring a change of topic. Haley had rehearsed in his mind a series of questions he thought would prove astute and shine credit on the cleverness of the American diplomats at the U.S. Embassy. "So, sir, if I may, I would like to ask—"

"*I lub Amedika too much*," the elderly sheikh interrupted. He gestured at the "tea boy," who was likely from India and in his mid-fifties, waiting in the wings to serve traditional Bedouin coffee to guests. The gentleman came running and poured out the scalding repast into small enamel cups. Haley noticed a blotchy, amateur tattoo in the shape

15

of a cross on his wrist when the man's sleeve retracted as he stretched out his arm.

"*I went small Messihi [Christian] school Saint Olaf, in Minn-ee-so-tah*," he interjected. His English was quite good but his accent, including the generous rolling of *rs* and confusion over *b* versus *p* sounds illustrated his being out of practice. "*I even went to chabel every week. I had pyu-ti-ful girlfriend. Blonde hair. I loved Saint Olaf too much. American family made me Thanksgiving meal. I had turkey, white botatoes, orange botatoes, stuff in turkey, cramberries . . .*"

Haley was a bit perplexed at the turn of conversation. He accepted the coffee, drank it, twisted his hand to indicate he desired no further beverage, and then attempted to re-enter the conversation.

"*Breadcorn, beas, blackeye beans, colored greens, turkey, botatoes, bie, bumbkin and becan bies, bread . . .*"

Haley realized Sheikh al-Ajmi was simply recalling a menu of every item he ate in the United States. This could be a long night.

"*Turkey, botatoes, gray-bie, bickles, and Saint Olaf my second home. I give $10,000 to the school to build Islamic brayer room. Maybe still go to chabel, but Islam students have new choice. I love Thanksgiving in Amedika too much,*" he concluded, looking at Haley.

During the menu's recitation, Haley took the time to get his bearings. He was in a long rectangular-shaped room. Lined along the walls was a series of fancy chairs and a mounted television screen broadcasting Qatar-based Al-Jazeera news network. The tea service was running the length of the room to ensure guests received the utmost in hospitality, including the coffee, chilled water, and a variety of fresh juices. Haley's favorite was the bespeckled, green, lemon-mint drink.

"Yes, sir," Haley responded. "Thanksgiving is indeed a wonderful and warm holiday and expresses a sentiment, though secular, that the United States government sets aside a day every year to thank God for His provisions." Haley congratulated himself on his eloquence and opening of the conversation to show America's softer, more meaningful side.

16

"I was here in Kuwait when Saddam invaded," Khalil rudely butted in. "The world didn't know what was going on here, but my brother, Sheikh al-Ajmi, and his friends joined the resistance to fight Saddam's troops."

Not sure how his conversation took this sudden turn, Haley tried to adjust course. "I haven't yet had a chance to read in on the events of 1990, but I'm sure it was a traumatic—"

"Amedika save Kuwait," interjected Sheikh al-Ajmi. *"George Bush was great man. Kuwait beeble lub him too much. Many Kuwait die. Many woman attack. Dishonor. They theft National Museum. Take all our treasure. Steal our 'arsheef' [archives]. Still gone. Our young men, executed in al-Iraq. Still no body."*

"Many Palestinians were expelled from Kuwait by the Kuwaiti government for collaboration with Iraq. Not true. I took food to Kuwaiti friends and even U.S. Embassy. My boss at that time drank water from the swimming pool and ate cheese macaroni and tuna. He gave me big award when Iraqis were gone," jumped in Khalil again. "I smuggled an apple into the embassy for him. It was the first fruit he had in months."

"I proud to be resistance to Iraqis. They destroy, rabe, steal. They execute hundreds my friends. They kill ruling family member, Al Sabah. He may be drunk, but he try to shoot Iraqi soldier. They kill him. Saddam execute his soldiers who kill ruling family—never spill blood of royalty—it's rule in war. Worse than army was civilian looters. They take everything. They burn everything. Never recover. They take my father's Mercedes," recounted Sheikh al-Ajmi.

Haley believed his role was now reduced to that of spectator, but he didn't mind. He clearly wasn't going to engage in issues of current relevance but understood the need to sometimes apply active listening as the best tool to gain trust. He learned this by watching how his father, a Presbyterian minister, nurtured his flock back in Walhalla. "Three fourths of communication is letting people talk," his father often said.

"I didn't realize that Iraqi civilians also entered Kuwait," Haley offered.

"Yep. Many civilians," said al-Ajmi, continuing, *"They destroy everything. They burn everything. Fernando go to church with them on Fridays. He see many of Iraqi Christian soldiers and civilians at mass on Fridays at big church combound. They take time for Friday brayers from their killing. Right, Fernando?"* he asked the tea boy with the cross tattoo.

"Yes, sir. Every Friday. The church was full of Iraqi and Indian Christians praying together," Fernando replied, wobbling his head while returning with more coffee. This time, he subtly adjusted his sleeve to cover his cross tattoo.

After about thirty minutes, Khalil stood up promptly and announced Haley and he needed to move on to another event. Sheikh al-Ajmi refused and insisted they both stay for dinner. After some arguing back and forth—just like his own father with someone over a lunch bill, Haley thought—they agreed, but new guests arriving at the diwaniya required that Haley and Khalil move down the room and away from the host so the newcomers could get face time with al-Ajmi.

As they conversed quietly, Fernando made rounds with an incense burner smoldering some type of resin, perhaps even myrrh. Following Khalil's lead, Haley "scooped" the smoke with his hands to flavor his personal space with the aroma. He noticed his Kuwaiti counterparts, generously drawing on the smoke, fanning it into their *ghutras* to maximize its essence into the fabric. It wasn't unpleasant but very strong and kind of strange for a bunch of dudes to be helping each other get their scent on, he thought. Haley also wondered how he would ever get the smell out of his suit and hair.

While scenting up, Khalil informed Haley about the church compound in which nearly 25,000 Catholics and Protestants a week visited and held worship services. Though the Christian community was comprised nearly entirely of Indian, European, Filipino, and North American congregations, some 300 Kuwaitis purported to be believers too. "Kuwaitis have a long history with American Christians. Your people set up a missionary hospital over a hundred years ago, and tended to the wounded ruling family members when they fought for their survival against Saudi backed *Ikhwan* [brothers] marauders. Since then, Americans and Christians have been welcomed here by Kuwait," Khalil conveyed.

They had a number of superficial chats with other guests, but as the jet lag set it, Haley found it hard to keep up with the introductions. He regretfully mentioned to his new acquaintances he had just arrived and had not yet had the chance to print business cards. He remembered briefly chatting with a gentleman who wore no necktie, until Khalil abruptly interrupted the conversation, pulling him aside to inform him that he should not be engaging with the Iranian ambassador to Kuwait, "Unless you're ready to make peace with him," he egged.

"Thanks for bringing me here, Nasser. I actually found talking to the sheikh interesting. It's very cool that he was part of the resistance. It must have been traumatic," said Haley, as the two found a few minutes at the end of the evening to chat with each other.

"Yeah, yeah," Khalil agreed. "It was a bad time. For everyone. Many people died. The Iraqis left me alone because I was a Palestinian, but afterward, the Kuwaitis deported some 400,000 of my people. I got to stay because I smuggled food to my Kuwaiti and American friends. My people called me a traitor because I didn't support Saddam. He had no integrity and neither did the Palestinians who joined in the looting. The Kuwaitis are simple, nice, generous people, but they want the bodies of their sons returned from Iraq. And they want their archives back."

"I get why it's important to return the bodies, but what's in the archives that's so important?" queried Haley.

"Allah yarif [God knows], my friend, but it's good that you brought your green American eyes tonight. Kuwaitis will like you. Just don't talk so much." Khalil smiled for the first time, but Haley surmised he could have misinterpreted this warm gesture as intended for him as he saw his friend's eyes light up with the arrival of a dinner, complete with standard Middle Eastern salads, bread, and a whole roasted lamb served on an enormous platter of rice.

Chapter 6

Kuwaiti National Assembly. The next morning, 7:15 a.m.

"You need to go to *Barlamen*. Special session. 8:00 a.m. I called motorpool for a driver," pressed Khalil over the phone. "I am already here. Bring your green eyes."

Haley was just completing the final wrapping and tucking of his necktie into a full Windsor knot. He thought briefly of how his Dad used to say, "Never trust a half Windsor man or anyone else who can't finish tying a necktie." This recollection was much more distracting than it was poignant. He shook his addled head to re-center his thoughts.

"Sure, I'll be there. Do I need to prepare anything, beyond just bringing my eyes?" snapped Haley, wondering if and when he might ever get to sleep. It had been after midnight by the time he arrived home the night before, and now he was off to "barlamen," which he assumed was the Kuwait National Assembly, or parliament.

Khalil had already hung up.

Forty-five minutes later, sans his morning coffee, Haley showed up at the rather modest, garishly white, yet futuristic in a past tense fashion, Kuwait National Assembly building. The architect clearly had a nautical theme in mind, but it wasn't clear to Haley if the edifice was designed to reflect a sail, a boat, or a wave—or somehow all three. He was dropped off in the VIP lane and made his way through the front door where

Khalil was awaiting him, with what the astute Haley perceived as his customary impatience.

"I have seats for us in the hall. We need to go now," hastened Khalil.

With his white, thinning hair, outdated suit, and his hyperactive and nonsensical mannerisms and irritable impatience, Khalil presented a decent adaptation of Alice in Wonderland's White Rabbit. Haley dutifully and urgently followed his lead into the grand hall of the National Assembly, scurrying in behind him to take seats in the balcony area reserved for the press and diplomatic community.

The MPs [members of parliament, or deputies] filed in and headed toward their seats. Haley did not know who the MPs were but could detect various groupings, largely denoted by facial hair, or lack thereof. He noticed the four women MPs chatting with each other, including the conservative women in their *hijabs*, or head scarves, and their more progressive or liberal counterparts with very stylish hairdos. Also grouped together were the clean-shaven, mostly younger men, whom Khalil said were part of the liberal bloc in parliament.

"And now the 'long beards,'" whispered Khalil loud enough for even some of the MPs in the gallery to hear, as evinced by their nods and grins. They approached Khalil from the floor and conveyed to him their customary greetings, checking on his health, his family, his concerns, his family again, and even his color, *"God willing."* Khalil never bothered introducing Haley, but they all seemed to know that he was parading yet another of his pet American diplomats in parliamentary show and tell. Haley was at first embarrassed, but realized he had entered Khalil's home arena, and thought best to continue following his lead. He noticed that the conservatives and progressives alike seemed to admire Khalil and their faces lit up when they saw him, even those with imposing dark, grim features barely visible behind their facial hair.

"These long beards," Khalil picked up again after his rapid-fire greetings, "include the conservative Shia. That one is Hezbollah," he gestured at one rather rotund gentleman with a massive beard. "That

21

one is "*Salafi [traditional or orthodox Muslim]*, and that one is Muslim Brotherhood," he added. "The Shia," he said, pronouncing the deeply guttural *'ein'* in the second syllable, "get along with the Sunni in Kuwait. They all came from Iran as merchants more than a hundred years ago. This is not like Iraq or Lebanon, or Syria, where people are divided by sectarian issues. Money makes friends. Lots of money makes lots of good friends. Salafis, you can distinguish because the hem on their *dishdashes* never touches the ground. Everywhere they walk is holy. These guys are more Muslim than Mohammed. They try to live their lives just like Mohammed did 1400 years ago, but I don't recall *ayat* [verses] in the Quran that spoke of him driving around in a Range Rover or Mercedes."

"And the Muslim Brotherhood. Here, these guys are harmless, and they're the best organized of all the groups, and the only MPs that unite around political issues. Everyone else here in this room was elected due to their standing in their tribes," again, Khalil's whispers approximated bellows, yet no one appeared annoyed or surprised at his indoctrination of young Haley.

"And the women . . ." he laughed, "You know the word for deputy in Arabic?"

"Umm, sure, yes, it's *naeb*, right?" muttered Haley *sotto voce*, a little taken aback by the question because deputy is not a known American term, nor is MP, given our bicameral congressional system. Plus, he tried to lead by example in demonstrating how quiet a whisper might actually be.

"Yeah, yeah. It's *naeb*. So, to make it feminine for the ladies, you simply add the *'taa mabuta [suffix, often turning nouns from masculine to feminine]* and make it *na-e-ba*, right?" tested Khalil.

"Yes. I guess so. *Naeba* would be the corrected feminized version of the word for MP, yes," replied Haley, wondering where this was going.

"Ha!" Khalil yelled his laugh. "*Naeba* is also the Arabic word for disaster, and Kuwait *barlamen* has four of them!"

Khalil enjoyed his little play on words immensely, and given his inability to whisper, shared this joke with those in the diplomatic seats and last three rows of MPs, most of whom understood English all too well and also found this tired joke amusing.

"Hush now! They're starting to deliberate," urged Khalil, again, more loudly than needed and directed at no one in particular, especially given that he was the only one talking.

The proceedings were entirely in Arabic. Haley's Arabic was decent, but not strong enough to follow the deliberations. He reached for headphones kindly made available by the parliament staff, but alas, the batteries were not charged. Khalil therefore summarized the proceedings as such:

"There is a split in *barlaman* over the issue of women's football. You call it soccer. The Kuwaiti women's team traveled to Abu Dhabi and was defeated 14–0 by the Palestinian women's team. The long beards, mostly the Salafis, are outraged. See the fat one there in the middle? He's the one raising a ruckus. He said it's heresy that women play sports and that they show skin, even if they wear a *hijab*. Everything is a heresy for him. He just wants a tent, goats, camels, customary four wives, and of course his $100,000 Range Rover. Everything else is a heresy."

"Shhh," hushed Khalil to no one in particular, since again, he and his loud whispering were the only noises being uttered from the balcony. "Now the counterpoint: The women MPs are outraged. They said it's a national disgrace that the Kuwaiti women lost 14–0 to Palestinian women. Kuwaiti women should win in international competitions, they said. They now ask for the funding of a new training facility and better coaches. These women are *naeba* disasters to the long beards."

Haley found it impossible to be embarrassed anymore and really loved the drama as it played out on the floor, with MPs from various factions yelling at each other. They seemed genuinely angry and upset, but he noticed during breaks how convivial they were with each other. "How much of the drama and theatrics was for real?" he wondered.

"Let's listen to the last item and then we go back to the embassy," said Khalil. "For this item, they wish to raise the issue of the long disappeared archives and national treasures, taken by Saddam."

According to Khalil, one of the more progressive MPs made an impassioned plea for the parliament to raise through UN channels the need to increase pressure on Iraq, to release the mortal remains of Kuwaitis taken by the marauding Iraqis, and to return all material and archives stolen back in 1990.

Part II

Chapter 7

Moroni, Grande Comore, Comoros Islands.

"I want him dead and I want him to suffer. I don't care how, but I want it to happen soon," an agitated gentleman, wearing a comfortable but expensive linen shirt untucked from fashionable slacks, hoarsely whispered to his companion. He was barefoot and reclined on high-end beach style furniture. He rattled the ice cubes in his glass, signaling his displeasure at the wait staff that his Glenfiddich fifty-year-old single malt Scotch whisky was running low. At nearly $30,000 a bottle, most people would be more frugal, but not Muhsin Bin Laden, who could not recall asking the price tag of anything, ever. Though surrounded by every comfort purchasable, Bin Laden felt secure but trapped on the Comoros Islands. And he was bored.

Muhsin was the scion of Mohammed Bin Laden, the developer who emigrated from Yemen to Saudi Arabia nearly a hundred years ago and then built his multibillion dollar construction empire, launched by refurbishing the holiest sites of Islam in Mecca, Medina, and Jerusalem.

No. Muhsin Bin Laden wanted for nothing except privacy and anonymity, mainly due to the exploits of his more famous and quite deceased brother Osama, but also due to his recent secret funding and scheming to re-introduce to the world the would-be Islamic Messiah. That plot, however, suffered a major setback a few months prior. A setback named Clayton Haley.

"I'm working on this, but you know, killing an American diplomat is no easy task. This *Glaiton Heely* is junior. He is insignificant, but should we kill him, it will bring much attention to your operations. He suspected, of course, your involvement in the Mecca incident during last *Muharram [first month of the Islamic calendar]*. He saw me in Iraq and somehow escaped plans I put in place to execute him," replied a nervous Ali Hussein al-Sadr, similarly attired, but being much more hirsute, appeared hotter and more uncomfortable. "I am sure that he informed his superiors of his suspicions."

Al-Sadr waved away the waiter who refilled Bin Laden's whisky glass, signaling his preference to drink Perrier. He looked out across the private balcony onto the beautiful beach scene below him. Palm trees laden with coconuts gently swayed in the breeze, while small breakers caressed the white sands. He was just far away enough to notice the time lag in viewing, and then hearing a second later, the white caps crash onto the ebbing tide. He could also see the emergence on the horizon of the moon, or *al-Qamar* in Arabic, for which the country was named.

He did not mind ordering the killing of the pesky American who had uncovered his plans to exalt Mohammed Abdullah al-Qahtani as the Mehdi, or Messiah, who had returned from forty years of absence, or *ghaibeh*, as it is known eschatologically in Arabic. The young man deserved a painful death and would receive it, *God willing*. Al-Sadr believed that with al-Qahtani's religious and historical credentials and the revelation of the prophet himself incarnate in a cloned young boy, he could usher in an era of Islamic rule, uniting both the Sunni and Shia houses of faith. Borders would no longer be relevant and the decadent House of Saud would no longer be the keepers of the keys to Paradise.

Instead of masterminding the return of Islamic greatness not seen since before the fall of Baghdad in 1258, al-Sadr sat in the Comoros Islands with a man he needed but did not respect. Bin Laden, he knew, like his older half-brother, thrived on chaos and hypocrisy. This "great protector of Islam" who received billions of dollars from the Saudi government for the upkeep of holy sites in Mecca and Medina, showed his true immorality here at the hotel on the pristine beaches of Moroni. He noticed Bin Laden was on his third whiskey, and with each sip, his ogling of the bikini-attired young ladies on the beach became less discreet.

"Regardless, I have tracked him to Kuwait. And I have dispatched al-Qahtani's nephews to finish what our friend Abdullah started in Aziziyah [Iraq]. With your permission, though, I believe we should make it look like an accident. If he is indeed targeted by our operatives, all attention will turn to his reports about what he discovered pertaining to our plans to introduce the Mehdi to the world," al-Sadr continued.

"Sure, it can be an accident, but it must be messy and painful, and I want him to somehow know that I ordered his death. It should be the last thing he is aware of before he dies," retorted Bin Laden.

"Now, go tell my hotel manager I need some private arrangements," Bin Laden continued, still looking at one of the more attractive beach farers. "And, tell him that I want the Comorian President to stop by after dinner. I need him to sign paperwork so that I might buy a bigger hotel, one with more such scenery.

Chapter 8

U.S. Embassy, Kuwait City, Kuwait.

Haley's first few weeks in Kuwait were a blur. He found that though thirty plus years younger than Khalil, it was hard to keep up with his incessant energy. He could not understand how a man in his early-sixties could work all day, be in the office as early at 7:00 a.m., and then go out to diwaniyas four to five times a week, staying out until after midnight. Haley discovered Khalil's secret later: He left work every day at 2:00 p.m. and took a four hour nap, ready to go again by the early evening. He and Khalil had a few run-ins from time to time, but Haley generally found that his admiration for his senior's knowledge and insight into Kuwaiti history and politics was matched by the older gentleman's feigned tolerance of him, and the two managed a constructive work dynamic.

Haley finished his orientation, settled his household effects, and got to know his colleagues in the consular, economic, commercial, military, public affairs, and other sections of the embassy. He also established his work requirements with Glennon and began networking, making calls on prominent politicians, officials, thinkers, and influencers. As he did so, he became more familiar with Kuwaiti society and culture and embarked on drafting a series of cables to Washington on political machinations in the country. It was a far cry from his consular work in Paris, and for that matter, the human rights work he did in Iraq. It kept him busy enough to continue the grieving process for his friends, Dr.

Ibrahim Mustafa and Paula Abrams, both murdered in Paris, largely, Haley still believed, because of a series of questions he pursued. He kept pictures of both of them on his desk as reminders of what he still attributed to his carelessness. He lost two other colleagues in Iraq and mourned them but not with the same intensity, given that he simply did not know them well. He still harbored bitterness over the callous nature of their senseless killing.

Meanwhile, though, he began to enjoy the freedoms of living in Kuwait and the many culinary options, ranging from food from the Far East, to American fast food eateries. He even checked out the famous Avenues Mall. At one and a half kilometers long and with over 1,000 shops, it was the second-largest shopping center in the Middle East. Given the oppressive heat and humidity, coupled with frequent dust storms, an indoor city such as the Avenues served as a gathering opportunity for the masses in a clean, cool atmosphere. Haley was overwhelmed by the sheer number of options for dining, though, and found going there a tiring experience, especially when home food delivery services were readily available.

He thought the Kuwaiti consumer market, which loved American fast food, was ready for a Chick-fil-A franchise and could have easily accommodated the company's policy of closing on Sunday, if only the Sunday could be substituted for the local day of prayer, Friday. Oh well. He did manage to determine that the Hardee's biscuit in Kuwait was nearly as good as the original, sans the pork sausage. The combination of eating heavy meals at midnight and grabbing fast food did not bode well for Haley's ability to stay in shape while in Kuwait, especially as his exercising was hampered by a left arm that was still rehabilitating.

He had read that Kuwait per capita was nearly tied with the United States in terms of obesity so realized that conveniences in the country were just a bit too . . . convenient. He also noticed belts did not accessorize the loose-fitting robes, or *thobes*, or *dishdashas*, for men, or *abaya*s for women. Given that the belt notches tend to mark progress on one's personal growth, so to speak, the lack thereof failed to send proper indicators that it was time to exercise and diet. The result was that like *muumuus* showcased in Walhalla's finest trailer parks, the Kuwaiti national dress code just seemed to keep expanding.

***

"I know you have a lot on you with the internal political file and covering sectarianism and tribalism, but I'd like you to run point on an ICRC program, alright?" asked Glennon in what seemed to be an order. He was leaning over the thin partition that defined the borders of Haley's office in the political section's small cubicle farm.

"Sure, but I'm sorry, what is ICRC and what would this entail?" replied Haley.

Glennon sniffed then cleared his throat in an indiscrete effort to clear phlegm, something Haley had noticed happened a lot. The humidity and dust levels in Kuwait were quite high, causing regular respiratory irritants for everyone, but Haley thought Glennon could show a bit more couth. "ICRC is the International Committee for the Red Cross. They've been running what they describe as a trilateral meeting once a quarter here in Kuwait. Not a big deal. Show up, punch the ticket, check the box, and then you're free for three more months. I used to cover it, but it's excruciatingly boring and a waste of time for me. Tag, you're it. You cover it from now on. There's a meeting tomorrow in one of the Sheraton ballrooms. Just go and listen; don't say anything and don't commit us to anything." He hocked again, asserting an end to the conversation.

"OK. I'll let you know how it goes," replied Haley, quite unsure of what he was now committed to.

Haley checked folders on the office's shared drive to see if he could find anything about this so-called trilateral ICRC meeting. He checked on both unclassified and classified systems, but keyword searches on

"ICRC" and "trilateral" yielded nothing. He was not surprised, however, given electronic files were supposed to be archived and purged every two years. He thought he might have a bit more luck thumbing through hard copy files in the safe. He opened the third of five drawers in the political section's shared safe and rifled through the files to see if anything relevant jumped out at him. When he had just about given up, at the back of the drawer, he discovered a file labeled "Tripartite Committee." Close enough.

In this folder, he found what appeared to be correspondence in English, Arabic, and French from the head of the ICRC office in Kuwait to the French, British, American, Kuwaiti, Saudi, and Iraqi Embassies. It looked largely to contain copies of some old military-style maps and minutes of meetings over the last few years. As Haley reviewed the material, he realized that the premise of the tripartite committee efforts was the recovery and repatriation of missing civilians and soldiers from the Iraqi invasion of Kuwait. It was also clear that this process was moribund and had not yielded any results in quite a few years. In fact, it was around 2004 that mortal remains of a number of Kuwaitis were recovered and returned to Kuwait. Not much had been done since then, and relations between Kuwait and Iraq were at an all-time low.

***

Sheraton Hotel Conference Room, First Ring Road.

"Ladies and gentlemen, I welcome you to another round of the Tripartite Committee," opened Luc Marc Chapelle, the head of the Kuwait-based ICRC. "Our agenda for this gathering is very light, so I believe we can move the discussion along and have us all out of the meeting within less than forty-five minutes. Our first order of business is to welcome the new American delegate, Mr. Clayton Haley," he added, pronouncing Haley's name correctly, albeit with a French accent.

"Thank you, Mr. Chapelle and fellow delegates to the committee. I'm glad to be here and I look forward to working with you," Haley said with his best professional voice, feeling a little guilty that he defied Glennon's admonition to not speak at all.

Chapelle appeared genuinely pleased to have the new infusion of input into the committee and introduced to Haley his counterparts from the other missions. "And to answer the question you haven't asked yet," he proffered, "the tripartite committee includes the Americans, British, and French. It was set up after the Gulf War, and the ICRC was asked to chair. We thought it wise to include Saudi, Kuwaiti, and Iraqi participants given their own vested interests. Until the fall of Saddam Hussein in 2003, the Iraqis never participated and never sought the repatriation of their young men who died in Kuwait. And, since we don't know the word for expanding a tripartite to six members, we held to the original name," he smiled at his playful turn on words.

"And, now on to our sole agenda item. Does anyone have any updates to our last meeting? Any progress on the file to find and recover those missing since 1991? If not, I'll adjourn the meeting and direct you to the coffee service. We'll plan to meet again in three months. Mr. Haley, might I get your email address to send you an invitation?" Chapelle concluded.

After self-service at the coffee trays and light banter, the small gathering dispersed. "No wonder Glennon offloaded this on me," Haley considered. "Someone needs to mercy kill this project."

Chapter 9

U.S. Embassy, Kuwait City, Kuwait.

Haley thought it useful to memorialize the rather uneventful gathering so decided to draft a brief spot report indicating simply that the meeting took place and covering some basic highlights. He knew there was not much about the event he could say beyond that. He was not able to secure business cards for the delegates, so he went back to the safe to research the names of the people present to include in his cable to Washington. While digging through the documents, he came across the old military maps again.

Per handwritten scribbles on the margins of the maps, they seemed to have been drawn up by U.S. servicemen in early 1991. They included strange notations, like "12 under the Camp Doha sign," "55 next to the burned out APC," and "500 next to the destroyed encampment." Each of the maps was crude in detail and contained six-, eight-, or sometimes ten-digit grid coordinates. "If our tripartite effort focused on the repatriation of mortal remains, I wonder if fleeing Iraqis killed in the liberation of Kuwait were ever returned to Iraq," pondered Haley.

He visited a number of websites detailing the liberation of Kuwait and discovered U.S. forces had killed thousands of fleeing Iraqis. Pictures were available on the internet that showed the destruction, in particular, on the "Highway of Death," in northern Kuwait near the Iraqi border.

He called ICRC Tripartite Chair Chapelle. "Luc Marc, I apologize for bothering you, but I have a simple follow-up question to our session today," he said, after re-introducing himself. "I found a number of old maps in the embassy that seem to point to the location of where coalition forces, in particular Saudi mortuary affairs soldiers, buried hundreds of Iraqi KIAs here in Kuwait. Were they ever recovered?"

"Thank you for your question, Clayton. To my recollection, no, because Saddam Hussein viewed those who died in Kuwait as traitors and did not want them returned. In fact, the ICRC handed over such maps to him personally in 1993, but he refused to take action," Chapelle responded.

"Now that there is a new government in Iraq, maybe the family members would like closure on this old and painful file. There may be thousands of bodies still here in Kuwait. If the Kuwaitis repatriated the remains, maybe this will spark some reciprocity from the Iraqis in finding the Kuwaitis still missing," said Haley.

"Let me check and get back to you. I must admit that I had not considered this angle before," replied Chapelle, quite pleased to have even a small ray of light shine on this long dead file.

***

Al-Abdali, Kuwait, near the Kuwait-Iraq border. Two months later.

It was Haley's sixth trip to the desert wastelands near the Iraqi border. Chapelle, true to his word, had indeed followed up on Haley's idea to revitalize the moribund tripartite file by flipping its mandate from finding Kuwaitis in Iraq to searching for Iraqis in Kuwait. He developed a strategy for doing so, circulated it among the six members of the tripartite committee, and secured their concurrence. Within a week, they met again to study the maps Haley provided. Turns out, much to Chapelle's chagrin, Haley's maps were only copies, and while rummaging through ICRC files, he discovered he actually had the originals, still unclaimed by the Iraqi government after all these years. He could only surmise the new leadership in Baghdad was either unaware of its sons still buried in Kuwait or uninterested in their recovery. To the Kuwaitis' credit, they were fully on board and eager to embark on any effort that might advance closure to this file.

The tripartite delegates drove north from Kuwait City to the al-Abdali district of Kuwait, abutting the Iraqi border. The road they took was the very same "Highway of Death," made infamous by strafing runs of U.S. Air Force A-10 Thunderbolt "Warthog" warplanes. These and other aircraft obliterated Iraqi encampments and marauders who fled in their retreat during the U.S.-led coalition to liberate Kuwait. It was one of many lopsided battles waged in the Middle East.

Prior trips to the area yielded almost no promising results, so Haley knew this would likely be his last foray into the field. The maps were almost useless. The listed grid coordinates should have been helpful but weren't precise enough. Searches with backhoes, provided by the Kuwaitis, continued to prove fruitless. Landmarks described on the maps were equally ineffective, as they had been removed over fifteen years prior. The landscape was simple, flat desert hardscrabble and sand. Certainly, there was no *X* to mark the spot to dig.

Haley was running out of reasons to join in on these fruitless searches. Glennon was irate first because Haley had defied him by contributing to tripartite committee agenda items—he had hoped that the effort would dissipate, not grow in interest, and second, because Haley was simply spending so much time outside the office, leaving him stuck with Khalil—the two of them were not getting along. Haley ensured that Khalil and he still made ample appearances on the diwaniya circuit in the evenings, so the distraction was primarily during the workday. Haley also kept up his reporting, managing much of it on the ride to the dig sites, which only occurred once a week or so, lending credence to Haley's argument to Glennon the burden was not onerous. He found it frustrating to find opposition to something he felt strongly about but to date had not been ordered to cease and desist. The ambassador and DCM were also not fans of this project; they only allowed it because of Chapelle's personal interventions with them—he needed a win and thought that Haley's proposal could deliver.

Haley did deliver.

During his fourth trip to the desert, Haley watched some of his Kuwaiti friends chase down a desert lizard of the *Uromastyx* variety, known in the local dialect as *dthub*. He could not tell which was more comical, a silly creature with a rather pronounced tail that could only run about twenty to thirty at a clip before exhausting itself or a Kuwaiti gentleman sprinting in his traditional *dishdasha* and sandals chasing one of God's ugliest creatures. The *dthub* lost the contest, and Haley was pretty sure he would end up at tonight's desert barbecue.

While watching the chase ensue, Haley noticed what appeared to be rags on the desert surface, windblown and nearly buried under rocks and sand. He lifted the edge of the material with his toe, half expecting another *dthub* to make his last sprint across the desert. Haley pried with his foot to dislodge the material. It was wedged tightly into the sand. He reached down and grabbed the cloth, and as he pulled on it, he noticed it shaping up to be a sweater or pullover. He grabbed it with both hands and yanked it, only to watch a shattered human ribcage cascade to the ground from what was left of the clothing in his hand.

The discovery was just the shot in the arm the project needed. The Kuwaitis ordered another bulldozer, and the team continued its analysis of the maps, hoping to better deduce the locations of potential mass graves. Haley held in his hand the map that provided an eight-digit grid reference and the handwritten annotation "55 next to the burned out APC." If he recalled correctly from his army days and land navigation courses, this map, if recorded accurately a few decades ago, should be precise within one hundred square meters. The reference to an armored personnel carrier, however, was useless, as it had long been removed.

At Haley's direction, the backhoes were already methodically making sample shallow digs as part of a sampling effort on a grid, hoping to find some indication of remains. Haley's British colleague was in one such ditch analyzing the dirt.

"Clayton, what do you think? See how this dirt has a different texture?" asked Nicole Carver, the head of the political office at the British Embassy in Kuwait.

"I see what you mean," Haley replied, wondering how he could have missed something so obvious. It looked like the earth had been scooped out and then refilled crosswise to the direction the backhoes were digging. "Let's dig to the right, just a bit," he asked of the driver in the backhoe.

The backhoe lurched into motion and reached out its arm to cut a streak down into the desert about a foot deep. As it loosened and scraped the packed sand, it became apparent to the excavators that a black bag was hooked onto the shovel. Chapelle stepped in to halt the machine and ordered the team to dig all around the site to allow better access. It became quickly apparent that this site bore real potential.

The dig subsequently revealed fifty-five body bags still clearly identified as belonging to the U.S. Army. Each bag was lined up parallel to its neighbor and reverently pointed toward Mecca. As the site became more accessible, Haley, Carver, and Chapelle instinctively stepped back, knowing that only Iraqi and Kuwaiti hands should actually recover the mortal remains that had lain unclaimed in the desert for so long.

Likewise, the Iraqi and Kuwaiti forensic experts on tap for this project knew exactly what they were doing and treated their patients with utmost care and respect. As they gingerly opened one body bag at a time, Haley knew that identifying these remains, which had "cooked" for so long in shallow graves in the desert, would be a huge challenge. In fact, most of the contents had degraded into what closely resembled soup, precluding any visual identification. Fortunately, many of the remains had wallets and identification papers, neatly preserved in sealed plastic bags. Haley was impressed at the systemic care provided by U.S. and Saudi servicemen in arranging for these hasty burials for enemy combatants so long ago.

The remains were carefully collected and accounted for and loaded onto a truck. Haley noticed the fifty-fifth body bag at the end of the row had more form than its counterparts in their advanced states of decomposition. As the pathologists opened the bag, and after the initial gag over the pungent smells emanating from the corpse, Haley detected a small round tube or sleeve, like what one would use to carry a piece of artwork. It was stuffed into what may have once been a pair of military style trousers and seemingly strapped to the deceased's left leg. It had suffered degradation, but it seemed possible that its plastic wrapping may have provided some measure of protection to its contents.

***

Discovering the mortal remains was a gratifying project, especially in watching former foes, the Iraqis and Kuwaitis, in a freshly dug trench working side-by-side. Carver joined Haley in solemn reverence, disturbed only by the clicks of cameras as they took pictures to memorialize their hard work.

"It's brilliant, isn't it?" Carver quipped. "To my recollection, this is the first time I've seen the Kuwaitis and Iraqis engaged with each other on anything. I think we've made history, my friend. I'm glad you joined the team!"

"I'm glad to have worked on this and hope this will jumpstart some searches in Iraq for the missing Kuwaitis. These families have been without any closure for too long. Without any information about what happened to their sons, brothers, and fathers," replied Haley, genuinely touched and surprised by his own glistening eyes. "If you'll excuse me, I better inform my ambassador."

***

"Ambassador, I have news for you," Haley said after dialing her mobile phone number. "We found the mortal remains of fifty-five Iraqi soldiers. They're all facing Mecca, all interred in U.S. military body bags, and all being recovered and prepared by forensics specialists for eventual repatriation to Iraq. I think this is a key development in Kuwait-Iraq bilateral ties, and I—"

"Does the British ambassador know?" she asked urgently.

"My counterpart is likely telling him now," Haley replied. "I'm happy to—"

"I'll call him," she interrupted again. "I want to ensure he doesn't break the news before I do."

"Maybe I'll suggest a joint press statement," the ambassador said to herself.

"Anyway, nice job. Can you please get back here and draw up some points for me?" she continued into the phone.

Haley had hoped to hang out in the desert to see things wrap up, but duty called, so he headed back to the embassy, about a forty-five minute drive. During which, he thought he could jot down some notes about how this would close a humanitarian file for some fifty-five families. He was pleased as he thought this could possibly bring two archenemies a bit closer together, especially at a time when Iraq needed Arab, not Persian friends. It also might be useful to research possible constructive angles regarding UN Compensation Committee claims filed by Kuwait against Iraq for reparations and a Kuwaiti injunction on Iraqi aircraft, pending resolution of various legal concerns.

He would follow up separately with Chapelle and the Kuwaiti forensics team regarding the contents of the fifty-fifth body bag.

Part III

Chapter 10

U.S. Embassy Kuwait City, Kuwait.

Haley dropped by Khalil's office to touch base on pending issues since he had been on the desert excavations. "Hey, Nasser. How's it going? Did you miss my green eyes?" joked Haley.

"*Blease* do not leave me with Don Glennon anymore," implored Khalil.

"Sorry, but what's going on? I don't understand," replied Haley, turning more serious.

"It's not important, but he's very, how do you say, *imbersonal?* He wants meetings, but he doesn't know how to speak to Kuwaitis. He interviews them but doesn't communicate. You, the Kuwaitis like. I don't know why," Khalil smirked.

"Well, I'm back, so you're stuck with me anyway. So tell me what you know about the Kuwaiti archives and its contents," Haley said and recounted for Khalil his curiosity about the fifty-fifth body bag, wondering if this could have been somehow connected to items reported stolen.

Khalil offered instead to do some research and set up appointments to learn more about the archives, including, at Haley's request, with Kuwaiti National Archives Director Dr. Hamad al-Marri.

***

True to Khalil's word, he came up with some rudimentary points for Haley, namely that unruly Iraqi civilian mobs, and likely some of the Iraqi troops who invaded Kuwait, ransacked the Kuwaiti National Museum, along with other public buildings and private residences. They looted or destroyed thousands of items and documents, which were reportedly part of Kuwait's heritage and history. Jewelry, gems, pottery, and original print, ancient Qurans, were stolen. In 2002, just before the U.S.-led liberation of Iraq, the UN reported that Iraq returned to Kuwait more than 400 boxes and over 1000 bags of documents or archives. The exact contents of these bags and boxes were never independently verified and were declared incomplete by the Kuwaiti government, so the Kuwaitis were compelled to continue to wait for their missing heritage.

He also set up an appointment for Dr. al-Marri for the following day to ask why the missing archives continued to vex the Kuwait people.

***

Kuwait National Museum.

"Thank you for seeing us on such short notice," said Haley to Dr. al-Marri. He gestured to Khalil for him to translate.

"No need for translation," replied Dr. al-Marri. "I speak English and you are most welcome. Please, before we begin, let me offer you Arabic coffee."

While awaiting coffee service, Haley glanced around at Dr. al-Marri's office, quite modest by Kuwaiti standards, but it did have an odd assortment of gold-plated baubles and artifacts. Stacked on the corner of his desk was the standard array of papers, much of which was yellow or dog-eared, very much what one would expect in the office of an archaeologist.

He accepted the coffee, as well as an accompanying date. The date, which he learned was harvested in Kuwait, wonderfully complemented the bitter and cardamom enhanced Bedouin style beverage. While he focused on his refreshment, Khalil and al-Marri became reacquainted, swapping notes about their families and Khalil's plans to one day be granted Kuwaiti citizenship.

"Thank you, sir, for the coffee and the date and for your valuable time," began Haley again. "Nasser and I hoped you might help us understand the importance of the lost archives, and if I may be so bold, learn what is still missing."

"Again, you are most welcome. And all of Kuwait is still grateful to the Americans for liberating us from Saddam's people. They devastated our country. They robbed and killed us, for what? Just some land and our money. God bless George Bush the father. He rescued us," Dr. al-Marri offered. He then recounted a number of anecdotes about his personal experiences and losses, even though he managed to escape hostilities by staying in London at the time.

"So Dr. al-Marri, it is clear that the trauma of the Iraqi invasion ran deep and still affects Kuwaitis today, but can you please tell me what archive items still await to be returned?" interrupted Haley, after al-Marri's rather lengthy monologue. "According to the UN and news accounts, gold, jewels, and artifacts were stolen, but I get the sense there were other items that may be even more valuable."

"Many items. Even I don't know what is missing. Many important papers and Kuwaiti heritage. It's very important that we have full accountability," al-Marri evaded Haley's question. "We hope the Iraqi people return what they took from us. Everything."

Chapter 11

U.S. Embassy Kuwait City, Kuwait.

"Nasser, what do you think?" asked Haley later that day, back at the embassy. He passed black coffee that he had just purchased at the counter of the mission's small cafeteria to Khalil. The coffee was hot and aromatic—and adequate—but not quite what one would find at the many American and European coffee shops throughout Kuwait. It was refreshing to buy coffee for an Arab, given their customary generosity and pride taken in demonstrating largese. For Haley, it was akin to the good manners he was accustomed to growing up in the Deep South. Though Khalil was not the gentle soul that was Dr. Mustafa Ibrahim, his dear friend from Paris, speaking to Khalil from the perspective of a student triggered deeply meaningful and sad recollections of the many hours he spent with the kindly professor. Haley had not spoken of his personal losses in France or Iraq to his new colleagues. It was a way of shutting out his grief, but somehow, he felt chatting with the elder Khalil reconnected him just a bit to his former mentor on his path of Islamic world discovery. "Why was Dr. al-Marri so evasive? Surely there must be some type of inventory of what was taken. Do you know why there is so much mystery surrounding this?"

"I'm sure it's something very sensitive. I've heard many rumors. Some say that the archives have embarrassing records, maybe land deals and arrangements the public shouldn't know about. Maybe arrangements made to agree with Saudi Arabia or Iraq about the borders with Kuwait. Some say maybe even the archives had financial records between Kuwait and Iran, in which Kuwait financed both the Iraqi and the Iranian governments during the fateful Iran-Iraq war," proffered Khalil.

"What do you think, though? What's your personal assessment? We know from online accounts, including from the UN, that Iraq returned to Kuwait lots of material seized during the invasion. Weirdly, though, UN and even the Arab League officials were never allowed to review the documents. Why the mystery?" asked Haley. "Why don't the Kuwaitis come clean with what was taken and what was returned? The whole world is sympathetic and would gladly help out."

"I think it's something very old. And maybe very damaging to Kuwait, or even the region. I think it might be connected to the old religious material Kuwait used to have. Some said that Kuwaiti archives contained first edition Qurans. Others said that when Baghdad fell to the Mongols, some religious scholars fled with early Islamic writings by boat. And if you take a boat from Baghdad, you end up not far from here," Khalil volleyed.

"The Mongols wiped out Baghdad," he continued. "Who knows? Maybe some Baghdadis escaped with treasure or material. There was nothing and no one here in Kuwait at the time but unfarmable land and a few merchants who ran trade between the north and India. There would have been no reason for the Mongols, or mongrels as I call them, to give chase to anyone coming to the south. There was nothing here at the time. You know that Kuwait was named for a small *Kut*, or as you call it in English, a shack or hut, but that was only when the current ruling family came here from Saudi Arabia some 450 years later and built the walls around the city, turning it from a shantytown into what it is today, a trade crossroad connecting the Arab-Persian world with India and beyond."

"Yes, I've seen sections of the old wall around the first circle part of town, near the Sheraton Hotel. Too bad those walls weren't around in

1990. Perhaps they could have protected the city from the marauding Iraqis . . . or at least slowed them down," said Haley.

"Those walls were built to protect Kuwait from a worse enemy. An enemy that shows its face every few generations—the *Ikhwan*, or Brotherhood. You probably confuse the *Ikhwan* and the *Ikhwan al-Muslimeen*, or the Muslim Brotherhood, which is the radical political group that comes from Egypt. Nope. The *Ikhwan* comprised Bedouin from the Arabian Desert. These were the original terrorists, and to this day, they inspire Al-Qaida, Da'esh, and many other terrorists. Their forebears caused the divide between Sunni and Shia Islam. Later, they were used by the House of Saud [Royal Saudi Arabian Leadership] to conquer most of the Arabian Peninsula, and when completed, the '*Sa-oodis*' turned on them. With the help of the British, they almost wiped them out. They almost overthrew the House of Al Sabah here in Kuwait and keep popping up from time to time. You won't know this, but they almost conquered Mecca in 1979," lectured Khalil.

On this last point, Haley remained quiet, as he knew this historical tidbit all too well.

Chapter 12

Qom, Iran.

Dr. Abulaziz al-Onezi was unhappy. He sat in one of many local coffee shops lamenting his poor fortune, and watched his son Mohammed tend to his onerous studies. He had dutifully moved to Qom, Iran, as instructed by his fellow Iraqi, Ali Hussein al-Sadr. Unlike al-Sadr, however, al-Onezi was Sunni, not Shia, and felt as comfortable living in Qom as a Southern Baptist might in the Vatican. On principle, he adhered to many of the same spiritual views of his Shia co-religionists, but he did not share their practices and traditions. He could not bring himself to use the *turbah* stones or other worship aids, for example, and he did not like the habit of delaying daily prayers by ten minutes as did Shia Muslims, just to show a bit of longstanding Persian defiance. Iranians, he assessed, still resented the fact that their "true religion," that of Islam, was passed to them via conquest by camel riding, unschooled Bedouin Arabs who crossed the Arabian and Iraqi deserts and conquered by sword the seats of power of multiple Persian empires.

"This Qom religiosity is fine for Ali al-Sadr; he's Shia," complained al-Onezi to himself. Hailing from a tradition of Sunni Arabs, many of whom had secular leanings, he found it hard to get caught up in their religious fervor. He did not like Qom and its nearly one million zealous twelvers, adherents who hold to the belief in twelve imams deemed the spiritual and political successors to Mohammed. It seemed there was a

48

Shia mosque on every street corner, but Sunni masjids were few and far between. Plus, he did not like the landscape or the food. He could kill for some Iraqi kebabs or *mazgoof*, a style of charred fish perfected by Iraqis since they were known as Mesopotamians, Sumerians, or Chaldeans. Iranian food was quite good but just not the same. Everywhere he turned, it seemed he and his little charge, Mohammed, a boy of about seven, were being plied with the excessively sweet brittle toffee known as *sohan*, or various Iranian nougats. "It wouldn't do for the world's next Mehdi, or messiah, to have tooth decay," he thought.

"Mohammed seems to have recovered from the trauma from a few months back," thought al-Onezi. It was one of the few times he was grateful for the child's epilepsy. He recalled that the boy had lapsed into a *grand mal* seizure at nearly the same instant the would-be messiah, Mohammed Abdullah al-Qahtani, was killed by an assassin's bullet in front of Mecca's holiest site, the Kaaba. This brutal incident proved a huge setback, as al-Qahtani had hoped to unite both sects of Islam under his leadership, and raise the child, Mohammed, under his spiritual tutelage, having just introduced the boy to the world as the incarnate clone of the founder of Islam and its most famous prophet, Mohammed.

Al-Onezi harbored his darkest secret—knowing of the failure of all of his attempts to reproduce an offspring from the prophet's genetic material. He felt shame and conflict that his work killed, maimed, or damaged young women across Iraq, all in the quest to find a suitable surrogate and mother for the return of the Mehdi. That he had given up on this and used his own genetic sample was known to none, as this revelation would have ended his life painfully and immediately. No one needed to know that he now had a son, one to replace the one lost to the Americans during their fateful 2003 invasion.

And now, he and his son, the presumptive Mehdi, were stranded in Qom, some 125 kilometers south of Tehran. His home, Baghdad, Iraq was roughly eight times that distance to the west, but with security hazards, nearly impossible to traverse. Little Mohammed was bright, but it seemed the Qom scholars expected mystic powers to manifest from the boy, given they thought he was their prophet incarnate. "This was unfair on two accounts," believed al-Onezi: "One, he was no more related to Mohammed than was the Ayatollah, and two, even Mohammed needed twenty-five years before he received revelations from Allah. In fact, many believed he was illiterate and therefore unable to scribe the visions revealed to him by the Angel Gabriel. It was instead his followers who many years later began documenting his heavenly encounters.

"No," reflected al-Onezi, "Qom was no Baghdad, nor was it even Tehran, which at least enjoyed some night life without the ultra-pious Qom-ites all seemingly intent on out-doing themselves in Shia service to Allah." Al-Onezi surmised Qom and Baghdad had in common only their brutally hot summers and the distinction of being wiped out by Mongols in the 1200s and then in the 1300s, by Tamerlane, a self-styled and Islamized Genghis Khan. The city also endured Afghan and later Russian invasions before it established itself as a seat of Shia Islamic theology, or marja'iyah. It took on renewed relevance in the 1900s as British mandates and occupations and regional rivalries precluded Shia populations from making their pilgrimages to holy sites in Iraq, Najaf and Kerbala, home to the tombs of the Muslim Prophets Hussain and Ali.

It was no coincidence, knew al-Onezi, that Ayatollah Khomeini started his 1979 uprising against the Iranian Shah in Qom. After his successful overthrow of the Pahlavi dynasty, the religious revolutionary remained in Qom before moving to Tehran. From there he claimed the seat of power, thus consolidating political and spiritual rule, as leaders did in the days of old.

He wanted to go home to Iraq, an Iraq that no longer existed to him. He was only in Qom because Ali al-Sadr compelled him so. And because he continued to claim it as necessary that the boy's "personal physician" be with him at all times.

Though not part of the planning for al-Sadr's large schemes, al-Onezi was intelligent. He perceived that just as the Islamic revolution and Khomeini's rise to power in Iran was largely conceived in Najaf, Iraq, he knew al-Sadr hoped the boy's status as the supposed incarnate form of Mohammed would launch the next revolution in Qom.

Al-Onezi wanted nothing to do with this plot.

Chapter 13

Kuwait City, Kuwait.

Abdullah Mohammed al-Otaybi and Ali Mehdi al-Qahtani sat at a coffee shop at Marina Mall, downtown Kuwait. They scoped various yachts docked in the harbor while nursing *karak* tea and *loqma* pastries. *Karak*, a strong, scalding tea mixed with evaporated milk and served in a demitasse, was very popular among young men throughout the Arabian Gulf. Just as popular was the round *loqma*, which looked like donut holes popularized by Dunkin Donuts. Though essentially just fried dough, *loqma* was sticky and served with drizzled syrup. The *karak/loqma* repast was a sweet indulgence indeed, but the two young men believed they deserved it.

Though actually Yemeni, they entered Kuwait from London on fake Saudi passports provided by Ali al-Sadr. Abdullah's pseudonym was Ahmed al-Rashid, while Ali traveled under the name Mohammed al-Dosari, both very common names. Given their Gulf heritage, they were easily able to blend in with the Kuwaitis and other Gulfis enjoying the dining and shopping scene in the small emirate. They garbed themselves in traditional attire, white *dishdashas* and headscarves.

"It's a simple boat. He's not an extravagant person. From his bank records, it seems he's quite poor. He comes from nothing. These Americans fool themselves in their belief that all are created equal and that family standing isn't important. You and I, we come from noble

Ikhwan families. We are destined for greatness," said al-Otaybi/al-Rashid.

"Yes. I see the boat. In slip number fifty-seven. Perfect for a brief excursion. And perfect for his long overdue accident. I've been looking forward to this day since we missed him at the coffee shop near the Sorbonne. He should have been there that day. I hate these cursed Americans," responded al-Qahtani/al-Dosari. "Heeley will pay for the death of our grandfather."

"And disrupting the arrival of the Mehdi. Everything was in place. His intervention is unforgivable. I only hate that we must wait. I am sure we could kill him in his apartment or on the road," retorted al-Otaybi/al-Rashid.

"No. Not an option. One, the embassy cars are bulletproof. There is no way we can ensure he dies in an accident. And our instructions are to ensure this doesn't look like a murder. The death of a healthy young man in his apartment could not be explained, so it can't be there or at the U.S. Embassy. We'll do it on the water, where accidents happen all the time," al-Qahtani/al-Dosari asserted.

"OK, but are we sure we can get him on a boat?" asked al-Otaybi/al-Rashid.

"Leave that to me," al-Otaybi/al-Rashid said. "I'm tapped into his phone. Per his WhatsApp exchanges, he likes to fish. He wishes to charter a boat for a few hours and has already made arrangements with the boat's skipper. They leave early Saturday morning. You need to hide on board ahead of time, and I'll retrieve you on a rented boat once you've killed him. Make it look like he fell and hit his head on the railing or something. Don't be gentle."

Chapter 14

Kuwait City, Kuwait

Haley's State Department issued iPhone signaled a call coming in from a close friend from his military days, Captain Nate Philson. Philson commanded a team of Operational Detachment Alpha, or Green Berets, in the region and came to Haley's rescue while in Iraq a few months back. These Special Forces elements were identified by their "18 series" occupation specialties, starting with the *alpha*, who of course, was Philson. His assistant detachment commander Chip Reims's skills as a sniper saved Haley's life and distributed some well needed justice to a brute named Abdullah. For that Haley was still grateful. The team sergeant, or "Dad," shepherded the unruly gang of warriors, including Tank, the energy drink sipping *bravo* and weapons specialist. Nimrod, the *Charlie*, was the ordinance expert, and resident loon. Doc, the *delta*, was an accomplished combat medic. He loved to regale the team with stories about keeping mauled goats alive as part of his training. He had also just finished the army's special forces scuba school in Key West, one of the toughest training courses available to warfighters. The *echo*, Joseph Smith, derisively nicknamed after the Latter Day Saints founder and a devout Mormon himself, ran the communications for the team, and Spook, was the team's *foxtrot*, or intelligence operator.

Haley derived great honor and entertainment from his association with these men and looked forward to seeing them again, but he had a special connection to Philson given their shared combat experience and Philson's staving off of Haley's imminent execution. His sudden intervention at the nick of time not only saved Haley's life, but his team's subsequent actions thwarted plans by a megalomaniac messianic figure from upending the Saudi establishment and instigating a wave of violence throughout the region. The two had been close since Haley's army days and his saving Philson's life from an improvised explosive device. Haley still bore the scars for taking the brunt of the attack. As such, Philson determined to be Haley's guardian angel.

"Hey buddy! Guess what? I'll be in Kuwait for a few days. My team is off on leave, so I'll be consulting with some ARCENT [Army Central Command, located in Kuwait] Special Ops guys at Camp Arifjan. Of course, they call it *Arifjail* because they hate being deployed to the region and stuck in a place with no action," said Philson.

Haley, genuinely glad to hear from his friend, replied, "Excellent. Anyone from the team or just you? Oh, and will they allow you off base? If so, why don't you hang out with me? I can certainly treat you to better food than the slop they have at the base."

"Sounds like a plan. In fact, I'll stop by the Base Exchange and get you some flat-nosed beef contraband. Pork is illegal in Kuwait, right? You want ribs or chops?"

"Both. I have room in the freezer. And I brought with me some good South Carolina mustard-based barbecue sauce. I'll be in hog heaven here in Islamic kosher country. And will you be here on Saturday? I've chartered a boat to try to catch some hamour; it's good, kind of like our grouper back home." Haley offered.

"It'll just be me, but yes, I can slip away on Saturday. Fish better be biting," Philson countered.

***

Haley was energized and looking forward to seeing his buddy again. Their friendship was forged in battle, and given what Haley had gone through over the last few years, Philson was one of the few non-family connections that he wholly trusted. It would be good to see his former commander and friend again.

He spent the evening unpacking his saltwater fishing tackle to get ready for the trip on Saturday. He also called Khalil to line up a meeting with a historian to discuss his questions regarding the archives. Hopefully, they could meet before the workweek ended on Thursday.

"I know just the guy. He loves me too much. We'll meet at his house at 9:30 on Thursday. Don't be late. Bring your green eyes," ordered Khalil enthusiastically.

Chapter 15

Bargouthi Home, Messilah, Kuwait.

Dr. Khalid Bargouthi did indeed seem to love Khalil "too much." They greeted each other with a litany of questions pertaining to health, family, status, color, family again, and quite a few cheek kisses, very common for men in the region. Seems like they are old pals, thought Haley.

Dr. Bargouthi also greeted Haley warmly, but clearly, Khalil was the main attraction. Bargouthi met them at the door of his palatial residence, wearing the while Gulf garb, but he somehow looked out of place. Khalil, seemingly reading Haley's mind, blurted out that Bargouthi was a Palestinian name, and their host, a political science professor at Kuwait University, had been granted Kuwaiti citizenship—a prize with considerable trappings for long term expatriates.

"My green-eyed friend wants to know about the stolen archives," Khalil blurted out, not affording Haley a chance to ask how Bargouthi gained citizenship.

"Yes, sir, I do," Haley quickly adjusted but slowed the conversation enough to allow their host to direct them to plush chairs in his majlis and to accept Arabic coffee, which seemed to materialize out of thin air. "I must first commend you on a beautiful home." They spoke in superficial terms about the residence, Bargouthi's education at Johns Hopkins, life as a professor in Kuwait, and how he managed to find himself outside of Kuwait during the Iraqi invasion.

"And the archives," Bargouthi came back to the point. "That's been a strong point of contention. Most of us can only speculate about what went missing and how damaging it might be to Kuwait or the region should they ever resurface. You've likely heard they could contain controversial land records, border demarcation maps, or even funding schemes for the loans offered to Iran and Iraq for their 1980–88 war. Yes, Kuwait played both sides of that conflict. No wonder Saddam Hussein wanted to conquer this little emirate."

"Yes, sir," Haley interjected. "We've heard all that. I'm curious as to what you think is missing."

"Are we off the record?" Bargouthi asked urgently.

"Sure, but I'm not a reporter. What I write is transmitted via classified channels to policy makers in Washington. I don't talk to the media," Haley responded.

"OK. I think the most sensitive documents that might be in the archives are from Yemen or perhaps elsewhere. And I think they may be religious in nature," he asserted. Seeing Haley's confusion, he continued, "Yemen has been embroiled in some twenty serious conflicts just since 1948. The poor Yemenis can't seem to get a break. What people don't realize is that Yemen played a key historical role in the establishment of Islam as a political power. It's only been recently that Yemen has been a poor country. It has an amazing and noble history, much of which has been overlooked or discounted by the West."

"For millennia the country served as a seat of empires or a transit hub for trade. The biblical account of King's Solomon's marriage to the Queen of Sheba from modern day Yemen also signifies the country's historical prominence. Some say that Cain and Abel are buried in the city of Aden, too. And it was important in Mohammed's day, as well. In fact, from my recollection, it was communities in Yemen, which also housed Christian and Jewish populations, that were the most welcoming of Mohammed and included a large number of converts to the new religion."

Ever the student, Haley settled into listening mode and nodded for Bargouthi to continue, adjusting only to sip on a small translucent glass cup of scalding tea, which a domestic worker had replaced for the coffee. He had in his lap his ever present scribble pad, but minimized his notetaking so as not to be distracting to himself or his kind lecturer.

"You must remember that the House of Saud has only been around for about 150 years, and only one hundred years of that did they enjoy any real power. Until the discovery of oil, the fledgling kingdom of Saudi Arabia was a backwater tribal mishmash. It became important due to one strong ruler trying to conquer the peninsula with the help of the *Ikhwan*, the terrorist progenitors to *Al-Qaeda* and *Daesh*."

"Yemen, certainly in decline, still shows the remnants of great civilizations and has significant heritage. Now sadly, the Yemenis can't take care of themselves, and over the last few decades, they have been moving bits of their legacy and wealth to more secure locations. You may have seen the YouTube video showcasing Mohammed's hair? Some purport that his hair was kept in Yemen for centuries but moved over to a museum in Dubai for safekeeping while war wages on. If Yemen had relics like that, what else might be out there? Can you imagine what types of treasures Damascus, or later Baghdad, might have had?"

Haley smiled, congratulating himself for having such a great job. A job that so easily engendered trust just because he represented a great and benevolent superpower. For all the criticism of U.S. policy in the Middle East, he'd found in his short time here, that people genuinely admired and trusted the United States. Dr. Bargouthi certainly seemed to welcome this opportunity to chat, and he seemed less guarded than Dr. al-Marri, the curator of the museum.

Haley asked, "Sir, I understand why you think Kuwait may have been in possession of prized material, but what makes you think that some of this would have been so religiously sensitive?"

Bargouthi answered, "If you'll forgive me, I'm a professor, so I cannot give you a short response. Bear with me, but I'll have to share some Islamic history with you."

Haley gestured that he should continue. He had an interest in history and thoroughly enjoyed this encounter with the kind gentleman. In some ways, the man's passion, intelligence, and genuine sincerity reminded Haley of his murdered friend, Dr. Ibrahim Mustafa, also a Palestinian, and someone who had generously invested into Haley's understanding of the Middle East.

Bargouthi continued, "Please know that I am a devout Muslim, so what I'm about to tell you should not suggest doubt in my own faith, but a practical, perhaps professorial, and academic approach to simple history. I wish others in your faith and mine took such approaches. Most of what we know about Islam, of course, has been passed to us in the Quran, and for we Sunnis, the *Hadith*, or sayings of Mohammed that were not included in the Quran.

"Much of the Quran, we believe, was written down by Mohammed's companions while he was still alive. The point being that Mohammed did not write his famous 'recitation.'" Bargouthi made the sign of rabbit ears with his hands, denoting the translation into English of the word *Quran*. He continued, "Though we believe that Allah revealed his message to Mohammed, Mohammed, who perhaps may even have been illiterate, did not write it down. His friends and followers did. As with your American Mormon friends, sometimes, the followers tend to be a bit more zealous than those chosen by God to receive the original message. And I suppose it's possible they may have taken a little extra zeal in their exercise of poetic liberties."

Haley opted not to reveal his own opinions that Mormonism, like so many other faiths, including Islam and Judaism, seemed to originate with strong overtones of sexual cultism. Their leaders tended to reward themselves with polygamy, certainly to consolidate power bases through marriage, but some took this way too far. Abraham, Jacob, David, and

Solomon came to mind from the Old Testament. Mohammed as well, as he was husband to more than ten wives, including a young child. And Joseph Smith was a special case too, and he may have been killed by his own followers who became angry when he took their wives unto himself. Haley thought it prudent not to raise these points at the time.

Bargouthi spoke over Haley's reverie. "The compilation of the Quran was not completed for many years after Mohammed's death. That said, most Muslims, namely the orthodox variety, believe every word of the Quran as dictated to Mohammed by Allah, as supposedly and eventually transcribed. No exceptions. That requires extraordinary faith in the precise memories of very fallible humans, in my humble opinion."

He paused. "Do you know the English word palimpsest? I would be impressed if you do."

"I'm sorry, but no. You said pal-im-sets?" Haley scribbled into his notepad.

"No. Palimpsest," corrected Bargouthi. "Let me get back to this word for you later. First, I'll explain. A number of German scholars went to Sana'a, Yemen in the 1970s to study historical texts and documents. Remember, Yemen, back in the day, was a great hub of political and religious scholarship. These scientists went simply to study some of the oldest texts in our faith."

"One scientist, in particular, named Gerd Puin concluded that the Quran, instead of a direct dictation from Allah, was more of what he described as a compilation of texts, and most concerningly, may have been written a hundred years before Mohammed. He noted in his findings that variations in spelling and word usage suggested some form of evolution of the Quranic language, putting him in strong contradiction to fervent followers who simply accepted the Word of God as revealed in its entirety during the lifetime of our prophet. I recall that in Christianity, you have a number of debates about rituals, liturgy, which gospels to include in your cannon, and various interpretations of end times eschatology, no?"

Haley nodded in agreement, impressed with Bargouthi's knowledge about Christianity. "Certainly, we've debated the foundations of our belief system to the extent of engaging in horrible wars and schisms. Even today, though most Christians tend to focus on what they agree on versus what they don't, one still finds significant gaps in biblical interpretations. And, we Protestants are known for, well protesting. They say getting us to agree on anything is like trying to herd cats."

"I find it amusing and healthy for people to discuss their beliefs. Often I find that both Christians and Muslims don't really have a strong foundation in their own faith. Instead, they default to their family or society structures which shaped them," Bargouthi asserted.

"And," he continued, "Most Christians don't realize that the Bible was translated into English for political expediency, and to, how do you say it? And to give the 'middle finger' to the Vatican's political power base?"

"Yep. That's how we would say it," Haley smiled. He recalled his college history courses that covered King James, hardly a devoted Christian, and his commissioning of the publishing of the first Bible in English. It was, he remembered, a bit of a struggle given that the transcribers had to draw from the English of the day terms to explain concepts from Greek and Latin that did not exist, such as the word baptism. The medieval English were hardly sanitary folks so were lacking in words requiring the spiritual cleansing that comes with water submersion, he mused.

Haley continued, "Most Christians still hold to the Bible being the inerrant, inspired Word of God, but allow for adaptations and even some evolution of text, to protect that truth, while adapting to linguistic changes that have occurred over the last two thousand years, like the formulation of my native language, English. God must know that His creation is way too lazy to study His Word in Latin, Greek,

Hebrew, and certainly not Aramaic. I find this discourse helpful in essentially underlining a big difference between Christianity and Islam, which tends to require adherents to learn the Quran in an outdated and extremely difficult Arabic. The Quran doesn't translate well, because it hasn't left the seventh century, one could argue."

"One could indeed argue that point, but it's best that one be a Muslim scholar or cleric, no?" responded Bargouthi with a devilish smile. "I will concede, however, that the Quran has not been subjected to the same level of academic scrutiny as has the Bible, and the Bible seems to have withstood the test of time. If you wish to numb your mind with a scholarly pursuit, I recommend the works of American academic John Wansborough. I don't agree with all of his findings but welcome his critical pursuit of truth. But let's get back to our German friends who studied some of the oldest Qurans in Yemen. Basically, Puin and his colleagues came to the conclusion that early Islam was essentially formulated as an errant Arabic Christian sect, one that opposed your notions of the trinity. They believed that Mohammed and potentially his precursors crafted a new faith to rehabilitate what they believed had become distorted since the onset of Christianity nearly six hundred years earlier. It was a Christian reform movement, to say the least, according to them."

"Puin, for his part, alleged that the original Islamic scribes weren't so original and took existing accounts and attributed them to the revelations that Mohammed received from the Angel Gabriel. His findings weren't so welcome, and the Yemeni authorities soon denied him access to the ancient manuscripts that he had been studying. What most people don't realize is that the Yemeni capital of Sanaa housed the oldest Islamic manuscripts in the world, and arguably the most important. The oldest Qurans are preserved in Turkey and Uzbekistan, but predating those are the manuscripts that were accidentally found in Yemen in the 1970s. They were almost thrown out with the rubbish. And the language in which they were written was *hijazi*, the Arabic dialect that Mohammed himself spoke!"

"And now, your new word of the day: 'palimpsest,' crudely put, recycled or repurposed manuscripts. In reviewing ancient Quranic writings, Puin discovered they were written on material that contained earlier writings, which had been wiped or rubbed off. In writing on such recycled material, early authors accidentally preserved pre-existing scripture. Puin using modern technology—or that of the 1970s—concluded that the Quran of today could not be the revelation Mohammed received from Allah. I don't agree with his findings, but my faith, challenged in my own academic and spiritual pursuit, can withstand some scrutiny," concluded Bargouthi.

"Wow. This is heavy and fascinating," offered Haley. "So if somehow these manuscripts resurfaced and or made it out into the general populace in less understanding capitals, this could be very upsetting to a lot of Muslims."

"The word I would use is incendiary," Bargouthi replied, adding, "If these palimpsests recording the origin of Islam existed in Yemen, just imagine what documents the Abbassid scholars held in Baghdad during the most glorious days of the Islamic empire."

Khalil, who had been asleep for the previous twenty minutes, snapped to attention, checked his watch, and ordered Haley and his green eyes on to his next appointment.

Chapter 16

"Clayton, are you sure that the fish are even awake yet?" asked Philson, yawning and toting tackle, gear, and a cooler and moving it onto a fishing boat. "Do we really need to be up at zero dark thirty to catch fish?"

"I thought that's when you did your best work," Haley smiled back. "If I recall correctly, your squid counterparts pulled in a pretty big haul a few years ago at half past zero dark thirty."

"Yep. They got due glory for that raid in Pakistan. Pretty sweet deal and accomplished with great precision. But that's what they do. We Green Berets tend to focus on the long game and insert ourselves more deeply with folks. We get to know them. We work, eat, and hang out with them so they trust us, and they are the ones empowered to effect change, not us. That's not to say that we don't also find time for aggressive proselytizing of democracy and the American way of life, but it's not usually conducted via urgent surgical strike like the Navy SEALS."

"Bitter much?" taunted Haley, loading the rest of the gear on the boat.

"*Wain al-asmak [Where are the fish?]*" Haley turned to the skipper, an elderly, weathered Kuwaiti gentleman in traditional, but stained and bedraggled Gulf *dishdasha*, who had a twinkle in his eye but seemed to be running a dental deficit, as exposed in his smile.

"*Asmak moujoodah, wayyid kathir, iza chunt mahzuuz. [There are a lot of fish here, if y'all are lucky],*" he grizzled back in Kuwaiti Arabic dialect.

Haley then remembered his manners and properly greeted the gentleman with the litany of customary Arabic greetings and introduced him to Nate Philson, who also exchanged some polite introductions. The man responded in turn, but showed a little surprise at meeting Philson, having met so few African-Americans in Kuwait. He poured piping hot tea for them, already prepared, as they arranged their gear in place. After a few minutes of getting things ready, including laying out the bait, comprised of frozen shrimp and squid and some mackerel, the captain revved both engines of the thirty-three-foot Bayliner 335 and moved slowly out of the harbor into the open sea.

"So, what are we gonna catch today?" yelled Philson over the boat's roaring engines.

"With my usual fishing luck, likely nothing," grimaced Haley. "It's called fishing, not catching, for a reason. I'm pretty content just being out on the water for a couple of hours, though. The level of dust is so much less out here, and it's just nice being out of the traffic and the rush of city life," he added, but then looked with annoyance at jet skis lined up, ready for customers to hit the waters offshore in the next few hours. "Who knows, we might bring in a hamour or two. They're excellent to eat and can be quite a lot of fun to catch. As an added bonus, we might see a dugong or two."

"What is a dugong? Some kind of bird?" asked Philson.

"Nope. It's a sea cow or manatee or some kind of seal. They're pretty ugly but also friendly. They're actually mentioned in the Bible, as their skins were used in the making of the tabernacle," Haley replied.

"Oh. Why do you even know that?" Philson rolled his eyes. "How's your love life?" asked Philson, suddenly changing the subject.

"To be honest, not of much consideration these days. Given everything that has happened over the last couple of years, I haven't seemed to be able to concentrate on anyone but me lately. I guess that's pretty narcissistic, but there you have it." He thought it way too premature to mention to Philson that a first-tour public affairs officer had caught his eye. He hadn't mustered up the courage to ask her out yet but noted they seemed to have found roughly the same convenient time to have lunch in the embassy cafe recently.

"Yep, you do seem to be into you of late. Makes for depressing loneliness, but I doubt anyone could stand you for long anyway. No offense, but you're kind of mopey," Philson egged.

Haley grinned back and shoved a three-ounce weight, two hooks, and a leader at him so that he might start outfitting his fishing rig. He also started breaking apart the frozen bait so there would be no delays once the skipper found the ideal fishing spot. "So how's your love life? Still maintaining a monogamous relationship with Uncle Sam, or are you finding time in your life for someone less dull army drab and who won't swoon over Jody [army slang for any man "who is with your girl when you ain't," referencing a large number of relationships that fail during long deployments.]?"

"I've got a girl back home. She's working on her master's degree. If she'll wait another couple of years for me, I'll propose to her. But I'm in no hurry, I'm having too much fun being a cowboy. This life is hard on relationships, and wouldn't be fair to her. For right now, the job has to come first, and I can't ask her to play second fiddle. When I'm ready to settle down, I'll ask her to settle down with me," Philson grinned. "But for right now, I need to hit the head."

"Alright. You do that. I'll finish getting the gear ready," Haley responded.

Haley finished tying off the rigs with a twisting knot his grandfather had taught him. He baited all four hooks on both rods and reels just as he noticed the skipper lowering the RPMs on the engines. They were slowing and circling some coral. The water was quite clear, and Haley could make out the panoply of colors on display from the depths. The morning sun was out now, with intense light already reflecting off the water. He grabbed his sunglasses out of his pocket and put them on. He then began fiddling with one of the rod and reel combinations, anxious to drop a line into the water. He noticed a boat in the distance following them, very likely, he presumed, coming to either fish or scuba dive around the same coral bed. Haley looked to what he thought might be due east and perhaps the landmass of Iran only a couple of hundred kilometers away.

The captain cut engines just west of the coral so they might drift across it in attempts to find the fish. Haley looked across the clear calm water to the north, just able to pick out the forms in the Kuwait City skyline through the morning mist. The ever present dust blurred silhouettes of the structures and gave the city an orange hue. He looked to the east, seeing distant shorelines, wondering just how close he actually was to Iran.

Philson emerged from the cabin, saying, "Next time I need to use the facilities on board, maybe you can remind me to wait until we stop. It was a bit rough keeping my bal—"

Philson suddenly collapsed, hitting the deck hard, blood already congealing on the back of his head. Behind him emerged someone wearing khakis and a t-shirt, holding a club in his right hand and a nine-millimeter caliber handgun in his left. Something about him looked oddly familiar, but Haley had no time for reflection. The assailant scurried up the ladder and clubbed the skipper as well. He too collapsed violently.

Haley was stunned and unprepared. He watched as the assailant slowly made his way down the upper deck to where Haley was standing. Still with fishing pole in hand, he stared at the man coming perilously close to him. Haley's sense of familiarity grew. He knew this guy from somewhere.

Haley's mind raced. This was a large boat but offered no cover or escape from someone with a gun on board. His eyes stayed on the young man who was less than ten feet away from him. Haley's peripheral vision detected no movement from the skipper; Philson was barely moving. Haley could make out the sound of a motorboat in the distance.

"Do you remember me?" asked the man.

Haley felt no compunction to answer a question fielded at gunpoint. He continued to stare while mentally screaming at his mind to formulate a plan of action.

"You should know me. My name is Ali al-Qahtani, and my grandfather was Mohammed Abdullah al-Qahtani. Before I kill you, Muhsin Bin Laden and Ali al-Sadr told me to—"

As al-Qahtani uttered his family name, Haley realized he was in a do or die situation. This was no time to contemplate. He knew he must act at that instant. He would not subject himself to kidnapping or certain torture and death. Lunging with the only weapon he had, he swung the fishing pole at al-Qahtani from left to right. Both men knew it was too short, but what al-Qahtani did not realize was that Haley had extended the fishing line and rig out about a foot or two beyond the pole. He had hoped to knock al-Qahtani in the face with the three-ounce weight. It would not seriously injure him but would buy Haley a split second of distraction to try to tackle his protagonist or die trying.

Instead, the fishing tackle missed and sailed passed al-Qahtani's head. It boomeranged on the back of his skull, however, and flung around slapping him on the left side of the face. The force of the action lodged both hooks firmly in al-Qahtani's face, including one in his left eye. The weight, given the velocity of the movement, knocked out a front tooth. The suddenness of the action terrorized the terrorist, and he emitted a high-pitched scream in pain and panic. Haley instinctively did what all good fishermen do when they connect with their prey; he yanked hard on the line and set the hooks, digging their barbs deep into al-Qahtani's cheek and eye socket. The baited squid still on the hooks gave the scene an extra added dose of gruesomeness.

Al-Qahtani panicked. Still screaming, he dropped his club and clawed at his eye with his right hand, while firing his sidearm blindly with his left. Haley tugged harder at the pole, jerking al-Qahtani's head completely around and tipping him off balance, making him drop the gun, while he grabbed helplessly at the hooks embedded in his face. Haley kicked the gun away. He knew that al-Qahtani would not be able to break the twenty-pound test line, and he was clearly in a great deal of pain. Haley kept the line taut. He felt squeamish about the injury he had inflicted but reminded himself this man was responsible for the deaths of Dr. Ibrahim Mustafa and his colleague, Paula Abrams. He should show no mercy to this dealer of death. Still though . . .

His brief reverie was interrupted as he saw Philson lunge with incredible speed to the side of the boat, grabbing an eight-foot fishing gaff stowed on the rails. In a single move, he launched the gaff over the rails and yanked it back, impaling a young man just under his left arm. He pulled him back with such force that the man slammed against the larger fishing boat, causing him to drop the gun he was carrying, and apparently aiming at Haley, harmlessly into the water.

Al-Qahtani, still howling, seemed to have regained a modicum of his composure and led by his still working right eye, lunged for the cutting board Haley had been using to cut bait. He grabbed the filet knife from the board and swung upward, cutting the line, and then he jumped between Haley and Philson, diving headlong into the smaller boat. The familiar-looking captain of the smaller boat must be Abdullah al-Otaybi, Haley surmised, as he saw him struggle free from Philson's long rusty hook, blood bubbling and running down his shirt. He gunned the boat's engine and pulled away at top speed from the Bayliner, with al-Qahtani writhing in pain on the boat's floor.

Philson and Haley looked at each other, stunned.

"You alright?" they asked each other simultaneously.

"Let's give chase," urged Philson, picking up al-Qahtani's gun, instinctively checking the round count by the weight of the magazine. Haley noticed his friend's countenance change. He no longer appeared to be the jovial fishing buddy. He had morphed into a battle-hardened killer, irate that he had been coldcocked but more furious that his prey was getting away. He had the look of many Fifth Group Special Forces soldiers inured to violence from their long and frequent deployments to the Middle East.

"I'm game but don't think this rig can keep up with the smaller speed boat," Haley responded and then added, "But let's see how the captain is doing."

"Oh. Yes, of course. Sorry. I'm still a little dazed," he responded while moving up the stairs, dabbing at the bloodied wound on his head. The fire in his eyes began dissipating.

After wrapping the head of the skipper in bandages they found in the boat's first aid kit, the two contemplated their next move.

"You still want to fish?" asked Haley.

***

Haley and Philson continued to tend to the boat's captain. As he eventually came to, they ascertained he likely had a concussion and, notwithstanding a nasty gash matching that of Philson's, he would likely be fine. They asked about their stowaway, but the skipper seemed genuinely at a loss as to how the assailant got on board. They noticed the boat had a compartment next to a bunk that easily could have hidden a man for a few hours. Given his "accident," Haley and Philson both urged the captain to turn the boat around and head for shore. He acquiesced and started back.

Philson reached for his phone to report the incident.

"Nate, can we talk about this first?" implored Haley.

"Dude, we gotta call this in. No way around it," he retorted.

"I know, but let's think about this first?" asked Haley. "The captain doesn't know what happened, and thank God, he only got knocked around a bit. Our two fish bait friends won't likely want to explain how they got hooked on fishing, so the question is: How do we report this?"

"What are you saying?" Philson asked.

"I'm saying that both characters—al-Otaybi and al-Qahtani—are on FBI lookouts. They're already wanted. We can let folks know through intel channels that they've been sighted, and perhaps the Kuwaitis can be convinced to compare immigration records to trace them and whatever name they used to get into the country. But like it or not, these guys will quickly be in the wind . . . and fast. They have money and resources. When we report this, I'll be fired again and on the first plane home. My reputation precedes me. My bosses have read the public accounts of me in Paris and Baghdad and think me an adventure seeking glory hound. When word gets out that my so-called troubles have found me out here in Kuwait, I'm toast. I need to speak to my good friend, Wilson Edger. I'll provide a proper report to our regional security officer at the embassy, but at the same time, I want to touch base with Wilson to build out the broader context. Plus, I think there might be something else brewing beyond simple retribution for thwarting their messianic plans in Mecca a few months back."

"Alright. But I'm gonna alert folks through defense intelligence lanes that the intel community needs to prioritize the elimination of these two knuckleheads. We were very lucky today, you know?" Philson angrily responded over the roar of the twin engines.

"Yep, lucky indeed," yelled back Haley. "It should be easier to track them now, though. One has a huge hole in his ribcage, and the other is gonna have a dickens of a time getting two hooks out of his face."

***

While the boat worked its way back to harbor, Haley called the head of embassy security to give an initial account of the incident. His colleague agreed to meet him at the wharf upon the return and ascertain what security and/or medical needs might need tending to. The head of security also said he would call Kuwaiti Coast Guard officials to be on the lookout for two grievously wounded seafarers arriving in port in the Marina Mall area.

Haley also sent a WhatsApp message to his pal Wilson Edger, who had been a source of useful collaboration, insight, and encouragement in Haley's navigation of the conspiracies surrounding the fateful attempt of the elder al-Qahtani to present himself as the Islamic Messiah, returned from "ghaibeh," or prophetic absence. Edger was kind enough to pray with Haley during his despondency over the death of colleagues and was instrumental in contextualizing events for department leadership. Haley remained very grateful. His message to him read as follows:

```
0825 C. Haley

    Wilson.  Plz  call  when  you  have
a  chance.  Urgent.  Two  old  friends
resurfaced,  tried  to  deepsix  me.  Lucky
I'm  a  fisher  of  men.  Think  it's  due  to
past  issues,  but  I've  run  into  new
conspiracies  i  need  to  run  by  you.  Call
me.  C.
```

Within twenty minutes, while still out to sea, Haley received the following:

```
0843 W. Edger
```

Groan. Hope you're OK and this is nothing serious. What's going on? Getting ready to board a flight. Can't call now. Will be in Amman soon. Can i call from there? How momentous is this? Where are you now, anyway?

0845. C. Haley

Yes. We can talk later. Plz do call from Amman. Got much to cover with you. Tweedles dee and dum showed up. Tried to settle scores. Lucky a pal with a green hat was with me. All ok now, but i think you and i should talk. Can do over secure line. Or you may wish to stop by while in the region. I'm in Kuwait. Have time to swing by?

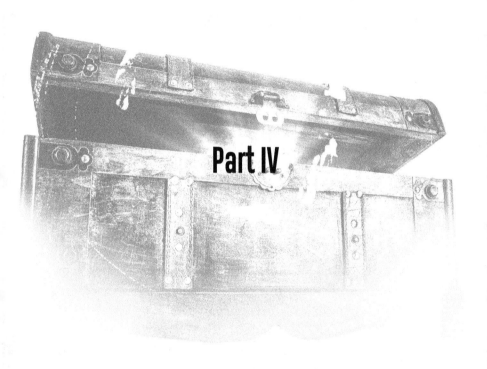

Part IV

Chapter 17

U.S. Embassy, Kuwait City, Kuwait.

The next few days were a blur. The security team, the ambassador, the DCM, the Department of Justice Legal Attaché, and others subjected Haley to a litany of questions, mostly implying—from Haley's perspective—that he somehow sought out the encounter on the boat and that he had not thoroughly coordinated his activities with the security team ahead of time, especially given the presence on board of Philson. Philson, for his part, was summoned back to his team of Green Berets and currently incommunicado.

Haley assured his interrogators he had sought out only a few hamour and possibly some other gulf fish. Nothing more. He certainly had no idea an armed assailant was on board and happily relinquished his phone to determine if it had been tapped. IT colleagues found no evidence of intrusion but did note that the battery life drained too fast. They noted this as a telltale sign of possible hacking.

The front office told him that a possible curtailment was a consideration, causing Haley a great deal of frustration. He wanted to argue against this, but he realized that the main concern of the embassy was the protection of his colleagues. Given that three State colleagues were dead and another traumatized due to their connections to Haley, he knew he was in no place to make demands. He relayed in his depositions his belief that the assailants targeted him due to the death of the elder al-Qahtani and the thwarting of their plans. He also believed they would not likely stay in Kuwait given their need for medical attention, including cosmetic surgery.

The front office told Haley that his future at post was under consideration, and he should coordinate all activities with security colleagues and plan no public engagements.

Haley found these new restrictions humiliating and wondered if he should simply agree to a curtailment. He chided himself on allowing his despondency to return. He wished Philson had stayed around. At least then, he wouldn't have had to endure the many questions thrown at him alone. And why no word from Wilson yet?

***

Haley wanted a cup of coffee. He went to the embassy cafe and ordered an Americano, no sugar. He liked how this drink, the Americanized version of an espresso, had a robust, burned coffee bean flavor, much more vibrant than that of a regularly brewed coffee. He recalled how Dr. Ibrahim lectured him on how coffee originally sourced from Yemen, which recalled to him his recent conversation on palimpsests. He pondered the potential veracity of German scientist Puin, and other scholars' claims that early Islamic writings predated Mohammed. If so, this would be earth shattering. Incendiary, as Bargouthi characterized it.

He also wondered if Kuwaiti archives stolen by the Iraqis in 1990 contained such pre-Islamic material. If so, he thought again, no wonder why the Kuwaitis were eager to have their archives back. And this would explain their vagueness in discussing what was in the missing material.

"I think your coffee is ready," nudged a soft voice next to him. He looked to his right and saw a beautiful young lady looking up at him. As with all women, Haley had no intelligent guess as to her age but believed she must be a couple of years younger than he. Jordan Cooper had mentioned to him over one of their chance lunch encounters that she had graduated from Penn State University three years ago and joined the State Department just after completing her master's degree at Georgetown. She worked in the public affairs section, covering cultural issues. She had completed her consular assignment, but Haley couldn't recall at which post.

"Um. Yes. I'm sorry. You caught me daydreaming," Haley answered, trying to snap back into reality and not appear transfixed with the details about her running through his mind. He paid for his coffee and hers in hopes of appearing chivalrous and apologetic for making her wait. He also hoped this might qualify as a date, without him having to actually make it official. "Want to chat?"

"Sure. I have a few minutes. Next coffee is on me, though," she said, smiling with her eyes, as they moved to a nearby table. "So what's going on? You seem distracted lately."

Haley flushed with a tinge of thrill that she had noticed him enough to know he had been distracted.

"Um, yes. I had a run-in with some old adversaries over the weekend. I got the upper hand this time, but our conflict remains unresolved," he said, as if describing an unpleasant office encounter instead of an attempted murder. He was under instructions not to divulge details of the attack.

"Oh, I see," she said. "I heard that the grandsons of the would-be Messiah tried to get revenge on you for the plot you foiled."

Haley was shocked at her forward response but pleased that she knew about some of his background. "You make it sound very dramatic and are amplifying the role I played in it, but yes, the men who attacked me don't appear to be the forgiving types."

Talking to her gave him the opportunity to look at her for the first time. He liked what he saw. The word "svelte" came to mind, but he couldn't recall exactly what it meant. She was certainly very attractive. She had long, full, dark hair, infused with blonde streaks. She had beautiful blue eyes and skin the color often described as olive. Haley had seen only green and black olives so thought this was an errant description. Her skin was indeed lovely, though.

Something about her features hinted at the Middle East, but he couldn't tell what. She smiled with her eyes, he noticed, again, finding it very inviting and at the same time disarming. She gestured a lot with her hands and seemed to tease her hair with her fingers when not gesticulating. She said something about Pennsylvania, but he didn't catch what. He enjoyed being with her and listening to her voice. It was quite the balm from having dealt with depositions and interrogations recently. A quick scan of her arms and ankles revealed no tattoos. For that he was thankful. He was not a fan of showcasing a blotchy, smudgy, blight on one's skin. "Wow," he thought to himself. He needed to rein in his mind and stop vying for the gold jump to conclusions in the mental Olympics.

She had been talking all this time, but Haley was too caught up in his distractions with her loveliness and his predicament—and his judgmental opining—to catch anything she was saying.

She noticed. "Thanks for the coffee, though," she concluded, starting to get up from the table.

"Wait, Jordan," he blustered. "I'm sorry. I have been distracted, and honestly, I find *you* a bit distracting but in a very nice way. Maybe we might find time to talk a little more, perhaps away from the embassy?"

"Sure. OK, but only if you promise to tell me what's been going on? You're a bit of a celebrity. Not many diplomats get so many media mentions."

Haley blushed. "Great. Just what I wanted. Notoriety."

***

Haley was frustrated. His mini-date with Jordan was less than inspired. Plus, he was likely to be subjected to more questions about the fishing boat account. He would rather simply be left alone so that he could do his job. It would have been nice if Philson could have stuck around to help answer some of the questions coming his way. And why didn't Wilson answer his messages?

He moseyed up to his office, half a cup of his coffee still in hand. It was already tepid. Oh well.

He entered the political office. Don Glennon waved him into his private office. There, across from Don, he saw Wilson Edger. "Wilson, what are you doing here?" he exclaimed.

Glennon quickly shot in, "Apparently you both know each other. Feel free to use the conference room down the hall, but if you're going to speak to events over the weekend, please bring me into the conversation. If it's the stuff from Mecca or Iraq, I have more important things to do." He cleared his throat again noisily.

"He's kind of rude and full of himself," whispered Edger to Haley as they departed the office.

"Yeah, but he's OK. He just doesn't like to be bothered by work stuff, you know, stability of the region, driving political motivations, end of times prophecies, you know, some of the tedious things about our jobs," quipped Haley, genuinely pleased to see Edger. "Why didn't you message, and how is it that you ended up here?"

Edger replied, "I'm embarrassed to say this, but I traveled without my charger and my phone died. I borrowed one in Amman but was tied up with meetings and research. By the time I had a break, I was already on a plane here to see you. I read some of the reporting on your weekend excitement. Given who these two nutcases are, I thought it good to see you in person to get your account firsthand. I'm on a task force trying to find these guys."

"Really. You might want to change some of the physical descriptions of al-Qahtani. He had a run in with some rusty hooks. His biometrics will have changed just a bit," insinuated Haley. "He's all right now, though, just like Buster," smiling and referencing a quote from "Arrested Development," a situation comedy television show.

Edger didn't get it. "Let's go grab some coffee," Haley said while disposing of the cup already in his hand.

On the way back to the cafe, Haley answered Edger's questions about the murder attempt and how fortuitous it was to have Philson on board. He looked around the cafe as they entered, hoping Jordan might be still lingering around.

"Yep, about that," Edger stepped in. "We've placed a request through military channels to have Philson's team assigned to Kuwait. There is plenty of work over at ARCENT HQ at Camp Arifjan, and they can slip up to Iraq as needed from time to time, but there is a growing fan base back home that sees you as a magnet for some pretty wild developments. It would be good to have some muscles nearby if you find yourself in a pinch again. From Philson's readout, though, sounds like you handled yourself pretty well. I can't believe you took on an armed guy with nothing but a fishing pole."

"Me either," muttered Haley under his breath. "I would have liked to have something more lethal, like a battleship, perhaps. So tell me, what is it that you've been working on?"

"Basically, your work," he jumped in. "Your reports and accounts from Paris, Aziziya, Mecca, and elsewhere have a number of folks spun up. We missed the Arab Spring and the buildup of ISIS or *Daesh*, and we're determined not to take anything for granted. We're exploring the potential for revival or other reunifications of the old *Ikhwan* groups and trying to look at these folks from historical perspectives. We're tallying leadership profiles and financial and political influences of these tribes. Some of them, like the *Rashaid*, number in the millions. It would not be good if they were disenfranchised or otherwise marginalized from their political leadership in countries across the Middle East. These tribes have family members in Morocco and Iraq and every country in between. There are the *Subaiey, Qahtan, Ajman, Utaiba, Onezi, Murrah, Bani Khalid, Dawasir*, and on and on. We're determined not to miss a big undercurrent that could bring about another wave of terrorism or unrest in the region."

Edger continued, pausing briefly while they ordered coffee. "Since you, um, stumbled on the web of conspiracies last year, we've been doing some in-depth research on just who the *Ikhwan* or Brotherhood are. It's been tough, as most folks wish to conveniently dismiss bands of radicalized tribes from a hundred years ago. Or many simply don't understand the distinction of the *Ikhwan* from the *al-Ikhwan al-Muslimeen*, AKA the Muslim Brotherhood. You and your theories have impressed upon me the need to dig deeper and consult more on who these tribes are and if they present a modern threat."

"Here's what I've picked up so far: The *Ikhwan* was essentially the network of militant tribes that Ibn Saud, the founder of modern Saudi Arabia, coalesced into his national army to conquer the Arabian peninsula a hundred years ago. After consolidating his peninsula power base, he kept these guys on as his National Guard. They were ravenous and quite effective at terrorizing and ripping out all pockets of dissent. Bent on religious fervor, they were at the beck and call of Ibn Saud, who established his newfound religious credentials as the custodian of the three holy mosques of Islam, including the Al-Aqsa Mosque in Jerusalem, before that edifice migrated to the care of the Hashemites in Jordan. Who were these radical tribes to doubt the Word of Allah as it appeared to come from Ibn Saud? They conquered, subdued, or converted all in their paths, namely the many Bedouin tribes that happened to traverse the borderless peninsula at that time."

Haley felt enormous gratification in hearing many of his own theories and the products of his reporting being summed back to him in such coherent precision. At the same time though, he took on a tremendous amount of responsibility in that his work seemed to have become policy. This made him very nervous and he fell under the attack of shards of doubt. What if he was wrong? What if his analysis misinformed or otherwise took government colleagues down rabbit holes of distraction when their focus should be elsewhere? He asked himself why any of this mattered and then recalled glimpses of al-Qahtani's honey-tinged eyes, which still haunted him.

Oblivious to Haley's mental wandering, Edger continued. "The *Ikhwan* with their religious fervor began to doubt the spiritual legitimacy of the House of Saud, however, as it began to institute political vice religious rule, and they turned against their masters. They were brutally put down by the Saudis, with help from the British. This was especially insulting to the *Ikhwan* as the British represented the worst type of infidels. Even so, these militants nearly overthrew the Saudis and almost conquered Kuwait and would have taken over modern day Jordan, if it weren't for the British dominance in artillery and its advances in aviation warfare."

"They've maintained a loose loyalty over the last hundred years, bought in large part by the enormous wealth derived from the discovery and exploitation of oil reserves in Saudi Arabia. And in turn, the political leadership of the House of Saud instituted a number of reforms to placate the *Ikhwan* tribes in their strict adherence to their conservative *Wahhabi* interpretation of Islam. Somehow, it ended up punishing women the most: no driving, no mixed gatherings, no travel without a male family member chaperoning, etc."

Clayton recalled a conversation he had a lifetime ago on the narrow streets of old Paris with Colonel Dave Richt, who blamed unequal treatment of women in Saudi Arabia on an outbreak of the "cootie germ."

"You might find it interesting that Juhayman al-Otaybi, *grandfather* of one of the young men who attacked you on the boat and leader of the 1979 siege of Mecca, was the son and *grandson* himself of those who had opposed, sometimes violently, Saudi rule. Juhayman's grandfather was killed by the Saudis. No wonder he felt just cause to upend the faux religious establishment, as he saw it, in laying siege to the Grand Mosque. He was prepared to die just like his grandfather. He did. They chopped off his head. And now his grandson seems willing to pay a high cost in sustaining the *Ikhwan* fervor. We need to watch out for these guys. No telling just what they'll do if they get behind a big enough cause!"

"Like the return of the Messiah? Or maybe the 'reincarnation slash cloning' of Mohammed?" asked Haley bitterly, having played a role in thwarting both.

"Exactly," replied Edger.

"Then I have some bad news for you about a new rallying call," warned Haley.

Chapter 18

"Yep," continued Haley. "This time, I've stumbled onto something more . . .'incendiary.'" He furrowed his brow trying to remember the word used by Bargouthi, which he recalled in Arabic also was a variant of the word holocaust, or محرقة *[muhraqa]*. "This time it won't be an old spiteful dotard claiming he's the Messiah come back from an 'absence,' or a little kid they supposedly cloned from Mohammed's bones. We Christians have been waiting for 2,000 years for the second coming of Christ. Our Muslim friends have only been waiting 1400 years. Why the big rush?"

Edger smiled, "But what is the big rallying call you mentioned?"

"Oh, this is where it gets good," Haley retorted. "There are some elements here in the Islamic world that don't like their faith questioned. Remember when the movie *The Last Temptation of Christ* came out in the United States? Remember the outcry and uproar over the notion that Jesus was married or wanted to be married? That was quite the controversy, with folks picketing and raising a holy ruckus. Movie theaters cancelled screenings and Hollywood tycoons received the message that the bottom line would be impacted by crossing certain spiritual red lines."

"Yes, and people were equally offended that the movie just wasn't that good, and that for some reason Willem Dafoe or other white Europeans could be cast as a Middle Eastern Semite," Edger shot back.

"Yeah, and the movie is still banned in a number of countries. Bottom line, though, is that the outcry was incredibly mild compared to how things get in this region when red lines are crossed. When religious sensibilities here are challenged, people die. Seems like we hear frequent cases of riots, beatings, firebombing, stoning, and certainly serious death threats whenever a Quran is burned, or irresponsible, intolerant statements denigrating Islam are uttered," opined Haley.

He continued, speaking quickly and not quite coherently as he tried to get his thoughts together: "My latest misadventure revolves somehow around the missing Kuwaiti archives and what may have been in them. I've learned a new word recently—palimpsest. This is a term that essentially describes repurposed manuscripts. Some of these manuscripts were used to write early editions of the Quran. Some of these Qurans are still around and kept in museums and in national archives. In Yemen, for example, historians and archaeologists studied several of these documents and reportedly discovered something that would shake the Islamic world to its core."

"What are you talking about?" asked Edger. "I don't follow. I thought the consistent thing about Islam is that its guiding doctrine hasn't changed or been altered, right? It's my understanding that the purists believe the word of Allah should only be read in largely antiquated Arabic, which you've told me is nearly impossible to understand by the majority of the world's Muslims.

"That's true. I marvel at the cohesion of belief in Islam when most Muslims hail from non-Arabic speaking countries, like Indonesia, Pakistan, India, Afghanistan, Bangladesh, and so on. That's why well-versed scholars and Imams play such an influential role in the spiritual guidance of the masses. They're the ones that keep this faith alive, by interpreting it for people who can't read its doctrine. Similar to Christian Europe in the dark ages, when so many people were illiterate," said Haley.

"So what would be controversial about old Qurans?" asked Edger.

Haley replied, "Nothing. It's what they were written on, these palimpsests."

"Sorry, but I just don't follow."

"Palimpsests are the papers, skins, or reeds, or whatever they used to write the Qurans on in the early days of Islam. The scientists who studied them in Yemen discovered the same material was used for earlier writings but were erased or somehow rubbed out. The earlier writings had various versions of the Quran, ones that weren't canonized, to borrow a historical Christian concept," explained Haley.

Edger, more confused, exclaimed, "Again, so what's the big deal? Sounds like the old scholars made typos and had to re-do some of their work."

"That's not what the German scientists assessed," Haley shot back. "Their studies reported that the old deleted versions, with verses from the Quran, predated the Quran, and in fact, predated Mohammed. The implication being that some or all of the complete revelation from Allah to Mohammed through the angel Gabriel may have already been written down, potentially before Mohammed's time. Should even a whisper of this get out and be exploited by the wrong sources, some folks won't take this news very well. Islam, to many Muslims, is meant to be the completion of faith, the final message or communiqué, to use a diplomatic term, from God to man, not merely a reform movement that simply took issue with the Trinity or other tenets of our faith."

"Good grief. This is terrible," said Edger as he finally put all the pieces together in his mind. "But is there some danger these notions and conspiracies might get out into the public?"

"The studies of the Germans are already known—you can find them on the internet—but regional governments have issued strong statements discrediting them, and they have prohibited the scientists from completing their work. I don't know," continued Haley, "but if influential folks wished to stir up unrest, not just in the Arab region, but in the greater Islamic world, this could easily be exploited. With the right spark, in a heartbeat, throngs of angry mobs could be compelled to take the streets and topple already unstable governments which espoused or entertained the notion the Quran wasn't immaculately inspired by visions from Allah. People will have to be on either side of this issue. No middle ground to allow for objective thinking."

"This is all very sketchy to me, but as I mentioned before, we don't want to get caught with our pants down again and miss another attempt to upend an already volatile region. So what is there to do?" shrugged Edger.

"I'd sure like to know what was in the case buried with the Iraqi we blew up in 1991 on the Highway of Death and if it was part of the missing archives stolen by Iraqi looters," responded Haley, who then narrated to Edger his account of the discovery of the KIAs in the desert near the Iraqi border.

Part V

Chapter 19

Moroni, Comoros.

"I have news for you, my prince," said Ali Hussein al-Sadr, accepting a chilled Perrier from the manservant of Muhsin Bin Laden. He paused until the "tea boy," as he was arrogantly and derogatorily referred to, left the room. While the elderly man, dressed in a slightly tattered tuxedo, lumbered out of the room, al-Sadr took in the suite's luxurious trappings. From the drapes to the enormous flower arrangement in the middle of the room, everything reeked of extravagance. True to his word, Bin Laden had met with the Comorian President and purchased a new luxury hotel, likely to launder funds from his many nefarious activities. Given the number of Syrians, Lebanese, Emiratis, and even a few Kuwaitis making appearances around the hotel, he suspected armed Shia militias loyal to the Iranian backed *Hezbollah* group had assurances they would make payroll for the next few months and likely have new weapons and ammunition to harangue Israel and various regional Sunni governments.

"Yes. Tell me your news, and it better be good," responded Bin Laden attired in a loose bathrobe over what al-Sadr hoped was more . . . attire.

"I have disturbing news. Steel yourself as this will make you angry. Al-Qahtani and al-Otaybi had major setbacks in their attempt on the life of Gleeton Heeley. Not only did they fail to even hurt him, they were grievously injured in the attempt. Al-Qahtani lost an eye and will need cosmetic surgery to fix his face and replace a tooth. Al-Otaybi suffered two broken ribs and a punctured lung. He is also dealing with tetanus," al-Sadr spoke quickly, choosing to get all the bad news out at once, while staving off the initial ill-tempered response of his boss.

"How could this happen? How could you let this happen?" Bin Laden roared.

"I don't know. I don't have the details yet. I only know that their carefully planned operation was thwarted by *Heeley* and a friend who joined him on the boat, and they had to be smuggled from the Kuwaiti harbor to Al-Faw, [Iran] where they received medical treatment before moving them to Tehran for further care. After which, I'll move them to Qom to reunite with Dr. al-Onezi," al-Sadr stated emphatically to show he was capable of making good executive decisions, all the while trying to hide his nerves in the context of delivering disappointing news.

"This is unacceptable," thundered Bin Laden. "Should this source back to me, there will be consequences."

"Understood," replied al-Sadr. "But not all the news is bad. We have a mysterious and positive development in Kuwait, one the accursed *Heeley* somehow had a hand in."

Bin Laden's sour expression adjusted.

"Our sources in Kuwait informed us that an international mission to recover war dead, buried in the Kuwaiti desert, found the remains of fifty-five Iraqi sons. You'll recall that just as you sent me to Medina in 1979 to recover the remains of Prophet Mohammed, *Peace Be Upon Him*, we dispatched my cousin, Hussein al-Sadr, to remove specific and sensitive documents of a religious and historical nature from the Kuwaiti archives during the ill-fated invasion some ten years later. You know, of course, that the American infidels rescued the weak Kuwaitis and chased my Iraqi kinsmen from the spoiled emirate. We never heard from Hussein again and never knew until now if he completed his mission. We had always suspected he may have succeeded, but we never recovered what he was assigned to take. We now have word from Kuwaiti scientists that Hussein may have been carrying preserved documents when he was killed," conveyed al-Sadr. "His mission may now be over and ours just beginning!"

"This is good news indeed. Bring the documents to me, along with experts who can verify their authenticity," said Bin Laden, adding, "This plan has been dormant for thirty years, but given all the arrangements made in the run up to the short-lived Messianic reveal in Mecca recently, we should be able to move on this quickly. If they are, in fact, what I believe them to be, we can move them to western scientists who will show no regard to religious beliefs of the people in the region.

"In fact, my brother Osama and I concocted this notion originally because cloning Mohammed was an impossible task thirty years ago. We knew that technology would not be available to us for at least a few decades. The material buried away in the Kuwaiti archives, if manipulated well by us, could cause an upheaval that would make the Arab Spring look like a spring soirée. This is good news indeed. If only we could have recovered this in the 90s. Losing track of your cousin Hussein was unfortunate," said Bin Laden dispassionately.

Bin Laden paused in his remarks and glanced at the news ticker in Arabic on an enormous 75-inch LED television screen across the room. The channel was set to *Al Ekhbariya,* a Saudi based satellite news network, funded and established by the Saudi government to compete with Qatar's Al-Jazeera programming for the Arab world. He pushed a button on his phone and the "tea boy" rushed in with tea service for Bin Laden and his guest. Once tea had been dispensed, the servant scurried out of the room.

"My half-brother Osama proved impatient," Bin Laden prompted. "Instead of taking my counsel to await the appropriate circumstances, he decided foolishly to poke the American tiger in the eye. He got what he deserved by launching too early. His dabbling with Al-Qaida is nothing compared to the rebirth of the *Ikhwan* I have in store. He threw our family money around in Lebanon, Somalia, Sudan, and Afghanistan to agitate people against their governments and the west, but failed to activate the real power base: our tribes, which under the right master can be wielded to an extent not seen since we repelled the crusaders. He never realized the real power at our fingertips, literally now, as we can excite the masses with only a few well-timed entries into social media.

"First, contact our network of Imams who are loyal to us. I want them raising dissent in Friday prayers across the region and recruiting young men to be martyrs in the upcoming holy wars. Second, I want tribal leaders who are loyal to me and my money to come and see me here. Not at once. Arrange them to come in small groups. This should include all the marginalized tribes, whose sons can't hope to get good jobs or pay their bills. It's time to revive the long dormant *Ikhwan*. They need to be ready to take to the streets and to overthrow American puppet regimes in the region. Third, check in on Dr. al-Onezi and our young prophet. Let's see how the boy's preparations are coming along.

"And let's redouble our efforts to kill the pesky *Glaiton Heeley*. He has lived too long," concluded Bin Laden.

Chapter 20

Kuwaiti National Museum, Kuwait City, Kuwait.

"Dr. al-Marri, thank you for agreeing to see me again so soon. If you don't mind, I would like to introduce you to my colleague from Washington. I've already told him how knowledgeable you are on the missing archives and your nearly thirty year search to bring them back where they belong."

"Yes, sir," interrupted Edger quickly and uncharacteristically. "It's good to meet with you. Clayton informed me of how helpful you've been, and it appears we have much in common. My name is Jason Johnson, and I am one of many curators assigned to the Smithsonian," he added, all in one breath. A Smithsonian business card materialized in his hand while he spoke. He transferred it over to al-Marri, who seemed delighted to speak to a fellow archive specialist.

Haley did his best to show no reaction to Edger's sudden identity swap.

"Dr. al-Marri, as you know, the United States played an important role in the return of many of the archives and material stolen from you in 1990 and 1991. In fact, colleagues of mine participated in a project called the Iraq Survey Group, which was tasked to comb through thousands of documents to locate information or intelligence on Saddam Hussein's weapons of mass destruction capabilities. In so doing, they came across material that belonged to Kuwait, and these were returned to you some years ago," said Edger/Johnson.

"I remember very well. I remember that when you occupied Iraq, you seized nearly 50,000 boxes of material in Iraq and moved them to your Combined Media Processing Center in Qatar to study. Of those thousands of boxes, we only received two small trunks from the American Embassy here in Kuwait, but alas, they were inconsequential," al-Marri responded. "But first, might I offer you *shai [tea]* or coffee? My staff here prepare a wonderful cappuccino."

Taking the recommendation, both guests of al-Marri agreed to the cappuccino. Their host slipped out of the room to track down the museum staff. Strange, thought Haley, as most officials in Kuwait important enough to have tea service typically had a button on their phone to order it. Dismissing the notion that it was odd, Haley shrugged his shoulders, and they sat back and waited on a comfortable sofa, with Edger giving Haley an apologetic "I probably should have told you I would be using a different name" look.

Al-Marri returned in less than five minutes. Behind him was a young Bangladeshi national wearing a tuxedo and carrying an ornate tray with three hot drinks. Cinnamon on the foam of the two cappuccinos somehow displayed a brown silhouette of two bulbous towers, the symbol and skyline of Kuwait.

Both guests commented on the cleverness of design and expressed wonder in how such a feat could be managed. Al-Marri smiled graciously but somehow seemed a bit uneasy and flustered, noticed Haley.

Al-Marri restarted the conversation. "Yes. We have recovered a number of archives but won't rest until we have a complete accounting of all that was stolen."

"It's odd, though, that we don't yet know what was stolen," said Haley. "Is there a reason that the government never issued a manifest or list of missing items?"

"It's very sensitive and part of our heritage. And very personal to our leadership," al-Marri deflected.

"I'm sure it's still very traumatic and painful for the Kuwaiti people to reflect on those events and what Saddam's rampages did to your country," jumped in Haley again. "And I was pleased recently to participate in the recovery efforts of the mortal remains of Iraqi invaders. Their families deserve to know what happened and lay them to rest. Many of them were just following orders, you must understand. You may have read about this in the news." Seeing his nod of affirmation, Haley continued. "And I understand that one of the bodies was buried with some kind of carrying case, potentially designed to carry maps, scrolls, or other documents. We were informed by the ICRC that this was turned over to you. Is this true?"

Al-Marri was visibly uncomfortable. "Yes. It is true. ICRC turned it over to us, but before we could open the case, someone stole it. We never got to see what was in it. It is a very regrettable loss. And if you'll forgive me," noticing that the cappuccinos were drained, "I must excuse myself to speak again to the Ministry of Interior to aid in the search for this item."

"Of course. I didn't realize. I'm very sorry for the intrusion. May we come back tomorrow to talk more about this?" asked Haley.

"I'm very sorry, but I have been called away urgently for a business trip. I don't know when I'll be back," al-Marri responded.

Chapter 21

U.S. Embassy Kuwait City, Kuwait

"I'm just spit-balling here, but instead of us pretending we're scholars, 'Mr. Johnson,' why don't we consult with real archivists?" Haley sarcastically asked Edger once back at the embassy. "I think we should speculate not on what might be missing from the Kuwaiti archives but what might have been there in the first place."

"Sorry about the name confusion, and thanks for not making it awkward. I thought he might be more inclined to speak openly with a fellow museum nerd. Clearly, I was wrong. He was either very upset about the theft of the material left on the Iraqi soldier, or he was hiding something," mused Edger.

"But what do you mean about what might have been there in the first place?" Edger switched tones suddenly.

"It's weird that no one talks about what was in the archives. Speculation has it that there were documents that pertained to potential Kuwait double dealing between the Iraqis and the Iranians during the 1980–88 Iran-Iraq war in which the Kuwaitis may have financed both sides. Certainly that would be embarrassing, but folks already believe that was true. Another speculation is that the Al Sabah ruling family had documents in there that pertained to sensitive arrangements and land deals used to keep the peace. I don't buy that either," posited Haley.

"What do you think it might be?" asked Edger.

"I have no idea but do know that in this region, the stuff you want quiet is anything that could challenge, one, the political establishment, and two, the religious endorsement of the political establishment, which gives certain families the right to rule. And above that, or three, anything that might challenge the religious thinking of folks. Leaders in this part of the world don't want folks questioning their divine authority," opined Haley.

"Sure, but what makes you think that there might have been something like that in the Kuwaiti archives? Kuwait essentially played no historical religious or political role in the region and only became significant in the last few hundred years due to its geographical positioning as a crossroads between Indian, Persian, and Arab worlds, and then later, the discovery of oil," retorted Edger.

"Yes, but I can't stop thinking about what they found in Yemen. Remember our discussions on palimpsests? Those documents had been lying around for centuries. But once scientists, *western scientists*, took a look in the 70s, serious questions about Islamic timelines arose. The answer from the Islamic world was not to study the manuscripts further, but to cease all study and to deny the scientists' access to the material. Case close. End of the matter. Convenient. When *The Da Vinci Code* book and movie came out, belief systems were challenged for sure, with folks taking one of three positions: Some simply accepted Dan Brown's not-so-original new theology, as it was convenient and fun to vilify the Catholic Church, an easy target these days. Two: Some Christians explored their own faith more deeply and debated the conspiracies in the book and movie as sensational or preposterous. Three: Some simply chalked the storyline up to historical revisionism or fantasy and enjoyed a smart, well-crafted narrative that tied historically unrelated symbols into a compelling bit of entertainment. Nicholas Cage's *National Treasure* movies did the same," Haley inadvertently lectured.

Rolling his eyes, Edger said, "Yes, I get it. Sometimes people want to believe in connections that aren't there. I don't get the tie-in to your

Yemeni *palimpsy* whatchamacallits, though. Your sequencing is all out of order. You argue that because they were discovered in Yemen, they might have made their way to Kuwait because Baghdad was destroyed some 800 years ago? This makes no sense at all. What's this have to do with Yemen?"

Haley responded, "Probably nothing. I only offer this as we're in a region that doesn't tolerate the mocking, ridiculing, or even questioning of its belief system. Kuwait's archives would have been as good a place as any to squirrel away some documents that were too important to destroy, and too 'incendiary' to allow into the public or into other arenas of scrutiny."

"Kuwait? Really? That's a huge stretch. Yemen, I get due to its proximity to Mecca and Medina, and to the fact that it historically played a key religious, political, and economic role in the region, certainly well before the Saudis came onto the scene. I'm sure that Cairo, Istanbul, Damascus, Baghdad, and other great capitals may have some historically sensitive and important manuscripts as well, as they also were seats of power during various Islamic Empires. Kuwait, though, was at best a desert outpost until the discovery of oil, only last century."

Haley countered, "All true, but if you go back in time, arguably, the greatest center for political, religious, and economic power for any of the Islamic capitals would have been Baghdad. If my history is right, Baghdad was famed for its scholarship, mathematics, astronomy, science, medicine, and religious studies. In fact, scholars from around the then known world traveled to Baghdad for enlightenment, while our ancestors were illiterate, being spoon fed religious doctrine by the Catholic political power, suffering from poor hygiene, and hiding from or joining in with the Vikings."

"Okay, okay. You've convinced me. Baghdad was important. So what? It must be 500 miles from Kuwait City. I still don't see how these two cities are connected and why 'incendiary' manuscripts of apocalyptic importance might have moved between the two," said Edger, on the edge of irritation.

"Does 1258 mean anything to you?" queried Haley.

"A late lunch time?" Edger lightened up.

"1258 was the year that Baghdad fell. Almost overnight. Arguably the greatest city on the planet fell at the hands of Mongol marauders in less than a two-week span. It's the equivalent of New York City or London being destroyed in a nuclear strike. I've been consumed by the archives and read up on a variety of possibilities that might connect Kuwait to Iraq. I'm convinced this might be it," rattled off Haley.

Edger said, "I still don't follow you—you're not connecting the two."

"Yes. But I know what does connect the two," Haley smiled. "Think about it. Let's say you're a scholar, a devotee of truth and discovery, and your beloved city is surrounded by the greatest and most violent army in history. This army of Mongols isn't known for mercy. It's not even known for conquest—it's known for annihilation. From Asia, across the Steppes, across Afghanistan, Persia, and all the way to the Mediterranean, the Khans razed and mowed down everything in their path. Knowing that, you would want to safeguard what you could. You would hide treasure and valuables or smuggle them out of the city. Again, some believe that early Islam was a Christian reform movement, not the start of a whole new faith entirely. I'll bet the scholars in Baghdad had compiled tons of scrolls of the early writings in Islam so that they might study the origins of their faith. Roads were blocked and guarded, and the trek to other capitals was hazardous and across treacherous lands and deserts. No. In 1258, the only way out of Baghdad was via the rivers. If you're lucky enough to grab precious items and people, and perhaps a boat, you likely hop into the nearest river around, the Tigris, and go downstream. Spoiler alert: Do you know where the Tigris would take someone looking to get as far away as possible from the Mongols and to a place not developed enough to grasp their attention?"

"Wait a second," said Edger, grabbing his phone to do a quick Google Map search. "Are you saying that the Tigris would take . . . someone . . . to—" thinking aloud while waiting for the map of Iraq to load.

"Yep," said Haley. "It would take a long time, but yep, one could float downstream on the Tigris from Baghdad and end up here in Kuwait. There wouldn't have been a city here at the time, but given its positioning as a strategic crossroads, there would have been enough of a community for survivors of the Baghdad onslaught to seek refuge.

"We need to talk to an Iraqi historian," said Edger.

Chapter 22

Kuwait University, Sabah al-Salem University City.

Unfortunately, Edger's home office called him back to Washington, so the two agreed that Haley should reach out on his own to an academic who might shed light on Baghdad, circa 1258. Given lingering distrust between the two countries since the early 90s, however, there were no Iraqi academics in Kuwait. Dr. Bargouthi, however, proved quite knowledgeable on palimpsests and Yemen's significance to the foundations of Islam, so Haley surmised he may be helpful in exploring Baghdad's stolen heritage to see if it might connect to Kuwait's. He frequently consulted with professors and appreciated their insight on tribalism and improving ties among regional neighbors. Connecting with Bargouthi on this matter was hardly a white lie, Haley reasoned, given his work on the ICRC file.

Given the Public Affairs Section's unique ties to academia, especially in promoting university exchanges, Haley thought it wise to include one of his colleagues from the section in the meetings. He had one particular colleague in mind. Perhaps Jordan Cooper might join him, he posed to her supervisor. Haley also consulted the security office.

He was annoyed that he had to ask permission, but since the attack on the boat, diplomatic security at the embassy had been especially vigilant in ensuring his safety and insisted Haley be accompanied by an armed escort from the Kuwait Ministry of Interior, just in case he ran into trouble again. "Great," thought Haley, "a chaperone on my second date with Jordan."

Haley looked forward to the meeting but felt tinges of doubt and apprehension that he might potentially be putting Cooper in danger. He still suffered enormous guilt his questioning led to the death of Paula Abrams in Paris.

Cooper, however, readily accepted his offer and even suggested they stop by a small shawarma joint for lunch on the way back to the embassy. Haley thought this an excellent idea and looked forward to both the meeting and the time with his rather attractive colleague. She also seemed keen on the engagement, but Haley suspected it was because she hoped to learn more about what had made him so "notorious" over the last few years.

***

"Dr. Bargouthi. It's so nice to see you again. Nasser won't be joining me today, but I brought another colleague who expressed interest in meeting you. Sir, this is Jordan Cooper from our Public Affairs Section," Haley said as he introduced her to Dr. Bargouthi.

"Sir, it's nice to meet you. As Clayton mentioned, I work in Public Affairs at the embassy. While some of my colleagues cover the media, I promote cultural and educational exchanges. We are delighted that Kuwaiti students study in all fifty of the United States," she interjected enthusiastically.

"It's good to see you again, Clayton, and I am honored to meet you, Jordan. I like your name, as it's shared with the country I grew up in," smiled Dr. Bargouthi, and led them into his spacious and well-kept study. Cooper and Haley sat next to each other on a plush sofa, while Dr. Bargouthi pulled a chair around from his desk.

"I have ties there, too," she added. "My mother is from a town near Amman called *Fuheis*. She met my father when they were both studying in the United States. They both loved *al-Urdon* so much, they decided to call me Jordan."

"I thought it was due to their devotion to the greatest basketball player of all time," weakly popped Haley, not at all comfortable joshing around with her yet.

Bargouthi, who had spent time in Chicago in the 90s understood and laughed at the reference. He also correctly assumed that Cooper's maternal relatives were Christian as *Fuheis* is one of the few Christian communities left in Jordan.

The three shared other courtesies and niceties, which continued over customary tea and coffee service. Haley thought to himself that Cooper and he had nice chemistry in the meeting. He wondered if he could arrange more such collaborative political and public affairs engagements. He was also glad the "chaperone" had decided to wait in the air-conditioned car.

***

"Dr. Bargouthi. In our last meeting you were very generous with your time and your insight on Yemeni palimpsests. I wonder if you might also be able to speak to some of the treasures of Baghdad that may have been removed or otherwise survived the Mongol devastation of 1258," finally inquired Haley, trying to sound very intelligent in hopes of impressing Cooper.

"You suspect some religious material from Abbasid caliphate somehow ended up in the Kuwaiti archives?" pressed Bargouthi, cutting to the chase.

"Well, yes, to be honest, I do," quipped Haley. "Is this even feasible?"

"Yes. Let's talk about Baghdad," Bargouthi replied.

Cooper started scratching on a notepad, but at a gesture from Haley, she stopped, understanding the cue that Bargouthi would feel freer to chat if he perceived this conversation for background, off the record.

"You recall from our last conversation that I allow for the belief that Islam had been subjected to less historical and scholarly scrutiny than that of Christianity and other faiths. I will also admit that some potential archeological evidence, which might have disproved notions in our belief, has been erased or otherwise removed. Challenges to the faith of many have often been viewed as inconvenient by those who wield power and this sometimes applies to your friendly neighborhood imams. In many remote areas around the world, the religiously influential continue to wield high levels of power. In Afghanistan, for example, you'll recall that the Taliban ruled the country in the late 1990s, until American led NATO forces swept in and removed them from power."

"Much like the Islamic Revolution that occurred in neighboring Iran in 1979, these theocratic rulers didn't allow for much free-thinking or other challenges to their leadership. They fight for survival and remove indications and symbols of life outside their narrow viewpoint. Thus the bombing of the giant buddha statues in Afghanistan by the Taliban, the removal of Bibles in areas dominated by strictly adhering Wahhabis or Salafis, and even the destruction of what some thought was the tomb of Eve in Jeddah, Saudi Arabia back in the 1970s."

Cooper raised an eyebrow, clearly having never heard Eve had a tomb. "Please. You're not trying to say that the world's first woman, essentially the grandmother of mankind, lived in Saudi Arabia?"

"I find this notion highly suspect and prefer simply to believe facts as presented to me," Dr. Bargouthi replied, adding, "I'll only point out that the etymology of the Arabic word *Jeddah* is indeed 'grandmother,' and until the seventies, there existed in Jeddah a tomb large enough for a giantess, at which pilgrims used to pray. And some believe the garden of Eden, or perhaps *Aden*, was actually in the modern country of Yemen. And before the House of Saud annexed its western lands about a hundred years ago, the people of Yemen laid claims to much of the *Hejaz* province, including the Holy Cities of Mecca and Medina. So no. She didn't live in Saudi Arabia. But yes, there is some indication a very large grandmother may have lived in Yemen, or what is now known as Saudi Arabia."

Haley suddenly recalled a rather ridiculous image of Shriners, men in their sixties and seventies, zipping through the streets of Walhalla on July 4th in go-karts, wearing red fezzes embossed with an Egyptian looking scimitar over a pharaonic image. Above this image was the word *Hejaz*. Haley promised himself he would explore the connection between go-karts and Islam's holiest cities at the first opportune moment.

"Meanwhile," Dr. Bargouthi continued, "Westerners argue that much of Islam has been corrupted because of the controls placed on it in the period between the revelation of Mohammed's visions to when the words of Allah were written down, potentially over hundreds of years later, much like the Bible, some suspect. And for those whom the Quran was not enough, Sunni Muslims adhere to the sayings of Mohammed, so-called the Hadith. This is rejected by Shia Muslims as they believe these further rules and regulations a bit too convenient and did not wish to abide by the dictates of what they believed were more politically than religiously based guidance."

"But you asked about Baghdad, and how it, as a political power, could have potentially housed religious treasures. Before its annihilation in 1258 at the hands of the Khans, Baghdad was beyond opulent."

"Baghdad was founded in the 700s, not long after the arrival of Islam in the 600s. The caliphate moved to Baghdad from Damascus, where the Islamic Empire was ruled by the Umayyads. These Umayyads oversaw the development of the Islamic schism between the Sunni and Shia, with the heart of the Shia world remaining in southern Iraq.

"The founder of Baghdad, Caliph Abu Jaffar al-Mansur, wanted a geometrically and spiritually perfect city, perhaps to reunite the two sects. He built it on the banks of the Tigris and brought in thousands of architects, blacksmiths, carpenters, and laborers from all over the territory he had wrestled from the Umayyads. He built a city in the shape of a circle, two kilometers across. In the center of the study stood the Great Mosque and the Golden Gate Palace. Also, according to a number of accounts, the Round City contained *Beit al-Hikma [House of Wisdom],* one of the greatest libraries and storehouses of literature in the world.

"The exterior perimeter walls were reportedly thirty meters high and forty-four meters thick at the base. This was one of the most impregnable structures in the then known world. These were some of the most remarkable buildings on the planet and invited scholars from all over to study and worship. This Great Mosque fell into disrepair over the centuries due to wars and to the elements, but portions of it were standing up until the 1258 sacking of Baghdad.

"In this circular city, two streets intersected and connected to spectacular gates named after great cities of the world, Damascus—due West; Kufa—due South; Basra—due Southeast; and Khorasan, due East, in Iran, and opening the gateway to all the *stans* and lands to the east."

Dr. Bargouthi stood up suddenly, and placing his thumb and forefinger on his face went behind his desk to a bookshelf. He muttered to himself and then exclaimed, "Here it is." He brought back to his seat a large atlas, turning the pages until he found a map dedicated to Iraq and its neighbors. He pointed slightly north of the marker for Baghdad, saying, "Most scholars believe the Round City to have been here." He spun the book around so Haley and Cooper could follow.

Though the map was in Arabic, Cooper traced with her finger a line due west to Damascus then due south to the city of Kufa. Haley placed his finger on Basra and asked, moving his finger to the east, "I suppose Khorasan is the old name for Iran?"

"Yes. And, I'm telling you this because Baghdad was designed as a wheel to be the hub, or center of the world, reaching out in trade and spiritual guidance to the then known important cities. I don't know if you care for symbolism, but it's incumbent on you to know why this city mattered and why its loss in 1258 is still felt to this day, nearly some

800 years later. One might argue that this is when Islam united with the sword, as the faith had to fight for its own survival. In one fell swoop, the Islamic world lost its political, spiritual, and financial center, at a time of devastating marauding from the east and European crusades from the west."

"Yes. Given Baghdad's location in the center of the world, and its Islamic religious and historical credentials, of course it could have contained manuscripts and early Islamic writings, certainly in the *Beit al-Hikma*. It would have contained great storehouses and libraries of scriptural treasures. No telling what would have survived the Mongol attacks. Very likely that some of the palimpsests did, though. And could easily have been smuggled down the Tigris. I hope to Allah they were because so much of our identity as a people was deleted and erased by the Mongols," he concluded.

Cooper gave Haley a "we have the coolest jobs in the world look" after they thanked and bid Dr. Bargouthi his farewell.

Chapter 23

Qom, Iran.

Through one of many burner phones kept by Dr. Al-Onezi, Ali al-Sadr ordered him to travel to Tehran and help with the clinical arrangements for Abdullah al-Otaybi and Ali al-Qahtani. Al-Onezi did not know the extent of their injuries but understood they had been involved in an accident and needed undetermined medical care, and in the case of al-Qahtani, cosmetic surgery. Al-Onezi tried to explain that as an *in vitro* fertilization expert, he was of no discernible use to the young men. Al-Sadr ignored his entreaties, however, and told him that he sought his help in making any needed arrangements and that funding would be provided in his Iranian bank account to facilitate any such arrangement with Iranian medical or government officials.

Notwithstanding, al-Onezi still did not know how he might assist. His *Farsi [Persian]* language skills were rudimentary at best. Obediently, however, per instructions from al-Sadr, he punched the name of Dr. Hashem Esfahani's plastic surgery clinic eponymously named Esfahani Clinic into his Snapp application on his Chinese made cellular phone. Per his car service application, he noticed on his screen scrawled in Farsi that the Esfahani Clinic was two blocks from the Tehran Royal Medical Center, near the intersection of *Valiasr* and *Valenizhad* Streets. He checked the address a few times as he did not trust his linguistic skills. He lamented his time in Jordan and his access to much more convenient and secure American technology, which operated in English, a language al-Onezi found more familiar given his training and boarding under the U.S. Medical Licensure Exam.

He felt troubled by leaving his charge, Mohammed, behind in Qom but knew the boy had plenty of religious scholars looking out for him. He only anticipated an absence of a day or so, which further mitigated his anxiety about separating from the child. He launched the application to call his car service and begin his brief ride to Tehran.

***

Tehran, Iran.

The hour-and-a-half ride to Tehran gave al-Onezi time to reflect on his personal grief in losing a wife and a son to both the Saddam Hussein regime and to the American "liberators" of his country. He resented the American notion of having to save Iraq from itself, though equally harbored hate for Saddam Hussein for bringing about the destruction of his beloved country through a senseless war with Iran and subsequent invasion of Iraq's erstwhile 19th Province of Kuwait. Al-Onezi didn't really care about the politics of these countries. He wanted his family back. And now, he had a son again. Though conceived in deceit, a secret he had to safeguard from Ali al-Sadr, he loved the boy and would protect him with his life. Yet, they both were trapped in a foreign land, at the beck and call of overlords who desired grander schemes for the boy, namely to present to the world a cloned or incarnated and returned from spiritual absence, *Mehdi* [Messiah].

His Snapp driver entered the city and tried to point out heritage landmarks for his passenger. Al-Onezi couldn't understand him and didn't care to break through the language barrier. He stared out the car window, hating Tehran. He noted the boring brownness of the city and its drab governmental edifices, also in dated 1970s-era practicality, countered by the plethora of colorful Shia mosques and kebab houses. Everything looked cheap and superficial.

Reflecting on his adopted home in Amman, which showed the wear and tear of hosting more refugees than it could bear, the bedraggled Jordanian capital seemed to take more pride in architecture and city layout. "These Mullahs here in Iran only think of prayer and dominating Arab capitals," al-Onezi murmured.

He was also disgusted by the hypocrisy surrounding him. Women were brutally punished for immodest attire, yet the city of Tehran was replete with fashion houses. "Did the Iranians wish to eradicate or emulate the West?" he groaned bitterly. In addition, he wondered at the dichotomy of Tehran being the nose job capital of the world. Given the rather large genetic endowments of noses Iranians enjoyed, he wasn't surprised at the numbers of rhinoplasties offered in Tehran, but he marveled at the contradiction of vanity and modesty: "Women were allowed to be beautiful," he mused, "but just not seen."

The masses, they seemed to him, couldn't withstand the oppression of the ruling theocracy, but the women certainly didn't mind expressing some rebellion in augmenting God's creation. Al-Onezi recalled that the former Ayatollah Ruhollah Khomeini issued a *fatwa [religious ruling]* permitting cosmetic surgery on women provided their care was performed by a woman. That seemed to open the floodgates, and Iranian women now sought out nose reductions at seven times the rate of Americans. They also seemed to favor the improvements further hidden from public view, with record numbers of women seeking breast augmentations. Al-Onezi scoffed at how the progeny of the greatest empires in history were reduced to the current religious rabble and their narrow and inconsistent interpretations of Islam. These iconoclasts established themselves as the bulwark, equally against both the spread of evil western liberalism and malevolent Saudi strains of extremist wahhabi Islam, yet all they produced were edicts on body sculpting, women not being allowed to spectate at soccer matches, and what type of music could be enjoyed.

It would have been comical, he thought, if not so dangerous. He recalled the trauma his uncle experienced in the 1980–88 Iraq-Iran war, in which he heard Ayatollah Khomeini inspired his revolutionaries to fight in their Holy War by giving young boys plastic keys, ironically made in China, to signify their deaths as minesweepers would usher them directly to paradise. His uncle, who led an Iraqi infantry company during that brutal war, kept a pair of those keys as war trophies, until he himself was killed during Saddam Hussein's brutal stamp down on a Shia uprising in southern Iraq.

Al-Onezi bitterly swore, wishing he and his son were anywhere else in the world.

***

Esfahani Clinic, Near Royal Medical Center, Downtown Tehran, Iran.

Al-Onezi arrived at the Esfahani Clinic. With no introductions, an expectant but wholly disinterested receptionist ushered him to the small operating theater, which he noted appeared to be sterile but ill equipped and outdated. Like the outside and facades of buildings, even the walls of the clinic seemed dusty and brown. The room was festooned with glamor poses by models, all of whom seemed to sport cute, upturned noses, and catfish style lips popular among patrons of cosmetic surgery. An oversized, grainy television was mounted shoddily to the wall with an extension arm, presumably so Dr. Esfahani or his staff could monitor surgeries on the screen.

Lying on the surgical bed was a surly Ali al-Qahtani. Seated uncomfortably in a corner on a wooden chair was his partner in crime, Abdullah al-Otaybi. Al-Onezi recognized the young men but didn't know them well, as both worked primarily through either their proxy—

and now quite deceased—Mohammed Abdullah al-Qahtani or the very much alive and in control Ali al-Sadr.

Seeing the young man recalled to al-Onezi the elder's demise, only a few months prior. They were at the Kaaba, in Mecca, Saudi Arabia, when an unknown assassin's bullet ripped through the elderly man's torso. The ensuing chaos and stampede allowed al-Onezi to sweep his son Mohammed into his arms and slip out of the holy site, which was revered in commemoration of the Muslim, Christian, and Jewish prophet Abraham and his eldest born and Islamically venerated prophet, Ishmael.

Al-Qahtani, the younger, was in no mood for reflection. He clearly was in discomfort. His face was wrapped in bandages, but his right eye remained open and intense with tears and what appeared to be a mix of rage and pain. A doctor unwrapping the gauze, looked up briefly, making an indistinct gesture toward al-Onezi, who interpreted this to be an invitation to sit down on one of the a black, rolling stools.

"How are you, Ali?" al-Onezi asked, while acknowledging Abdullah al-Otaybi for the first time with a nod.

"I'll live, but *Aqsam billah [I swear to Allah],* he will pay." There appeared to be no need to explain who "he" was, given al-Otaybi, al-Qahtani, and al-Onezi all understood Clayton Haley was the subject of this conversation. Esfahani was either unable to follow the conversation in Arabic or simply disinterested.

"How did this even happen? How did *Ha-i-lee* do this to you?" al-Onezi asked.

"We miscalculated," muttered al-Otaybi, speaking through clenched teeth. "The *ibn sharmouta [Arabic epithet]* had a bodyguard with him onboard the boat. We planned the attack perfectly but could not account for the extra defensive measures in place."

Al-Onezi sensed a bit of bluster unbalanced this account but knew not to press issues or allay blame on two young men thwarted in attempted murder. "So what's next? Do you know why I am here and what our instructions are?"

"You are simply to pay the good doctor and help administer any follow-on treatment he prescribes," re-engaged al-Qahtani. "It may be that my mishap will require some surgery and recovery time. We will join you in Qom, and help you watch over the boy to ensure he is getting the education he needs."

Al-Onezi suddenly felt very crowded. Instead of being able to plot his and Mohammed's way out of their predicament, he now worried he would be nursing two demanding and violent patients back to health. While he pondered this, he watched Esfahani finish unwrapping the bandages from al-Qahtani. Al-Qahtani's left eye appeared destroyed and beyond rehabilitation, and it oozed blood and pus, suggesting painful inflammation. Similarly, his left cheek was swollen and infected. Stitches, antibiotics, and new beard growth would help him regain some of his old self soon. His eyes, however, were worrisome. His left eye was blinded, and his right one, and both of al-Otaybi's, would be on al-Onezi constantly.

Chapter 24

Moroni, Comoros.

Kuwaiti National Archives Director Dr. Hamad al-Marri's direct flight from Kuwait International Airport touched down without incident on one of its seventeen weekly connections to Comoros Prince Said Ibrahim International Airport. The airport was named for a former leader of the country, who attempted to balance the post-World War II growth of his country in developing relations with Saudi Arabia, France, and regional African powers. He had a special kinship and perhaps protective relationship with then Saudi Arabian King Faisal, until the Saudi king's assassination in 1975. As evidenced by the poor state of affairs in the country, the Comorian leadership had not bonded well with the right source of benevolence since then and languished under poor governance.

Al-Marri glanced at his ticket, noting the International Civil Aviation Organization designation code for the airport as FMCH. He also noticed on the overhead monitor that the airport was located in a small town of *Hahaia*, roughly a thirty-minute drive from downtown Moroni and the cascade of beach hotels on the city's corniche. As he witnessed on the video screen onboard maps on the flight, the small archipelago of islands comprising Comoros was nestled in the Indian Ocean between Mozambique and Madagascar.

This was al-Marri's first visit to Comoros, but he knew it to be a popular destination for a number of his countrymen. He proudly stayed out of political and financial intrigues but was aware wealthy investors from around the region frequently connected here in questionable business activities, out from prying eyes of international banking regulators and compliance officers. In fact, he knew by accents on the plane that Syrians, Lebanese, Kuwaitis, and not a few Emiratis joined him on the flight to Moroni, largely, he suspected to move their money around the region undetected and well laundered. He also suspected that financial fealty supplanted political and tribal loyalties, believing Shia Hezbollah and Sunni Al-Qaida idealogues alike found common ground for conducting business transactions on Comorian soil.

Al-Marri, a simple curator, as he prided himself, would steer clear of political intrigue, and only provide his personal assessment of the material he studied recently to those who financed and summoned him. His interest was solely that which was found on the remains of an Iraqi corpse, identified by his compatriots as "Number 55," who lay buried in a shallow Kuwaiti grave for nearly thirty years.

***

"Hamad, sit please. Make yourself comfortable," Muhsin Bin Laden directed at al-Marri as he entered the opulent penthouse hotel room suite. They moved to plush chairs set in a majlis fashion around a coffee table. Al-Marri knew to whom he was talking. The Bin Ladens were, of course, a very famous and enormously large family. He knew not to judge the family by the actions of the unrestrained Osama, but all the same, it was a bit intimidating meeting Muhsin. Other than being tall and thin, there was not much family resemblance between Muhsin and Osama. Al-Marri had not expected it, though, given the two were only half-brothers and among more than fifty sons. Their late father, Mohammed Bin Laden, must have believed it a religious command to populate the earth, which he did with a revolving door of wives and concubines.

"Thank you, sir. It's an honor to meet you," he said as he shook hands. Then he glanced in the direction of Ali al-Sadr, "And, you sir, must be Ali al-Sadr, the gentleman who summoned me?"

"I would hardly call it a summons," responded al-Sadr with a smile, adding, "Just an invitation. You are most welcome here in Comoros. My friend and benefactor Mr. Bin Laden and I find these islands conveniently 'off grid' and easy to conduct sensitive business matters."

"I can appreciate that but must state first off I am not accustomed to being ordered to travel to another country for such business matters. But more importantly, I am not at all comfortable with my role in removing archives from professional study. And I do not like being questioned by the American Embassy," complained al-Marri.

Both Bin Laden and al-Sadr flinched at this. "Who did you speak to and what did you say?" Bin Laden demanded.

"Two young men," he said, retrieving from his pocket business cards. "One Jason Johnson, a curator with the Smithsonian Institute and Clayton Haley, a political officer at the U.S. Embassy in Kuwait," he added, reading from their cards.

"Under no circumstances are you to talk to either of them again," Bin Laden ordered, his voice sinisterly low. "Ali, I need you to find out who this Jason Johnson is, and please, don't fail me again regarding Haley's demise. I don't care how messy it has to be. As soon as the boys are healthy, send them back in to finish the job."

Al-Sadr nodded.

"I told them nothing," al-Marri fibbed and then abruptly changed the subject to more relevant concerns regarding his role, trying to remove himself from what clearly was a murder plot. "The material you had me take needs to be studied in the confines of a proper laboratory, like the one I have at the Kuwaiti Museum. The more movement it suffers, the more potential damage it faces," said al-Marri.

"I am willing to take this risk," interjected Bin Laden. "You brought the material with you, correct?"

"Photocopies," al-Marri replied. "As you instructed, I removed the document from the museum and secured it at my villa. No one can find it there. As you may or may not know, an effort led over the past few months by the Red Cross resulted in the recovery of some fifty-five mortal remains of Iraqis who invaded my country in 1990. They were killed by the Americans and then buried in shallow graves by Saudi mortuary affairs units until they could be repatriated to Iraq. Saddam Hussein declined all offers to reclaim their bodies. This is all in the Red Cross report I sent you."

"Yes. We've read it," al-Sadr chimed in. Tell me about the so-called number fifty-five."

"Of course. This is what was not included in the report. As you know, the remains were all enclosed in U.S. Army body bags. In the decades of cooking in the hot and humid Kuwaiti summer, the corpses . . . dissolved. There was nothing left of them but bone fragments, pieces of uniforms, and I'm sorry to be crass, a blended soup of what had once been a body. It was not at all pleasant to see," said al-Marri.

Al-Sadr remained stoic, but pressed, "Yes, but tell me about number fifty-five."

"Yes. I'm getting to that," responded al-Marri. "For most of the bodies, we'll need to compare DNA samples with family members in Iraq who placed themselves on a registry looking for lost ones from conflicts of old. Some, however, actually had identification on them, preserved in sealable plastic bags. It seems that the Saudi mortuary officials took great pains to protect papers found on the bodies. Some of these documents included drivers' licenses, military identification cards and orders, and passports. Your mysterious fifty-five was one such victim. Here, I brought copies of his material for you to review."

As he spoke, he dug through a worn leather satchel befitting a curator. He retrieved a Manila folder containing five photocopied pictures.

"Hussein Mohammed al-Sadr," al-Sadr read. He thumbed through the other pages briefly but looked up at both Bin Laden and al-Marri. "Yes. This is my cousin. This is the one dispatched by you, Muhsin for your mission," al-Sadr said with a hint of resentment, continuing, "Just as you selected me in 1979 to steal items in Medina, my cousin Hussein did his part in Kuwait eleven years later. Unfortunately, he was never heard from again."

"Not to be too insensitive," interrupted Bin Laden, shrugging toward Ali al-Sadr. "Tell me what else you found in his body bag."

"I found a carefully preserved sketch. Your cousin Hussein," al-Marri looked toward al-Sadr, while unrolling a large laminated printout, "removed an old map from the Kuwaiti archives. The only reason the Americans didn't recover it was that it was concealed, wrapped around his legs and under his trousers."

"A map?" gesticulated Bin Laden. "I dispatched him to retrieve ancient religious relics that could agitate the masses and, if possible, documents relating to the Kuwaiti financial backing of both Iran and Iraq during their 1980–88 war. I sought this to prove Kuwaiti duplicity while the war raged on. Saddam told me personally, many times, of his suspicions of this double-dealing and toward the end of the war, he asked for my assistance in uncovering proof that he could show to the world how this tiny emirate deserved to be absorbed back into Iraq. It was part of his plan to restore Iraq's greatness. He really believed himself a reincarnated king of old, but as history proved, he sorely miscalculated the Americans and their ridiculous love of what they call the 'underdog.' My half-brother made the same mistake. So did our revered Messiah Mohammed al-Qahtani. All paid with their lives. I'll be more careful moving forward," uttered Bin Laden in a rare and snide monologue. "Show me this map and help me understand how he failed in his mission," he continued.

Al-Sadr slid the map photocopy he had been staring at across the coffee table to Bin Laden. He also showed him what looked to be an ancient cast iron key.

"What is this? It's just a circle next to a river! It could be anywhere! Why was he carrying this?" asked an incredulous Bin Laden, apparently still angry at the perceived failure of his late emissary some thirty years later. "This is worthless."

Al-Sadr shrugged his shoulders.

Al-Marri posited, "I would hardly deem this worthless. We can't know how he knew where to look for this or how he knew its value, but our dear departed Hussein understood that he carried a treasure, perhaps more valuable than he could have ever guessed."

"What are you talking about?" queried Bin Laden through his teeth.

"You brought me into this because of my expertise. Though you did not allow me the proper time to study the parchment upon which the map is drawn, I can tell you that I have studied many such papers, and I believe this map, or at least the material upon which it is sketched, may be nearly one thousand years old. And this key also bears intense study. I'm convinced it's medieval."

"Again, so what? We have a rusty key and a map that looks like a wheel next to a river with some indecipherable Arabic text, perhaps some unknown tomb?" a growingly exasperated Bin Laden said, while studying the photocopy. "How can this be valuable or important?"

It was al-Marri's turn to become annoyed. "Again, you should have let me properly study this paper. Now that you've required me to steal it, I won't be able to. And I certainly won't be able to publish any findings about it. Just how many cities have you ever heard of that were perfectly round?" he snapped sarcastically and rhetorically.

"This was, of course, the famed 'Round City of Baghdad' before it was destroyed by the Khans in the thirteenth century. And this is important because it was part of our national archives that were stolen by Iraqi looters," chastised al-Marri, this time with an accusative glare at al-Sadr, who happened to be both Iraqi and Shia—two counts against him in al-Marri's book.

Al-Sadr appeared unbothered.

Then, seeing that Bin Laden was losing interest, al-Marri said, "And it's important because it was in our secret vault of our most highly treasured archives. This is no simple map and key. As curator of the museum, I, along with only a handful of senior officials, am privy to the items that were in this vault. This was our equivalent to the Americans' Area 51," he paused for effect.

"Only five living people have knowledge of and access to this inventory list. As curator of the museum, I have always known what your countrymen stole from us," he said looking at an indifferent al-Sadr. "This is proof that, potentially, some remnants of the legendary 'Beit al-Hikmah' remain. And according to the file code under which this map was stored, it was the property of one of the few survivors of the siege of Baghdad in 1258. The man's name was unknown, but according to secret files I perused in the late eighties, he seemingly escaped the devastation of the siege and managed to salvage or otherwise rescue some stored treasures, perhaps early Islamic writings or other scholarly works. The supposition is that he secreted the material somewhere in Baghdad and then fled to the south and safety, while leaving the great city to its new masters."

Bin Laden, clearly intrigued by the twist, retorted, "This is interesting, and from your scholarly point of view, I imagine this is the find of the century for you, but how is this relevant to our aims of uniting the region's tribes under the banner of *Umma* [Islamic nation community] to set aside political leadership created or owned by western powers?"

"Sir, with respect, that is up to you, the silent Mr. al-Sadr," replied al-Marri gesturing at al-Sadr, "and your agents throughout the region. I saw on the plane coming here and in the hotel lobby you already have your financial networks established, and I've seen and heard on social media and in the mosques how you have your *imams* attuned to messianic messaging. Now, it would seem, you only need a catalyst. I've seen the YouTube clips of the aborted introduction to the world of the young boy, Mohammed. I suppose you were behind that? No matter. It seems you have a Messiah at the ready. So what would spark the revolution you have lined up?" Again, he paused for effect.

"There is no telling what our ancient friend may have saved from the Khans, but we've seen time and again the rise of challenges to our faith. We, especially the Saudis, have been adept at squelching or otherwise silencing this. It's no coincidence that we described pre-Islamic history as the era of ignorance. You and I both know that this *'jahaliyyah'* is not meant to describe the people of that era; it is meant to describe our modern day cognizant choice to remain ignorant about our faith's origins. In fact, as recently as the seventies, German historians sought to disprove the foundations of our faith by claiming the Quran was essentially written before our prophet's revelations. I would suggest that if there are *Beit al-Hikma* treasures that survived, ones that shed doubt on traditionally held Islamic chronology, perhaps we invite more Western scrutiny and publication of them. In so doing, we unfetter the organic uprisings against them and their puppet rulers over our region," concluded al-Marri.

Bin Laden looked at al-Sadr. "I want you to provide our new friend whatever he needs to see what we might do to restore *Beit al-Hikmah* to its glory. Perhaps we may find treasures that will inspire the masses to return to the true Islam."

Chapter 25

U.S. Embassy Kuwait, Kuwait City.

"Thanks so much for having me come along in your meeting with Dr. Bargouthi," said Cooper while taking her seat in the small embassy cafeteria.

"Well, technically, university professors tend to be public affairs contacts, so I should be thanking you," replied Haley, pulling two neatly wrapped shawarma sandwiches from a paper bag. He passed one to Cooper. He had wanted to dine outside the embassy with her but thought it a bit awkward to go on a "date" while Herman, the embassy driver, and their ministry of interior minder, waited for them. Instead, he had the kindly driver swing by one of several favorite shawarma stands. Haley and Cooper both tried to impress each other with their Arabic while ordering their sandwiches but embarrassingly learned the vender was actually Indian and spoke little Arabic beyond basic greetings. They simply made their purchases in quiet, with Haley insisting on buying an extra one for Herman, and made their way back to the embassy.

"Well," Cooper continued, with more than a little flirt, "you still owe me some scoop on why you're so famous."

"I'd be happy to talk about my first two botched assignments at some point," Haley said, clearly evincing discomfort. "But can we pull our thoughts together on today's discussion first?"

Cooper sensed she had touched a nerve and adjusted her demeanor, "I'm sorry. I didn't mean to be inconsiderate. While I am interested in your backstory, I also realized that you've had some unpleasant experiences. I don't mean to pry."

"No, no. That's okay," Haley quickly and sincerely replied. "It would be nice to talk to someone about what happened. I just have no idea where to begin, and it will take a while."

Cooper, reading him, replied, "Let me suggest we start today and work backwards. If or when you're ready for a deeper dive, let me know? And, stop hogging the tabouli," she flirted again, eyes smiling. "And tell me what the deal is with these *plimsy* thingees."

Haley wished Edger was there so he didn't have to try to sound convincing. "These *palimpsests* are ancient manuscripts that contain what many believe are original Quranic writings. The problem is, some scientists from the 70s believe these documents were recycled, with even older, pre-Mohammed Quranic writings on them that were later rubbed out."

"Wait. You said pre-Mohammed Quranic writings? Do you know what you're saying? Islam is based on the singular belief that the Quran was revealed to Mohammed in its entirety. That would undermine one of the key elements of Islamic belief! This kind of thing would shock the Muslim world to its core," exclaimed Cooper.

"No doubt, but evidence exists this is the case. It's just that scrutiny of this evidence was shut down, maybe because it might have been very inconvenient to the masses of folks whose faith is interpreted for them by Imams. You'll often hear the broad explanation that the time before Islam was simply labeled *jahaliyyah*, or era of ignorance," explained Haley.

That's quite convenient," quipped Cooper. "But why does this matter and what is the U.S. government's interest in this? Why not leave well enough alone?"

"I sure wish I could leave this alone. I wish I'd never heard of Mohammed al-Qahtani, some nut job who wanted to be a Messiah and start a religious revolution. Hardliners like this guy have no value for human life and certainly don't mind offering up their co-religionists as martyrs so they might achieve their ends. I feel an obligation to pull on this palimpsest thread because this is the kind of thing that could be easily exploited. And the folks who exploit religious beliefs are dangerous people. I have some first-hand experience with this," he noted, subconsciously rubbing his left arm.

"Ummm. You have a tabouli smile," Cooper smiled at him while tapping her tooth with her finger.

Haley smiled back, further exposing a large piece of parsley caught in one of his front teeth. Growing up, his mother used parsley as only a garnish, but Haley found the Lebanese and others in the Levant used the herb, along with tomatoes, onions, bulgar, lemon juice, and olive oil, as a key ingredient in this delectable and mainstay salad. "Maybe I should use parsley more sparsely," he said in an utterly failed attempt at humor.

"It's your jokes that need cutting, not your herbs," Cooper quipped, while Haley squeaked his teeth clean with a napkin.

"Plus," Haley added, reverting to his earlier thought, "I find eschatology interesting."

"Escha what?"

"Eschatology. You know. End times prophecies. Growing up in the buckle of the Bible Belt, I heard my whole life about how Jesus was coming back any second, the saints would be raptured, the thousand years (or is it seven?) of tribulation would take place, the anti-Christ would appear, Israel would be saved, death and destruction to all non-believers, you know, judgment day. Lots of folks are obsessed with this, and there are whole series of faith-based books prognosticating the exact timing for the end of the world. Of course, every few years, the same folks have to retool their prophetic predictions. My dad preached a simpler message: Live every minute anticipating Christ's imminent return, but don't be afraid to make long-term plans."

"I can't help but wonder why so many folks are in a hurry for eternity." Haley continued, enjoying talking to Cooper. "I also find it interesting that other faiths have similar beliefs. I read somewhere that Mohammed's tomb in Medina, Saudi Arabia contains his body and that of two of his followers but also has an extra room for Jesus for his return. It doesn't make sense to me they believe Jesus would come back only to die and be buried. I'm not sure how that works. I'm only a novice at comparative religions," went on Haley.

"Xxxxxcccckkk," sounded a vivid and gross throat clearing nearby. "Clayton. What's all this nonsense about *escha-whoosits?*" accused Glennon who had listened in on the tail end of the conversation. He sat down without being invited and placed his plate of *saag paneer* on the table, an Indian dish made regularly at the embassy cafeteria. Haley hadn't tried it yet, as he found the bright green spinach and cheese mix could only be described as a Dr. Seuss-esque *oobleck.*

"Oh, you know, end of times religious fervor," remarked Haley.

Glennon rolled his eyes. "Not this nonsense again. Don't you have better things to work on?"

"Yep. I have a cable draft for you on the latest round of parliamentary interpellations of the prime minister. I entitled it, 'National Assembly Grilling, More Fizzle than Sizzle,'" Haley smugly said, while smiling at Cooper. Glennon sniffed again and then launched into an oblivious and lengthy diatribe on cables he wrote in previous postings, believing that both Haley and Cooper were impressed.

Both knew their first proper date had come to an end.

***

"Nasser, would you please scour the press and let me know if you track any odd trends about tribal unrest or discontent with regional governments? And on a hunch, might I ask that you also explore social media as well to see if folks are generating any online buzz about false messiahs?" asked Haley of Khalil back in his office suite once lunch concluded.

"You will have *pyu-ti-ful rebort* in the morning, but *blease*, no more digging in the desert. You can't leave me with Don Glennon anymore. He makes strange noises in his nose in front of my Kuwaiti friends. You must stay with me. I'll find you another messiah," implored Khalil, with a mischievous smile.

***

True to his word, the next day, by 8:30 a.m., Khalil had emailed him the following daily news summary.

- *National Guard Units Strike for Extra Pay, Benefits (Al-Watan—Saudi Arabia):* In a rare sign of discontent, members of several Saudi National Guard Units protested low pay and benefits. Ringleaders were rounded up by local police and Ministry of Interior forces.
- *Friday Prayers Announce Mehdi has returned from Ghaibah (El-Ghad—Egypt): Imams* report the arrival of the Mehdi, having returned from years of absence. Sightings still unconfirmed.
- *Sunni Tribes Push Regime Forces to the Outskirts of Idlib (Al-Thawra—Syria):* In a rare show of cooperation, tribes in Syria launched an offensive in Idlib that pressed Syrian President Bashar al-Assad's forces to the outskirts of the city. Meanwhile, Iran's Islamic Revolutionary Guard Corps moved troops into the city under the cover of Russian air support.
- *Vanity is Skin Deep (Al-Ittihad—United Arab Emirates):* Social media reports Iran now has the highest numbers of nose jobs per capita in the world, replacing the United States. Despite

tense relations between the UAE and Iran, Emiratis, both male and female flock to Tehran clinics for custom-made surgeries.

- *Gathering of Imams in Comoros Raises Questions about Connections to Illicit Finance (MEMRI—Israel):* A confab of Islamic scholars in Comoros raises questions about financing schemes among wealthy Arab supporters of Hezbollah and Al-Qaeda.
- *Potential Mehdi in Waiting Excels at Holy Quran Recitation (Ettela'at—Iran):* A young boy, Mohammed, seven years old, recites the entirety of the Quran in Arabic. Qom scholars rejoice and openly speculate he may be the long awaited Mehdi.

Khalil also included a sundry of loosely translated social media clippings he scoured from the Internet:

Social Media

#ALRASHEEDSUDANI: Long have our tribes been divided and allowed the illegitimate oil barons of the House of Saood [sic] control our wealth and holy sites. #FREEMECCANOW.

#QOMYOMALIQAMA: Qom update: Young Mohammed shows piety, recites the Holy Quran in perfect Quraishi Arabic. Allah the most Merciful save and protect him. Is the Mehdi returned from Ghaibah?

#ALOTAYBIALASHEERA: Son of Grand Mosque martyr betrays family in swearing allegiance to Saudi National Guard. He shames the legacy of his father and grandfathers, both martyred by BeitSaud.

#FOLLOW$ALIRHAB: Hezbollah and Al-Qaeda funding sources converge on small East African archipelago. How can diametrically opposed ideologies share funding streams? What is the role of Gulf financiers in Dubai and Riyadh?

#KUW-ARSHEEF: Iraq has held our Kuwaiti martyrs and our archives too long. Return them now. What are you hiding?

Part VI

Chapter 26

U.S. Embassy Kuwait, Kuwait City, Two months later.

Cooper had been busy working on a series of events with the commercial section promoting Discover America Week highlighting U.S. imports into Kuwait, so Haley hadn't been able to follow up on another date. Plus, he didn't want to formalize the relationship in official terms, such as date, relationship, or couple, so as not to grab attention from rubbernecking embassy colleagues. He gave her space but tried to conveniently run into her in the cafeteria from time to time. She seemed genuinely glad to see him on those occasions, but with other colleagues lurking about, the two didn't seem to connect. He noticed her long hair had changed tint a little, and she now looked especially vibrant with new blonder streaks.

Things were quiet on the Edger and Philson fronts as well. He sent a few emails and some WhatsApp messages to both but received no reply. The embassy Haley minders, including the security office, Glennon, the deputy chief of mission, and the ambassador, all seemed to relax standards as well, even allowing Haley to go out to meetings on his own sans interior ministry security details. Even the ever-lurking spectral presence of al-Otaybi and the cycloptic al-Qahtani seemed distant. For the first time in over two and a half years, Haley relaxed. He would have taken a deep breath but found Kuwaiti air too humid and dust-filled, so he knew better than to inhale too deeply unless in filtered air conditioning.

Even work with Khalil had become routine. He enjoyed partnering with his self-appointed elder statesman. He was just as impetuous as ever and condescended other embassy employees he believed weren't as important or didn't work as hard. He clearly believed his work, and his work alone, shaped the dispensing of policy power of the United States in a way that benefited the people of Kuwait, including the majority of the population comprised by third-country nationals. Khalil was a proud Palestinian and regularly regaled Haley with distant memories of his childhood in *Khalil*, known biblically and currently in Israel as Hebron. His family had been among the population forced out "to make room for the Europeans and Ethiopians," according to Khalil, and as such, found refuge in Jordan. He carried a Jordanian passport but claimed an impossible Palestinian citizenship.

Haley enjoyed hearing his accounts and always listened attentively. He marveled at how Khalil equally blamed Israelis, Americans, those he characterized as corrupt Arabs, "Gulfis," and others who dabbled in Middle East politics. He wasn't resentful or bitter, though, just highly opinionated, thought Haley. His teaming with Khalil brought back many fond memories he had of Ibrahim Mustafa, who from Haley's recollection was much more rational and less of a "big personality." The two enjoyed lunch stops at a new favorite restaurant, a family style Lebanese joint across from the bulbous twin towers, and Haley was honored to have Khalil's oldest son Yousuf join once or twice as well.

Khalil remained surly in the workplace, however, as his disposition was set at a cantankerous default, but Haley learned to appreciate the gentleman's passion for his work and that he stayed on top of the Kuwaiti political and tribal scene. As a consequence, they were able to put out a number of useful cables about the roles tribes played in maintaining a balance of power in the Kuwaiti National Assembly among the liberals, *hadhar [civilized]*, Bedouin, conservatives, and ultra conservatives. Haley found his interviews with the Muslim Brotherhood and Salafi MPs the most interesting, as it reminded him of politics back in Walhalla, where folks there also worried about the evils of rock and roll music, immodest attire, school dances, alcohol, and so on. Haley recalled how some of his favorite jokes back home played nicely in his new surroundings:

Question: You know why Southern Baptists oppose premarital sex?

Answer: They're afraid it might lead to dancing.

-Or-

Question: Do you know how to tell the difference between a Southern Baptist and an Episcopalian?

Answer: *"Whiskey-palians"* will wave to you at the liquor store.

He swapped out Southern Baptists with Muslim Brotherhood or Salafi in retelling the joke at several of the more liberal, progressive diwaniyas and always got a resounding laugh. Perhaps it wasn't fitting for him to make light of either belief, but it helped him connect to the local denizens and gave him a real appreciation for their efforts to build a faith and family first society, and he genuinely respected the wholesome environment in which Kuwaitis and Muslims writ large raised their children. It saddened him to reflect on drug use, underage drinking, teenage pregnancies, and other potential destroyers prevalent back in his hometown. It also made him value and appreciate even more the faith environment in which his parents raised him and his siblings. He recalled having to depend heavily on Providence recently, while enduring torture and what he believed was imminent and painful death.

During this moment of reflection, Haley decided to follow up on a nagging question regarding the repatriation of the Iraqi remains. Al-

Marri's previous nonchalant quip that the item buried with the fifty-fifth corpse was stolen bothered him. While sitting at his desk, he called Luc Marc Chapelle at the ICRC who confirmed the disappearance but believed it more of a bureaucratic error and that "it would show up." He was nonplussed by the matter, saying, "everything was handled by the Kuwaiti and Iraqi forensic specialists. I'm sure they have full accountability for this and it's likely sitting on someone's desk awaiting further study. Besides," he added, "we have a copy of it. I think it's some antiquated map, perhaps of old Kuwait City, demarcating the original city walls. As you know, Kuwait is built on concentric circles. It seems to be an engineering plan for drainage or something. Nothing of significance, just an old sketch wrapped around a very old key," he dismissed.

"Might I get a copy of the sketch?" asked Haley, miffed reports of the theft of the document had not been circulated to various parties.

"Sure," Chapelle replied, "I'll email you a version later today, once I get to my office."

***

Two hours later.

Haley chastened his mind for thinking more of this than was due. Chapelle was probably right. The dead guy in grave number fifty-five was probably some looter lucky to have grabbed a souvenir from the national archives and unlucky enough to pick up a useless civil engineering or sewage map to the city. Still, he wanted to see for himself just what might have cost the man his life, courtesy of U.S. Air Force Warthog or other aircraft that strafed retreating Iraqi looters on the Highway of Death.

He was away from his desk, grabbing a hurried coffee with Cooper, who had instant messaged him to see if he had a moment. Grateful for a reason to fend off conspiracy notions, he hustled down to the cafeteria to see her.

"Whatcha up to?" she asked, grabbing a hot drink so full of whipped cream, milk, sugar, and various trendy flavors, Haley imagined it no longer matched the definition of coffee.

"Same ole, same ole," he responded, grabbing his black, no sugar Americano, somehow feeling just a bit more superior and patriotic by doing so. He sensed something off with Cooper.

"I've been busy lately and putting in long hours with our media promotion work and thought it good to maybe touch base. I've missed hanging out with you. Remember, you promised that when the time was right, you'd help me understand what you've gone through," she said.

"Sure. I'd like that. I don't think that can happen here at the embassy, though, with Glennon skulking around or my green eyes being constantly summoned by Nasser Khalil. Mmmm. Would you be open to . . . maybe having dinner?" Haley asked, embarrassed that having experienced combat, personal injury, torture, and threat of death, he found asking this simple question terrifying.

Haley flinched while Cooper paused.

"It's about time, Clayton. I thought maybe you had lost interest and would never invite me to dinner," she said quietly, and she too seemed nervous. She had really pretty eyes, and they smiled warmly, Haley noticed.

"No. I haven't lost interest. I just wasn't very hungry," he quipped, regaining his courage and this time landing a bit of humor. "And if you like good, blue collar Lebanese food at affordable Palestinian prices, I'd be happy to take you to my new favorite haunt. Tomorrow night?"

"It's a date. I'll meet you there at 7:00?" her eyes smiled again.

On the way back to his desk, Haley found it difficult to focus. He forgot what he had been working on and for that matter, wasn't sure if he had appointments he was missing. Glennon barked at him as he walked by his office, "Clayton, please ask Khalil to get me an appointment with the foreign ministry American Affairs director for tomorrow? I lost his number."

"Sure thing. I'll ask him right away," he replied, assuming the task sourced from Glennon simply not wanting to speak to Khalil himself.

He sat at his desk, called Khalil with the request, and opened his email. Buried in his inbox was a note from Chapelle with an attachment. The note itself only read:

"Clayton, as requested, please see a copy of the map sent over by the forensics team. You'll see it's a crude drawing of what I suspect was downtown Kuwait about a hundred years ago. Based on the identification papers found in the body bag, our deceased was someone named Hussein al-Sadr. Best, LMC."

"Hmmm," thought Haley. He was painfully acquainted with an Ali al-Sadr, remembering back to Aziziyah, Iraq and subconsciously massaging his left arm. Even in his world of conspiracies, he knew trying to connect the two al-Sadrs was an enormous coincidence. "Besides, there must be tens of thousands of al-Sadrs," he concluded.

Haley looked again at the screen and clicked on the attached PDF. It appeared to be a cell phone photograph of an unscrolled, crude map. It was faded in places, with some script on it impossible to read. Haley enlarged the photo so he could study it. He noticed it was indeed a circle—in fact a series of concentric circles, but oddly, they were perfect. If this was drawn by a Kuwaiti city planner, he never realized his vision as old Kuwait City walls were roughly round but never in a perfect 360 degree circle. It did appear to be a city, though, but not of much use to an engineer. It was too basic. To the east of the circle lay a river. Four equidistant marks on the circle seemed to depict gates, two in the north and two in the south. Arabic script above those gates was either illegible or just barely legible. Haley could only make out one, to the north west of the city: باب الشام or Bab al-Sham, otherwise known as Syria or Damascus Gate.

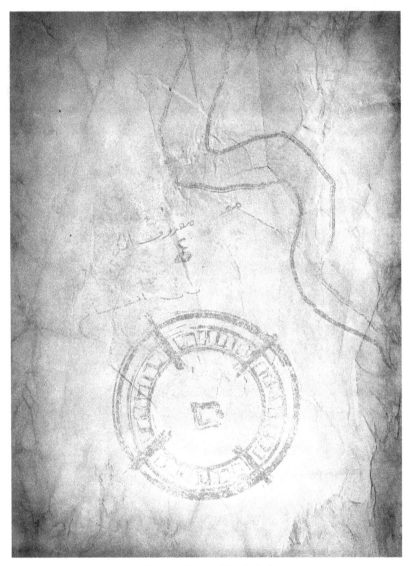

Round City of Baghdad

That again didn't rule out Kuwait because the Shat al-Arab riverway did indeed flow to the east of the city and Damascus was mostly northwest of Kuwait. But Haley knew this couldn't be Kuwait. And Kuwait had no need for gates to the south. He had heard of a perfectly round city, with concentric circles demarcated by walls and fortifications and west of a river. "That city was upstream a few hundred miles and about 800 years from here," recalled Haley. He realized he was looking at a map of the fabled Round City of Baghdad, nearly completely destroyed in 1258 and finally razed by the Ottomans in a city infrastructure rebuilding project in the 1800s. He also noted markings on the map, roughly equidistant from the city center north to the Tigris River, including incomplete words scribbled in Arabic:

مقب معروف الكر

[Mqb... Maroof al-Kar....]

He found the script very hard to read but thought he could make out the above letters. He performed a quick Google search with keywords Baghdad, round city, and house of wisdom. *M-q-b*, he knew, formed much of the root of the Arabic word for cemetery or tomb. *Maroof*, however, wasn't going to be helpful, as Haley knew this to mean simply the word "known" in English. He would need to have more information than simply a "known tomb," as he could only imagine thousands of graves and cemeteries in and around Baghdad. "Still," he thought, "why not expand the internet search to include 'known' cemeteries in Baghdad?" As he input the Arabic characters, he also opened a search for a map of Iraq.

To his utter surprise, the search in Arabic for the "known tomb" revealed a shrine dedicated to *Maroof al-Karkhi*, seemingly a saint who converted to Islam from Christianity, who was buried around 815 AD. He was also key in the development of mystic strains of Islam, which transcended both Shia and Sunni sects.

Haley reminded himself that in addition to the translation of the word "known" in English, *Maroof* was also a rare, but "known" first or family name in Arabic. Haley clicked on the pin that popped up marking his shrine and noticed it was south and west of the Tigris River, in downtown Baghdad, and not far from the oxbow that encompassed the Green Zone and the U.S. Embassy. In fact, as he explored the city map, just south of the expansive *Maroof* cemetery, he noticed a perfect circle, marked on the website simply as "Grand Mosque," which apparently was under construction. It was clearly an enormous undertaking and Haley could make out in the satellite photo building cranes of the type used for high rises and skyscrapers. He mentally overlaid the map he received from Chapelle on the screenshot and was convinced that he was looking at the same image, removed by nearly 800 years. The Grand Mosque site's perfect circumference must be the same location as the center of the Round City. And nearly equidistant north to the Tigris River was the *Maroof* Cemetery.

"What did this mean?" he wondered, while pushing CTRL and the Print button on his keyboard to keep copies of both maps.

***

Haley also checked his secure email account to see if he had any traffic or need to follow up on messages at higher levels. "When it rains it pours," he snickered to himself as he saw an invitation from Wilson Edger for him to join a videoconference the following day. Parties were expected to dial in via secure phone or video channels. There was no agenda, but the title of the conference was listed as "Latest Middle East Regional Tribal Rumblings." It sounded very interesting. There were approximately twenty names on the invitation list across the U.S. government interagency, and Haley was delighted to see a few Department of Defense names he recognized, including Philson and Reims. The conference would take place tomorrow, he noted at 5:00 p.m., local time. If it finished at 6:15 or so, he clocked, he would have just enough time to meet Cooper at the restaurant.

Chapter 27

Conference Room, U.S. Embassy Kuwait, Kuwait City. The next day.

Haley had participated in a number of videoconferences but always as a backbencher, or note taker, never as a principal participant. It made him nervous to think he might need to speak up to a crowd of faces on multiple screens on a television. Also, the blurry images and sound delays often proved distracting. He felt relieved he wouldn't be expected to speak, but just in case, he thought it wise to draw up a rough outline of issues that had impacted his life since he joined the department.

He hastily scribbled down some memory joggers and then recalling an interview he had with the ambassador in Baghdad, decided he better type out his thoughts so he wouldn't have to depend on his scrawly penmanship.

He jotted in large, 14-font notes key names, issues, and some chronologies he thought might be useful to recall if needed:

- *Mohammed Abdullah al-Qahtani—visa applicant, would-be Messiah, killed by Saudi Spec Forces last year. Did all conspiracies die with him? Who was the kid and the man at the Kaaba with him? Incomplete recordings from that day suggested the kid was a clone?*

- Juhayman al-Otaybi—henchman, ringleader of siege in 1979, beheaded, his father executed by the Saudis. His son now in Saudi National Guard, grandson—Abdullah Mohammed al-Otaybi, hooked by Philson

- Abdullah Mohammed al-Otaybi and Ali Mehdi al-Qahtani—visa applicants, and relatives of above. Likely murderers of Dr. Ibrahim. Attackers from the boat

- Ibrahim Mustafa, ME professor Sorbonne gunned down because he suspected al-Qahtani's return from Ghaibeh, and believed the theft of Mohammed's remains in Medina tied to his father's murder

- Ali Hussein al-Sadr—possible ringleader of cloning effort. In hiding now. Whereabouts unknown. Connected to thug-Abdullah now deceased

  - Shia. Likely the guy agitating for regional tribal conflict.

  - Possibly he has a sugar daddy? Muhsin Bin Laden? Maybe he's calling the shots? He was part of the 79 siege and was never prosecuted.

- Why did cyclops and Otaybi try to kill him on the boat? Was it revenge? Complete thug's job? Or was he asking too much again?

- Mortal remains—is this connected? What's the deal with #55. Al-Sadr? Significant?

- Palimpsest (don't mention, but this issue could easily be exploited if folks wanted to turn conservative tribes against the political establishment. Apocalyptic—repeat—don't mention. This isn't fully cooked!)

Haley felt a bit more assured he might be able to coherently order his thoughts if folks on the screen asked him any questions. At least he wouldn't stumble over the names of the various miscreants who had so impacted his life. "Edger better do all the talking, though," he told himself, looking forward to getting past the call and to the dinner with Jordan.

Haley punched in the dialing codes right at 5:00 p.m. Two or three outstations were already online, as evidenced by their "Hollywood Squares"-like boxes on his screen. He didn't recognize anyone so tried to look official and disinterested at the same time, only offering a quick glance at the soulless, never blinking, and inescapable camera lens. He shuffled his notes and doodled a bit. He cleared his throat, and in panic, looked up to confirm the mute button was on the screen. Suddenly, high pitched "beee-boops" rang, signaling the entry into the conversation of several other participants, including the host. Haley noticed Edger on the screen in an official setting back in Langley, but to his delight, he also saw Philson and several of his Green Beret teammates, who instantly broke the stoic decorum:

"Waddup, Clayton!" yelled one of the soldiers who had saved his life seconds before he was to be executed on the outskirts of Aziziyah, Iraq. His name was Nimrod, named after the legendary and ancient warrior ruler. He was especially full of himself once he found out his faux namesake's origin was Iraq, where he had served in multiple combat tours. His teammates mischievously insisted, however, on inserting the second person pronoun in front of his name, as in "you Nimrod." Haley also recognized Doc, Tank, Dad, Spook, Chip, and Joseph Smith. Modern day Vikings, to be sure, but loyal, professional, and just the team one would want if one found oneself in a pinch, as Haley had not long ago. Haley knew Philson by his given name but joined the team in using the monikers bestowed on the others.

"Shut up, you Nimrod!" predictably ordered Dad, the Team Sergeant and highest ranking non-commissioned officer. "We're on TV. Try to be respectful."

"I am being very respectful. I even put on shoes for the occasion. Look at Spook, he's wearing flip flops and brought a beer to the meeting," said Nimrod.

Spook raised his beer in toast to Haley.

"Who are all those loser stiffs out there in the suits?" Nimrod continued. "I thought we were gonna chat with Clayton."

"Yea. And why do their shirts have sleeves?" asked Tank who was wearing a bright pink Chi Omega sorority tank top. His massive arms and chest made the petite top look ridiculous. By the look of Tank's distended bottom lip, akin to a duck's bill, he was working on an ample supply of snuff tobacco. He placed his "spit cup" on the table next to Spook's beer.

Haley smiled broadly, genuinely happy to see the wacky crew of what he believed to be the best warfighters on the planet. Most were shabbily dressed in tee shirts and cargo pants—a far cry from regulation uniform—and sported beards and magnificent hair. He smiled back warmly, on behalf of the "stiffs" on the video conference, and pointed at his ear, informing Philson and crew they were on the air.

"Awww, sh—" the sound suddenly dropped as Tank reached across the table to hit the mute button. The move jarred Spook's beer, and he elbowed Tank hard, knocking him to the floor, just after he accomplished his mission of turning off the sound.

Haley loved the show and was disappointed the sound was cut, though acknowledged if it were allowed to continue, would likely need censorship. Philson shook his head in embarrassment and shuffled himself to the seat in which he could lead the discussion, while Dad cleaned up the mess behind them.

"Apologies for the delay, folks, but let's get started," Edger suddenly chimed in, ignoring the Green Beret dramatics. "Thanks for dialing in.

Glad you're all here. Looks like we have DOD, State INR [Intelligence and Research] in Washington, Agency, DIA, and State in the field, via Clayton Haley. For those who don't know me, my name is Wilson Edger, and I'm assembling a task force on following what we're describing as tribal rumblings across the Middle East. I invited all of you selectively to join in, as you are all familiar about recent happenings regarding the attempted rise to power of a faux Messiah. The same individual who stormed the Grand Mosque in Mecca in 1979. I have no idea how he stayed in what some religious scholars call "*ghaibah,*" or absence all these years, but he did. And he almost returned in a way that could have unseated the House of Saud, a key ally. If he had succeeded, he might have unleashed a whole wave of tribal violence that would have made the Arab Spring look like a picnic. He didn't. He didn't because of the good judgment, intelligence, determination, and not a little luck—most of which was bad—of Clayton Haley, whose efforts nearly cost him his life."

Haley was unsure of how or if to respond to such accolades. It made him very uncomfortable, and he hoped someone would change the subject quickly. He saw Joseph Smith throw something that looked like popcorn at the camera in the small screen occupied by the Green Berets. "They brought popcorn to a video conference?" Haley pondered incredulously.

"My determination is that we need to keep up focus on tribal concerns and the potential for the activation of these groups," continued Edger. Through Haley's efforts, we've seen that only a hundred years ago, bands of tribes under the name of *Ikhwan*, or brothers, ravaged the Arabian Peninsula and surroundings. These guys were every bit as bad as Al-Qaeda and ISIS, only without social media. We need to be mindful of what could unite, agitate, or provoke them. The possible cloning of Mohammed was one such thing, but thanks to Haley, with some help from our rather unorthodox Green Beret team, we thwarted their plan."

Haley noticed more popcorn. Haley cringed as Spook accidentally picked up Tank's spit cup to toast Haley. Haley hoped he wouldn't take a sip. He also noticed Dad had his head back and was clearly asleep.

"We need to be mindful of other things that could also spark them," Edger continued again. "One such concern is that we don't know if they succeeded in cloning Mohammed, and if they did, where the boy is now. You'll recall pictures of the boy and his father or doctor in the background pictures of our successful operation that took out al-Qahtani. Saudi intel counterparts told us he slipped away. We need to track him down to get his story and determine what plans people have for him. Also, we need to track down Muhsin Bin Laden and Ali al-Sadr, both uncovered by Haley, both mysterious, and both also in whereabouts unknown. Until we know they don't have designs on marshaling up a new Messiah or other leader to rally the masses, we need these guys on our radar."

"We also need to track down the rather violent minions of the newer generation al-Otaybi and al-Qahtani," Edger restarted after flipping through his notes. "Yet again, we find Haley in the middle of things, as most of you are aware they tried to attack him in Kuwait."

"Clayton ripped the dude's eye out with a fishhook!" abruptly inserted the Nimrod, who had slammed the talk button, cheered on by his team. Even Dad seemed to wake up for the celebration.

Haley sunk in his chair, wondering if anyone would notice or mind if he suddenly exited the conference, his finger hovering precariously close to the "hang up" indicator on the remote control.

"Yes," Edger rejoined. "Haley, with help from Philson, was able to get the best of his attacker. For that we're relieved. But what's next? What else should we be looking out for? We'll go out to the outstations for questions and commentary, but first I'd like for Clayton to provide his thoughts on the latest threads he's been pulling. Clayton, can you please provide us an overview?"

Haley was stunned and embarrassed and had expected to not be seen or heard. He had no idea what to say but was glad he had taken notes. He looked down at them hoping smart words would magically manifest.

"Um. Thanks, Wilson. Um. Hello. It's good to see you. Um," he knew he was off to a horrible start. He didn't quite know how to restart. He resented Edger's throwing him under the bus. He tried to gain some composure but noticed that Edger was pointing at his ear, signaling that the mute button was on. Haley smiled, realizing he had a second chance. He pushed the button, turning the icon on the screen from red to green.

Relieved, he now had something to start with. "I'm sorry. I didn't know the mute button was on. User error. Thanks for your kind words, Wilson, and it's good to see some familiar faces out there. To be clear, despite Wilson's rather generous assessment of my contributions, a lot of what we've uncovered should rightfully be attributed to guesswork and dumb luck, and more rightfully, help from our friends. It's good to see Nate Philson and his team of merry bandits out there."

More popcorn. Philson gave a slight salute and Dad was asleep again. Spook was on his second beer.

"I don't have much to tell you other than odd coincidences, but I would offer to you that through open sources, we're hearing rumblings of the arrival or impending arrival of the Messiah, or *Mehdi*, as he is known in Arabic. Seems to me that the boy who was portrayed by al-Qahtani as Mohammed incarnate may have been whisked off to Qom, the seat of Shia power. I have nothing to support this but a few odd news reports and suspicions. And common sense would suggest that the two assailants al-Otaybi and al-Qahtani may have ended up in Iran. Both needed extensive medical attention after our little run-in, and they wouldn't have risked it in Kuwait. Iran isn't far from us here, so I suggest putting out feelers. Is there anything else of interest from my end that I can help with?"

Edger jumped in quickly, "Yes. I believe we've missed key developments like the civil war in Syria, the Saudi war against the Houthis, the rather silly Saudi and UAE 'mean girls' embargo of Qatar, the rise of ISIS, and other events because we didn't pay attention to what was deemed insignificant at the time. I'd like the group to hear what you've been up to. Tell us about the retrieval of the mortal remains."

"Um. OK," replied Haley, not expecting this to be of importance. "Sure. Short version of the story is that I led an initiative to exhume and repatriate the mortal remains of Iraqi KIAs from the Gulf War on humanitarian grounds but also to help restore ties between Kuwait and Iraq. We found fifty-five bodies lined up, facing Mecca and are in the process of returning them to their families in Iraq. The last guy in the group had the same family name as one of the guys present in my getting roughed up in Iraq last year, and he had on him a map of what I believe is the fabled Round City of Baghdad, which per legend, contained the *Beit al-Hikma*, or House of Wisdom. Some historians suspect this was an ancient library that contained literary treasures held over from the Arab and Muslim conquests but also contained writings dating back to Christian, Roman, Persian, Greek, and other civilizations. It was one of the best libraries in the world until decimated by the Mongols during their attack in 1258. This is wild speculation, but I believe the map in the possession of our mystery corpse points to a cemetery in Baghdad. Reports I've read suggest that the Mongols were superstitious. If you wanted to hide some of the greatest treasures on earth from their rampage, I offer to you that a tomb might suffice."

One of the screens chimed in, "What type of treasure do you think could have been hidden in the tomb?"

Haley presumed the caller was with DIA, as he couldn't connect him with other participants. "I have no way of knowing. I have uncovered reports on the internet that indicate that early edition Qurans, along with a vast heritage of scholarly materials were kept in these great libraries so can only imagine that if folks were fleeing Baghdad and wished to preserve anything from the great infidels that were the Mongols, they would have likely grabbed everything they could. You gotta remember that in addition to Baghdad being the London, Paris, and New York of

146

the era, it was also the MIT and would have had the greatest annals and volumes of science and medicine in the world. These were the guys who led the planet in astronomy, chemistry, mathematics, engineering, and so on. They even invented algebra and developed the concept of zero."

"And they learned to manufacture paper for these books, so they were better preserved. I read somewhere that they learned the process for making paper from some of their Chinese POWs and began mass producing this about three hundred years ahead of their European counterparts. They had to. For the first hundred years or so of Islam, the Muslim pioneers were compelled to memorize the oral accounts of Mohammed's vision. He used to tell them what he saw, they memorized it in its entirety, and then they spread the word to whomever they could, by mouth or by sword. This was fine, I guess, until a particular battle saw the loss of some seventy of these scholar warriors. At that point, it became imperative that their holy writ from Allah be preserved and disseminated across the world. How else could Islam spread to the non-Arabic speaking world? And how else could scholars at the time verify the reliability of Mohammed's visions from God? Enter Yousef Bin al-Hajaj, a brutal but efficient governor of Iraq, who ruled at the behest of the Umayyad Caliphate while it was still in Damascus, just before the Abbasid Caliphate set up in Baghdad. It was he who harmonized the Arabic language, including how to pronounce and standardize the structure for writing and reading Arabic. This was essential to the masses learning to read and recite the Quran," concluded Haley, a little surprised to hear how congealed his thoughts were becoming.

"This is interesting in a National Treasure context, but sans Nicholas Cage, what are we supposed to do with this information?" retorted the same anonymous suit.

Haley was annoyed. He did not wish to be subjected to an interview or deposition. Edger should know this. He had no way of verifying any of his rather cockamamie notions so did not appreciate trying to defend them. Time to throw Edger under the bus, he thought, saying, "I don't know. I'm just being responsive to Wilson's request."

Wilson interjected, "Clayton, go ahead and mention your latest theory. You know, the one about the palimpsests."

Haley paused, knowing that what he was about to say would cause significant eye rolling. "Yes," he started, "Palimpsests. It turns out that according to scientists from the early seventies, some original Qurans were written on material that may have been repurposed from earlier writings, writings that may have predated Islam. This is all found on the internet. You can only imagine how such material could be distorted and used to motivate tribal masses across the region, already disenfranchised from the ruling establishments, and potentially prone to revert back to their *Ikhwan* roots."

"I don't know," Haley continued. "No one thinks this is crazier than I, but I would note that someone stole the original map of what I believe to be Baghdad's Round City before it could be properly analyzed. I'm lucky to have received a photocopy. Perhaps the 'thief,'" he made the rabbit ears gesture, "was just souvenir hunting or maybe it simply got lost. I only offer this in deference to Wilson's call to mention other various strains and details, no matter how odd or insignificant. I leave this for your consideration."

Edger wrapped up the call, thanking Haley for his intervention and mentioning that he would draft a readout to memorialize the conversation. He also mooted to arrange another call in a month to see if others had thoughts or developments to raise. Haley noticed that Spook, Tank, and Doc had all joined Dad in his slumber.

Chapter 27

Lebanese Restaurant, Downtown Kuwait, an hour later.

Haley arrived at the restaurant about fifteen minutes late so felt harried and annoyed with himself, and Edger, for his delayed departure from the embassy. He didn't want Cooper to wait for him and certainly didn't want her to think he stood her up. He parked just outside the restaurant and made his way to the entrance, hoping she wasn't there yet. He had sent her a text alerting her he would be late and pinging the restaurant's address to her but wasn't sure she received it.

He found her waiting for him in the restaurant lobby, and she looked lovely and forgiving. Haley was still wearing his suit from work, but Cooper had managed to change out of her business suit to a more comfortable outfit, white form fitting pants and a modest navy blue blouse. Haley noticed a gold necklace supporting either a medallion or amulet, but he wasn't sure of the difference between the two items and didn't want his gaze to linger too long on her neck, especially when her eyes were so inviting.

"I'm so sorry for being late, Jordan. I got held up in a videoconference with some folks in D.C. They seem to forget that we're seven hours ahead," he offered, extending his hand and immediately regretting his gesture. They were colleagues and friends, perhaps more, so it was odd to shake hands. He wasn't about to give her the European or Arab greeting of a kiss, however, as this was a bit too intimate, while being superficial at the same time.

"And they forget we have a different weekend. I can't tell you how many calls I get on Fridays, but I bet they don't want me to call on Sunday when our work week starts," she responded accepting his hand but not knowing what to do with it.

Haley sensed she enjoyed or at least hopefully forgave his awkwardness. "Should we get a table?" he interjected rhetorically. He approached the maître d' but before asking him for service, noticed a sign denoting that the restaurant had two sections, one for men and one for families. He kicked himself for not anticipating this and feared they wouldn't be allowed to dine together. He didn't want further interference in their date so quickly debated positing a white lie that he and "his sister" might be joined by their father shortly, allowing them access to the family section. He prayed God would preemptively forgive the falsehood but then relaxed as he realized there was no need for fabrication. The waiter ignored Cooper and nonchalantly escorted them to the family section, likely as he did all westerners. Haley realized the virtue laws were mainly in place to protect the locals; Westerners were already doomed as morally bereft and un-savable.

"I hope you like this place, Jordan. It's pretty blue collar, but I find the food quite good. It passed Nasser Khalil's high standards for Levantine fare. Maybe you'll approve, too," Haley said.

"I'm sure it will be fine. And I thank you for dinner. I've been looking forward to this, Clayton," she responded.

Haley noticed she pronounced the *t* in his name. Most people, especially in the south, took the lazy path of substituting the letter for a glottal stop, resulting in a *Clay-'un* sound. He liked the way she said it and smiled at her.

The waiter directed them to a table in the back of the family section where there were other couples dining, so Haley didn't feel too conspicuous by being on a date. Kuwait was accustomed to westerners and had a great affinity for Americans since President George H. W. Bush assembled the nearly global coalition to expel Iraq from Kuwait in 1991. Haley recalled that Yemen and Jordan were among the very few detractors, as they had registered complaints that no one came to their rescue when Saudi Arabia annexed large amounts of real estate from their countries, including the holiest sites of Islam.

Haley shook his head, ordering himself to stay focused on his beautiful date and what he hoped was a budding romance. Their table was quiet and secluded but fell short of romantic, as evinced by the plastic table cloths and the presence on the tables of boxes of tissues instead of proper napkins. "Maybe I should have picked something more elegant for a first proper date?" he doubted to himself. The smells of fresh bread and prepared meats emanating from the kitchen, however, assured him he had chosen well.

"This looks wonderful. In fact, it reminds me of some of my favorite restaurants in Jordan. I grew up on Shami [Levantine] food, and my mom makes a mean *'jajja freeka'*," she added.

"I have no idea what that means but can only imagine it's some crazed form of dancing," Haley jibed.

"It's Jordanian for chicken freekah," she rolled her expressive eyes, which Haley finally identified as a bluish-silver hue. "Freekah is the burned grains of green wheat folks in the Levant have been eating since the world's civilizations have been conquering us. Once the Romans, Greeks, Hebrews, Persians, Babylonians, Israelis or other empires razed our villages, to survive, the townsmen and women would scrounge up whatever they could find from the fields, even if it wasn't harvest time. We still eat it to this day. It's very tasty and healthy."

"Us?" Haley asked, while needlessly thumbing through the menu. He knew what he would order—essentially a smattering of salads, falafel, and some grilled chicken.

"You remember from our chat with Dr. Bargouthi. My mom is from Jordan. She met my dad at Penn State when they were there as undergrads. I spent most of my childhood summers in Jordan, around Amman. I hope a hick from the sticks like you doesn't mind hanging out with an Arab-American," she smiled.

"I'll make an exception, just this once," he smiled back. "And not to be too preachy, but I don't like using hyphens in describing fellow Americans; they look too much like minuses." Haley felt a sense of elation at his cleverness and open-mindedness.

"Whatever appeals to your white guilt, gringo," she smirked. "Should we order? The talk about *jajja freekah* has made me hungry," she flashed a devilish smile at him.

After placing their order, both using impressively good accents in pronouncing the Arabic delicacies, she queried him on his background and what drew him to the Middle East.

"Honestly, it was the army that chose the language for me and sent me off to the Defense Language Institute in Monterey, California. Since then, I've developed a real interest in the Middle East, the people, and the food," he opened his hands in a gesture toward the food which was beginning to arrive. "But also, I have a lot of questions about how our belief system in the United States, especially across the conservative and evangelical parts, is influenced by or tries to influence developments in the Middle East. My parents were always pretty open, but so many from my community were set in the belief of supporting Israel at all costs, without much consideration for the impact on Palestinian Christian and Muslim communities. I've never quite understood how or why we actively supported the large scale displacements of peoples based on their race or religion, even when they matched our own," he preached.

"You're preaching to the choir, brother," Cooper quipped back. "My mom is Jordanian, but her parents are Palestinians from the West Bank, pushed out due to expanding Israeli settlements. As a U.S. federal official, I support our policies and our actions, and I admire the Israelis and the nation they've built, but I can't help wondering how much of our policies are borne of political, or even emotional expediency." Haley liked her even more.

The full salad course arrived. Nervously, he asked Cooper if she wouldn't mind if he prayed over the food, stating this was part of his family tradition, adding, "Sometimes with my mom's cooking, it was mostly a precautionary measure."

She readily agreed, and said she would like it very much. After which, like pros accustomed to the cuisine, they attacked the hummus, baba ghanoush, tabouli, and slightly bitter green and sweeter black olives, ripping the piping hot pita bread into small sections with which to grab the food. Neither needed utensils.

"So yes, growing up in the South seemed an odd entree into the Middle East, but I found so many folks consumed with eschatology, end of times prophecies, the rapture, the Anti-Christ, and other sensational, and to some folks, terrifying events. Seems that much of this hype comes from modern day so-called prophets, not the Scriptures themselves. I honestly don't understand the relevance, but like you, as a government official, think we are compelled to live in the here and now in the implementation of our policies . . . some of them aren't necessarily that bad," he noted.

Then, changing the subject, he added, "Do you know which country, after Israel, gets the most mentions in the Bible?"

"I suppose Jordan?" she asked.

"I'm sure the river gets lots of mentions, but no, not the country. It's Iraq, otherwise referred to as Babylon, Shinar, or Mesopotamia. I'll bet you didn't know that according to Genesis, Adam and Eve were created in Iraq, and the Garden of Eden was there, too. Though, Yemenis also claim having the garden in Aden. Noah built the ark in Iraq, according to accounts. Babylon, of course, was famous for Nimrod, the great grandson of Noah, and his famous and prideful tower and the world's subsequent linguistic confusion and dispersal. Plus, Abraham sourced from Ur, in southern Iraq. So did his daughter-in-law. Jacob spent twenty years there working to marry his "Iraqi" brides, Rachel and Leah. Jonah was from Iraq, and the story of Esther took place there as well. Assyria, which conquered the ten tribes of Israel that splintered off and never returned? Also Iraq. Daniel and the lion's den? Iraq. Shadrach, Meshach, and Abednego? Iraq. Ezekiel preached in Iraq. The famous "writing on the wall?" Iraq. Grass-fed Nebuchadnezzar? Iraq. Even Peter supposedly went to Iraq on one of his missions. The Babylon referenced in Revelations? Iraq. In terms of history and the prophetic future, Iraq has always been at the forefront of God's plans for his people. I have no idea what any of this means but find it very cool to ponder," Haley posited.

"Yes, and I heard that Sylvester Stallone planned to film movies there, starring himself as *Iraqi Balboa* and teaming up with super spy hunters *Iraqi and Bullwinkle* to fight *Ivan Drago, Boris, and Natasha Creed,*" she added with a put on Russian accent. "Yes, I can tie obscure connections together, too," she flashed her devilish smile again.

Haley liked her, readily and willingly ceding his loss to her in a battle of wits. He relished each morsel of food and conversation, already planning to order dessert and tea to ensure the evening drew out as long as possible. Despite his earlier jitters, he enjoyed talking to her, and even more so, delighted in listening to her.

Chapter 28

The meal had been excellent, the company exquisite. Haley couldn't recall enjoying an evening this much in a long time and marveled at how easy it was to connect with Cooper over so many issues of common interest. He dreaded seeing the bottom of his cup of *shai bilna'na' wa alsunober [hot tea with mint and pine nuts]*, a delicious import from North Africa to the Levant and the Persian Gulf.

He suddenly and inexplicably felt uneasy. Not sick, not worried, just unsettled and uncertain. Blackness descended on him, clouding his awareness and ability to focus. The sounds in the restaurant became muffled and then rose to a cacophony of roaring, breaking, crashing, scattering, screaming, and shooting. Shooting. More screaming. More shooting. Automatic gunfire. He could hear nearby thuds of bullets forcing their way into and through nearby walls. Through tables and windows and the ceiling. Sickening thuds meant perhaps bodies as well. He removed the thought from his mind and forced himself into quick response mode.

He looked at Cooper. Her beautiful eyes were alight with fear but more inclined toward action than panic. Haley looked around, seeing an unfamiliar setting. He had been so absorbed by her company he failed to take into account his surroundings, safe he felt enrapt in her. A hasty glance revealed that in the family section, he was buffered slightly from the room accommodating only men. A cultural oddity from his Walhalla perspective for sure but one that bought him valuable seconds and an invaluable warning of the calamity in the restaurant.

His glance informed him of only three possible egresses, one that led to the main part of the restaurant and danger. A second was marked as an emergency exit, also undesirable in case assailants lay in wait for just such an escape. A third way remained available through swinging doors and the kitchen. It was roughly ten meters away, across the middle of the dining room. He chose door number three, instinctively assuming it the best of the options, knowing it would provide more cover and potentially some utensils or knives that might double as weapons or projectiles.

Haley grabbed Cooper's hand, pulling her away from the table and the poor cover it provided. "Let's make for the kitchen. We need to get out of here!" he urged. She leapt with him moving quickly toward the kitchen. They covered half the room as doors to the private salon burst open revealing an assailant dressed entirely in black leather, as if adorned for a ride in a motorcycle gang. His face was unidentifiable as he wore a black balaclava. Over his shoulder was a strap connected at both ends to what Haley quickly recognized as an AK-47. He was aiming it recklessly at tables in the room, occupied by patrons not yet decided on the multiple escapes. As the muzzle of the weapon flashed in angry spurts at the nearest table, the eye of the miscreant flashed at Haley and Cooper still making ground toward what they hoped was succor. He ripped away a magazine, which had just spent its quantity of 7.62 caliber rounds, reaching into his satchel for another clip.

Haley had been pulling Cooper along as they moved to what he presumed was the kitchen. As they neared their destination, he grabbed her with all his might, lifting her bodily in an airborne tackle that propelled them both through the swinging doors and into the kitchen. He hoped he wasn't too rough, but he would rather her endure bumps and bruises instead of the full on military style assault that was waging in the dining room. He also hoped he had enough time to get them both, and other patrons, out of the restaurant and to safety before the attacker reloaded. Cooper was on the floor struggling to get up, unable to gain traction as her heels scuffled on wet tile.

The lack of the resumption of firing worried Haley. He feared the silence as much as the sounds of the attack. He stole a glance into the dining room from the edge of the kitchen door jamb. In less than an instant his mind took in a widely disparate panoramic scene, from left to right. In the foreground, he noticed the hinge on the door slightly off kilter, likely resulting in a squeak each time the waiters entered and exited with orders. Scanning right, he noticed patrons cowering and whimpering under tables, some were holding children tightly, all crying and supplicating in prayers.

In the middle of his view, he saw the attacker in the process of loading another clip and staring directly and only at Haley. A balaclava disguised the identity of the assailant, but Haley noticed, in that instant, that his left eye was covered or otherwise blackened. Haley sensed familiarity, making him more wary. His eye never blinked and stayed focused on the door jamb that hid Haley. To the right of the killer, Haley saw devastation: tables were overturned, bodies with limbs awkwardly askew lay where they had fallen, and blood pooled in puddles. He couldn't estimate the body count in the glance but thought it must be four or five. Some lay still moving, others praying and begging the gunman to spare them. And completing the analyzing look, Haley saw the pockmarked trim of the kitchen door, riddled with bullets perhaps meant for Cooper and himself during their flight to safety.

Having taken in the scene and analyzed it, he made the decision that action was needed or, one, the gunman would kill more in the dining room, or, two, he would come into the kitchen after Cooper and him. Weapons that lay within his reach were scant, only a soup ladle on the counter, a broom, a dusty fire extinguisher, clearly expired, and a light switch. He hopelessly grabbed the ladle and the broom.

Haley took action, hoping and praying that a man armed with an automatic weapon didn't expect resistance. He forewent the extinguisher as too heavy and potentially dead weight, turned off the light, which proved largely ineffective, only barely reducing his silhouette as he lunged low into the dining room and headed directly at the malefactor. The gunman, still focused on the kitchen, expectedly fired at the movement but anticipated it at a higher level and unloaded his rounds harmlessly into the door behind Haley as he dashed toward him. Haley launched the broom, handle first like a spear, at the assailant. It went by his head harmlessly but distracted him enough to raise his aim even higher, especially as the weapon discharged its automatic fire.

Haley continued his low charge, slightly adjusting to come at the gunman from the right, where his vision was impeded. Haley felt a painful tug on his shoulder. It stunned him but not enough to slow him down. He closed in on but clearly miscalculated the distance he had to charge, and realized barring a miracle, he had only set himself up for an execution at point blank range. The action slowed dramatically in his mind. He could hear his breathing, his elevated heart rate, and even the Muzak playing in the background: He thought he detected the saxophone riff in George Michael's "Careless Whisper," and became despondent for a second. "Really? I'm gonna get shot in the face during this song? I hate this tune," he moaned internally.

The miracle happened. Haley didn't know how or why, but the attacker began flinching and ducking. Haley kept up the momentum in his own attack, still low, and off to his own right in the darkened room. He closed in. Armed only with the long soup ladle, he swung widely and upwardly at the face of his nemesis, who seemed to still be swatting at projectiles. The scoop part of the ladle connected to what seemed to be the sightless left eye of the murderer. The contact did more damage to the ladle than to its target, bending it significantly and ensuring it would never dip soup again. It did, however, stun the assailant long enough for Haley to lift up from his crouch and grab the firearm, directing it toward the ceiling where it could do less harm. Haley's momentum led him into a football style tackle, knocking his enemy onto his back, with Haley tumbling after, still wrestling with the gun.

Haley now had the upper hand. He had both hands on the weapon, and adrenaline surging through his veins made him the more powerful of the two. He wasn't going to lose possession of the gun and determined it would not be used against innocent civilians again. He ripped it away with all his might; even the strap on his opponent's shoulder offered little resistance, as it cleared the length of his arm, such was the force used by Haley.

In the same instant, Haley noticed the source of the miracle that had bought him a precious split second. A shoeless Cooper had been lodging various projectiles, including her own shoes, at the assailant from the kitchen. Restaurant patrons had followed suit, throwing knives, forks, glasses, and even a vase of flowers. It was a good team effort.

Haley adjusted his advantage over the gunmen, grabbing the rifle in his right hand and jamming his left knee into his gut. His left hand went to his throat, which he squeezed with all his might to force a full submission. The man clawed at Haley with his hands. Haley clocked him hard in the head with the broadside of the gun, slamming the right side of his face into the carpet. He struggled more. He hit him again with the rifle, harder, then with an anger he had never known, began smashing the weapon repeatedly against the head of his opponent. He wouldn't relent until a more powerful force stopped him.

"Clayton," the more powerful force, now at his side, quietly said. "That's enough."

Haley felt a gentle touch on his shoulder. Cooper had joined him and was now signaling to him that he had done enough. Haley's rage turned into exhaustion, a tiredness the likes of which he had never experienced. He felt drained. He looked at what he had done to the man on the floor. The balaclava was still in place, and though black, was clearly bloodied and torn. White shards showed through the material, perhaps bone or teeth. The body was motionless, but Haley didn't believe him to be dead. Haley had no idea how many times he struck the man or how long he had pounded on him. He only knew that his victim must be prevented from making other victims.

As he calmed, he reached down and grasped the apex of the mask and ripped it off callously. Gruesomely, he snagged on some of the shards. The left side of the assailant's face was damaged beyond recognition. The right side, however, when Haley turned his face toward him, clearly revealed that of Ali Mehdi al-Qahtani. The sinister but pained face of the man who had tried to kill him on the boat and had likely killed Paula Abrams and Dr. Ibrahim Mustafa, looked up at him with vile hatred. He was still very much alive but would need more plastic surgery.

"Wain saddiqak al-mal'oon al-Otaybi [Where is your cursed friend, al-Otaybi]?" Haley uttered quietly, looking into an eye full of contempt. *"Rooh aqtilahu kaman [I'm gonna kill him, too]!"* Haley had subconsciously moved the business end of the weapon to inches away from the left eye of al-Qahtani. Al-Qahtani's hatred turned to fear. He looked into the eyes of Haley and for the first time, realized that his opponent was not someone who kept getting lucky, as he had long surmised, but someone who would continue besting him. Al-Qahtani, who had thrived on terrorizing people, found he had a knack for killing the defenseless. While the aspirations of his grandfather, Muhsin Bin Laden, and Ali al-Sadr gave him purpose, he had never encountered someone with equal resolve. Now he was eye to eyes with someone who appeared determined to end him.

Haley fought every natural urge to simply squeeze the trigger and rid the world of someone who made no positive contributions to it. It would have been so easy. Something stayed his hand: his father's voice, reciting words Haley was made to memorize when he was little, from the Gospel of Luke. "Love your enemies, do good to those who hate you, bless those who curse you, pray for those who mistreat you. If someone slaps you on one cheek, turn to them the other also."

"Thanks, Dad," groaned Haley sarcastically. He really wanted to kill this guy. Cooper's hand still rested on his shoulder. The fire in Haley's eyes diminished, moving from rage to pity. Al-Qahtani's expression similarly transformed from fear to shame, mixed with intense pain from his injuries sustained by Haley's relentless attack. He squealed and cried out. Suddenly, with no provocation, two shots rang out, converting al-Qahtani's face into an unrecognizable mass.

Standing over his bloody corpse was Haley's ever present but rarely noticed ministry of interior minder. A wisp of smoke emanated from his handgun, which hovered only a few inches over al-Qahtani's lifeless corpse. The minder uttered an Arabic phrase that Haley was unfamiliar with but likely sent the unrepentant al-Qahtani on his way to *al-Jaheem [Arabic for hell]* to join his grandfather.

Chapter 29

Farwaniyah Hospital, Kuwait City. The next day.

Haley wasn't sure how he ended up in the hospital. He felt fine. Better than fine. Very relaxed. Blissful. Peaceful. Something was wrong. These were feelings at odds with the traumatic experience he had just endured and was now starting to remember. He looked around the room, his eye catching on an IV drip, the apparent source of Haley's new sense of well-being.

Haley felt alone. The hospital room was appropriately sterile, both in decontamination and lifelessness. It was well lit but with no direct sunlight. The Kuwaiti heat was too intense to allow natural light, so blinds and blackout curtains were set up to fend off the severity of the elements. Inside were the typical medical fixtures and accoutrements one would expect in a well-developed society. Missing, thought Clayton, was the comfort of friends and family. He wondered if he might call home to let his parents know he was okay. He was okay, he presumed, glancing toward the IV and the good feelings it dispensed.

"Hello, Mr. Klaytoon, sir. My name ees Esmerelda. You are here at Parwaniyya Hosbital. You came in late last night, sir," said a nurse forcibly as she entered the room.

"Hello, Esmeralda. *Kamustaka?*" asked Haley.

"Ma bute, sir, ma bute," she replied with a wide grin, pleased that Haley greeted her in her native Tagalog. Identifying her as a Filipina

162

was easy for Haley as nearly all Asian staff in healthcare in the gulf were from the Philippines and largely regarded as very competent professionals. Many of them were subsequently highly recruited and granted employment-based immigration visas to work in hospitals in the United States and Canada.

"Esmeralda, do you have details about the attack at the restaurant last night? Do you know how many people were, um, hurt? And there was a young lady with . . . aughh," he grimaced. As he spoke he adjusted himself to try to sit up, experiencing torrents of pain shooting through his left shoulder. He had been subjected to considerable pain before. During his military service, he took shrapnel in his leg from an improvised explosive device detonation for which he was awarded a Purple Heart. He had also suffered a brutal beating as a civilian at the hands of a thug named Abdullah while impaired with a broken arm. Both experiences occurred in Iraq.

"*Young lady is pine, sir. Just pine. She has pruises and pumps, but she ees okay. She wants to see you, sir. I tell her to wait,*" said Esmeralda.

"I would love to see her, but can I have my clothes?" asked Haley, feeling very conscious wearing only the flimsy hospital gown in which he somehow found himself attired. "Who had taken off his clothes?" he wondered.

"*No clo-these, sir. Too much blood. You need new clo-these,*" she replied.

Haley moaned. He went to the restaurant from work, wearing one of his suits. Yet another one destroyed in the line of duty, he sighed. He only had five suits and hadn't replaced the one he lost in Iraq during his encounter with the elder al-Qahtani. He hoped Jos. A. Banks Clothiers had another big sale soon.

"*I tell young lady to come een. She bery bretty,*" Esmeralda said slyly, while checking the drip and glancing at his chart.

A few minutes later, Esmeralda opened the door, waved down the hall, and then ushered in Cooper.

163

"Hey, Clayton. How ya feeling?" Cooper said. She smiled but seemed very subdued. Haley thought she looked beautiful but troubled, and rightfully so. They had shared a traumatic experience, and he didn't know how she would view him after seeing the violent side of him. Haley had still not reconciled his actions with himself from last night either.

"Hi Jordan. I'm okay," he winced as he tried to sit up, even more self-conscious of the scant attire he wore, covered only by the thinnest layers of sheet and blanket. She approached the bed to steady him and prevent him from trying to sit up. She gently pressed his good shoulder back with her right hand. Her left hand grabbed his. It felt warm and comforting.

"I'm so sorry about last night. I hope you're okay. I never meant to expose you to danger. I only wish—" he started.

Cooper interrupted, "You saved my life. If you hadn't have thrown me in the kitchen, he would have killed us both."

"Yes, but you saved my life when I was stupid enough to charge at him. You've got quite an arm. If it wasn't for you and the folks at the restaurant, my charge of the light brigade would have ended like the original, in utter defeat," Haley said quietly.

"Your actions saved a lot of lives," she said.

"How many were lost or wounded?" he quickly asked.

"Seven died. Including two children. Four others have critical wounds, like yours, and two more are in intensive care. It was terrible. And it was savage. A few others have scrapes, bumps, and bruises. It's horrible what he did to those people," she replied, having difficulty speaking. "It was like a scene taken from a horror film," her lips quivered involuntarily downward, and her already red eyes filled with tears. She was clearly exhausted.

"I'm sorry you had to see what I did to him. He deserved a good beating . . . but not that way and not from me. I lost my mind when I

164

saw the danger he had put people in and then went completely insane when I recognized him," he asserted, struggling to speak.

"I know. I was scared for my life during the ordeal, including when I saw what came over you. You were as terrifying as he was, but I knew your violence was directed at the present danger. I'm glad you calmed down when you did, and that it wasn't you that killed him," she said softly.

"Me too," he responded in similarly low decibels, "But it was you that snapped me out of my rage. I'll never forget your voice speaking to me as if in the middle of a storm. Thank you for rescuing me from me," he said, enjoying holding her hand. Then Haley urgently asked, "Did I do that to you?" as he noticed bruises on her arms and neck for the first time.

"Well, I think most of my injuries were caused by the kitchen floor, door, and counter," she said smiling. She had a beautiful smile, he thought again, and realized this was the first time he had seen her without makeup. He found her entrancing and felt enormous guilt for what he had put her through. He hated the topic and location of conversation but enjoyed spending time with her, even if in a hospital.

Sounds of commotion interrupted his thoughts about Cooper. He heard shouting, some swearing, and what he thought might be barking and possibly a howl just outside of his room. He was completely helpless, injured, in a hospital bed, wearing a flimsy gown, and saw not even a ladle or fishhook in sight to defend himself.

"I tell you we are family. I'm his brother Larry. He's his brother Daryl. He's another brother, Daryl, and he's his cousin, the Nimrod. We're here to check up on him. Don't try to stop us or we'll go Saddam Hussein on your heinies," said a boisterous voice.

Haley noticed poor Esmeralda valiantly trying to stem the invasion of men Haley knew all too well. Accompanying his friend Nate Philson was his entourage of Green Berets, apparently checking up on him. He signaled to the nurse that it was fine to let them in. She acquiesced but commanded, *"Pibe, sir. Only Pibe."*

"You heard her, you knuckleheads, only five. Nimrod, bring the bag, Doc, Spook, and Joseph Smith, you're welcome to join. Chip, can you and the others make up an excuse for the department of justice and embassy security guys to hold them off? They'll want to speak to Clayton, but I want us to check on him first," said Nate Philson, to the warm relief of Haley.

The small horde of Vikings entered the room, beaming at Haley, who smiled back.

Nimrod said in his uncomfortably loud voice, "Waddup Claypot? Who's the hottie? She available? *Ahlan wa sahlan [Well, hello—in Arabic],*" Nimrod continued, addressing Cooper in his smoothest Lando Calrissian tones. "That's how they say *kaif halik [How are you?]* to the ladies in Arabic."

"No, it ain't, you Nimrod. It's how they say hello in Arabic. Wonchu just *ikhras [Arabic, for "shut up"]* your pie hole and let me check on our boy. "*Sabah al-khair, ya anissa [Good morning, miss]*, please forgive our resident Neanderthal. He has no manners." Doc shook Haley's hand while casting Cooper an appraising look and a wink. He then went quickly to review Haley's chart.

"Hey, y'all. Good to see you. Could have used your help last night. I found myself in another dust up. Good thing my colleague Jordan Cooper was there. Some quick thinking on her part distracted my cycloptic friend long enough to get his peashooter away from him. Jordan, say hello to my Green Beret friends who helped me out of a scrape back in Iraq," Haley introduced. She warmly shook hands with the group and skillfully managed to avoid a hug from Nimrod.

"GSW [trauma vernacular for gunshot wound]. Through and through. Close range. Some tissue damage. Gonna need some time to recover. Won't play badminton any time soon. No high fives either," said Doc, holding his hand up to Haley for a high five.

Haley instinctively tried to reciprocate, but painfully realized he couldn't, eliciting a rare smile from Doc. Spook was eating the meal set out for Haley. Haley didn't care. He genuinely appreciated the company the way a child would a circus.

"Seriously, are you available?" insisted Nimrod.

"She's out of your league, you Nimrod," said Spook. "Can't you tell she's sentient and walks upright?"

Philson finally managed to cut through the histrionics of his team. Haley knew he allowed quite a bit of questionable behavior because these men were highly skilled in their warcraft and just the soldiers one needed in combat. They had served with valor in Iraq, Syria, and Afghanistan, and meted justice out to a large number of terrorists who had worn out their welcome on the planet. Haley felt honored and touched by their friendship.

"How're you, Nate? It's good to see you," said Haley sincerely.

"I'm the one checking up on you. Seems like we almost lost you last night. From what I gather, you seemed to have taken out our old friend with a ladle? I guess you couldn't find a rod and reel in the restaurant?" joked Philson, covering up his concern and worry.

"Nope," quipped Haley. "From now on, only seafood restaurants," and then, after a pause, said, "Jordan tells me it was pretty bad at the restaurant—seven dead and two in ICU. I think we were really lucky."

"Only the good are lucky," said Philson. "You saw action was needed and took it. That, and, I've long suspected the Good Lord isn't done with you yet. And neither are we. I have a plan I need to discuss with you, but you need to get well first, okay? We can't stay here long. Pretty soon, the hospital staff will realize we're not family and your embassy colleagues are hankering to get dibs on you to find out what happened."

"Sure. I'll look you up when I get out of here. I'm curious about your plan and would like to hear more. By the way, al-Qahtani tends to run in pairs with his cousin, al-Otaybi, the guy you hooked on the boat. I wonder why he wasn't part of the attack last night?" pondered Haley.

"Turns out he was but was chased off by the rather alert interior ministry guy charged with keeping you safe. He and al-Otaybi scuffled at the door, which allowed al-Qahtani to gain entrance and wreak his havoc. Al-Otaybi is on the loose. I gave his description to your security folks and their Kuwaiti counterparts but fear he's long gone again," replied Philson.

"And by the way, I had Brother Joseph Smith swing by your apartment for some clothes so you don't have to walk the halls in your muumuu," Philson added, gesturing to a soldier placing a bundle of clothes on the bed.

"Thanks. That's very thoughtful, but how did you get into my apartment?" asked Haley.

Philson grinned toward Joseph Smith, who simply shrugged, while giving Haley a pat on his good shoulder.

"He had to give you his own magic underwear because yours all had skid marks in them," jibed Nimrod.

"*Ikhras*, you Nimrod," said Joseph Smith and Haley in unison. Nimrod yelped in pain as Doc injected him in his butt with a vial he withdrew from his bag. Nimrod, in turn, swung at Doc and they tussled onto Haley's bed and onto Haley, and he began writhing in pain.

Cooper then ordered, "Out! Unless you're helping Clayton. Out!"

She was surprised at their simple obedience, as they all made for the door.

Nimrod asked as he exited, "What was in that shot you gave me? I can't feel my heinie!"

Doc replied, "Just Teamocil. I've been issuing this to the whole team. It's actually Dr. Fünke's 100% Natural Good Time Family Band Solution, which is now partnered with the U.S. Army to induce a sense of well-being. You'll thank me later." He left the room singing the words from a jingle made popular by the television show "Arrested Development." "*There's no 'i' in teamocil, at least not where you think—*"

"Okay, Ms. Cooper. We read you loud and clear. I'll move this zoo along. Before I go, I just want to say two things to you. One. Thank you for saving his life last night. Clayton is top brand, one of the finest soldiers I've ever known, but above that, one of the best men I know. And two. Please look out for him when I'm not around? He keeps finding himself in scrapes and makes great friends and worst enemies. He could use a guardian angel like yourself," Philson said earnestly. Both Haley and Cooper blushed.

"But lastly," he continued. "Please call your parents and let them hear your voice!" I've spoken to them four times since last night, and they're worried sick."

Cooper rifled through her purse to find her phone. Haley's was lost in the battle the previous night.

Chapter 30

Farwaniyah Hospital, Kuwait, Kuwait City.

Haley spent the next few days recovering from his wounded shoulder. Though painful, as Doc diagnosed, the round went through muscular tissue, fortunately missing organs and bones. His prognosis predicted a painful but an eventual full recovery, with the assistance of dedicated physical therapy. Esmeralda and her colleagues at the hospital provided him with excellent care and service, and he enjoyed daily visits from a variety of friends, including Philson, his teammates, and colleagues from the embassy. The ambassador and the deputy chief of mission swung by, as did Nasser Khalil and members of the locally employed staff at the embassy. Dr. Bargouthi stopped by as well. In addition to social calls, a number of security and investigative types visited him in the hospital, peppering him with questions about the attack. Also present was a rotation of Kuwaiti interior ministry officials who policed the hospital corridors to ensure no further attacks.

Cooper, unfortunately, seemed rather absent to Haley, even when she stopped by the hospital to check on him. He feared the trauma they endured together may have driven a wedge between them, and he couldn't blame her for wanting some distance. He selfishly wanted her near him, as her presence comforted him, but he experienced self-loathing over the notion that being near him put her in harm's way. The thought of her becoming yet another victim of his carelessness induced waves of despondency.

Given the steady stream of visitors, however, he didn't have a chance to explore his feelings with her, and meanwhile, her attention to him when she showed up seemed more perfunctory, or even duty bound than affectionate.

Also weighing on his mind was the uncertainty of his future. Per conversations with the ambassador, paperwork was being filed for his imminent curtailment. Haley, of course, was discouraged but knew a threat to his life remained ever present, and by extension, he was a danger to colleagues in the mission. He would rather lose his budding friendship with Cooper than expose her to further danger.

***

Thawrah District, Iraq. Three days later.

Ali Hussein al-Sadr had just arrived in the *Thawrah*, or Revolution District, as it was formally known, of Eastern Baghdad. As his driver moved him to his temporary accommodations in the middle of the district, he reflected on the city and how it had changed since his childhood. What had started in 1959 as a massive housing project to move displaced portions of the majority Shia population, now looked to him like a rundown ghetto. The locals, the U.S. military, and western press in 2003 renamed the massive slum, which hosted more than one million inhabitants, Sadr City. The district derived its unofficial name from one of Iraq's most famous Shia residents, Ayatollah Muhammad Sadiq al-Sadr, who along with two of his sons, was executed in 1999 by Saddam Hussein. He was survived by another son, Muqtada al-Sadr who, attempting to wield the spiritual credentials of his forebears, seemingly served in the self-appointed capacity of hero to the downtrodden.

Though Ali al-Sadr enjoyed opulence abroad as a key, personal agent of Bin Laden, it felt good to be home, even if for only a short period of time. This joy was diminished, however, by the dread he felt over the impending call that needed to be made to Bin Laden about yet another failure to kill Clayton Haley.

He made the call while in the car, and as he surmised, his benefactor wasn't happy. The silver lining, he thought to himself, was that given the potential for the communication to be traced, Bin Laden knew to be careful with what he divulged over the line and restrained himself from demonstrating his full wrath. He ordered al-Sadr via cryptic tones to continue trying "to carry out his mission," which al-Sadr clearly understood to mean killing Haley and recover whatever Dr. al-Marri suspected remained of the ancient treasures, potentially still located in the Baghdad surroundings. Al-Sadr doubted he would get another chance at Haley while he remained in Kuwait and under the careful watch of Kuwaiti security officials, not many of whom he could buy off. He had waited forty years in plotting the messianic return from *ghaibeh* for Mohammed al-Qahtani so consoled himself that he could wait a few more weeks to kill Haley.

Al-Sadr was glad to be back home but resented the mission. He saw no utility in pursuing the fool's errand that was the hunt for so-called treasure, written scrolls or otherwise. He doubted this project would yield anything of interest or value, assuming that if anything of worth had ever existed, it certainly would have been recovered by now. And he didn't like or trust Dr. al-Marri and certainly didn't want to be his errand boy. Still though, being "home" was certainly much better than being confined to the, albeit luxurious, presence of the increasingly erratic and lecherous Muhsin Bin Laden. Sadr City was his hometown and backyard, and despite answering to both Bin Laden and al-Marri, al-Sadr knew he would call the shots and determine the outcome. "Perhaps, al-Marri might meet with an accident," he mused, knowing just how dangerous Baghdad could be to an outsider, especially a Kuwaiti national.

Al-Sadr assessed he needed some help and decided to track down Abdullah Mohammed al-Otaybi, who had returned to Iran after his disastrous and thwarted restaurant attack, and order him to join him in Sadr City. Al-Sadr also determined he would no longer underestimate Haley and needed al-Otaybi to help design what he hoped would be a foolproof plan for when he was ready to resume operations against the young American diplomat who had proved so resilient and inconvenient.

***

Qom, Iran. Same day.

Al-Onezi heard the mobile phone ring in the next room and surmised that al-Otaybi was talking to al-Sadr. Very few people had his number. Plus, the young man had no friends other than his cousin. In fact, al-Onezi reflected he had only ever seen al-Otaybi with al-Qahtani. The two had been inseparable, and now al-Otaybi returned from his most recent assignment alone and in a very sour mood. Al-Onezi and al-Otaybi had a relationship best described as transactional; certainly there was no love lost between the two. Al-Onezi cared for al-Otaybi as would an indifferent medical professional tend to a patient. Al-Otaybi, for his part, simply ignored al-Onezi, a welcome exchange for the latter. Now, however, al-Onezi perceived a solution to his problem lay with "caring" more for al-Otaybi.

Al-Onezi's life had become more complicated since the younger man's return to Qom. Al-Otaybi, Saudi by nationality but with Yemeni origins and raised in France, did not blend in well among Qom's pious elite. He spoke no Farsi and made no attempt to learn the language. Without invitation, he moved back into al-Onezi's modest apartment, which was housed above a *hussainiyya [Shia gathering hall]* so young Mohammed could get to his lessons early. The apartment was large enough and adequately furnished to accommodate other guests, but al-Onezi didn't like having al-Otaybi around, fearing his proclivity to violence. Plus, he was a constant reminder of the control various masters had over al-Onezi's life.

And al-Onezi grew weary of Iran and its contrived and governmentally ordered religiosity. As a life-long Sunni Islam devotee, al-Onezi tired of the Shia iconography, especially the ever-present portraits of the prophet Hussein, always with what he thought was a tasteless black velvet backdrop. Al-Onezi sought a rescue from his confinement.

"How long do you think you'll be here?" asked al-Onezi of al-Otaybi when the younger man emerged from the next room after completing the call. "And do you think your cousin Ali will be joining you as well?" He hoped engaging the younger in conversation might shed light on his plans and how long he would have to cope with his unwelcome co-guest.

"Not long," al-Otaybi uttered. "Ali is dead. Killed by the American. *Sij wallah [I swear to Allah—Gulf dialect].* I will kill him myself."

"Allah yerhamuhu [May God have mercy on his soul]," replied al-Onezi, not out of sympathy or concern but because it's the phrase said upon hearing of someone's death. More superstition than faith or devotion, especially in this case.

Al-Onezi had a number of questions about the death of al-Qahtani but intuited his new roommate had no interest in talking about it. He opted to return to the default in their relationship, asking, "So what's next? Do you return to Kuwait?"

"No. I have to wait to kill the American. I'm summoned to Iraq. Sadr City, to be precise."

"This is excellent news, as Mohammed and I have also been summoned to Iraq," al-Onezi concocted and delivered his lie simultaneously, intentionally leaving out the details of who might be summoning him and why. "Tell me when you're ready to leave, and we can leave with you. We can be ready within a few hours."

"I've not been informed about this. I was only told to make plans for myself. Who exactly told—" started al-Otaybi.

"I'm not responsible for what my masters tell you or don't tell you. I only know if the boy is who everyone hopes will unite the Islamic umma [religious community], he'll need to continue his studies in Najaf and Kerbala, the real seats for global Islam, at least while the corrupt House of Saud controls Mecca," interjected al-Onezi urgently and then quickly adding before al-Otaybi could refute, "And it will provide me ample opportunity to check on your chest wound. You suffered significant damage to your rib cage and your lung during your mishap on the boat. You still need medical care."

This bit of faux concern seemed convincing, and al-Otaybi shrugged in indifference.

"I'll pack and prepare for our transfer while you make arrangements for crossing the border into Iraq," said al-Onezi.

Al-Otaybi shrugged again, "Sure. We leave tomorrow morning at first light. I'll get us across the border, and then we'll link up with al-Sadr when we get there. Be prepared for a long drive. We'll cross at the small town of Khanaquin, in Diyala governorate. The guards on both sides of the border will wave us through provided we're generous with *baksheesh.*"

"It's ironic you used the word *baksheesh*," replied al-Onezi. "You know, of course, this word for bribe derives from Farsi and is one of the many foul byproducts of Persian civilization."

"I don't care," rudely retorted al-Otaybi. "Just have cash ready."

Chapter 31

Camp Arifjan, Kuwait. Three weeks later.

The following three weeks were a whirlwind for Haley. Not only were his curtailment orders cut, meaning the duration of his tour at Embassy Kuwait City was significantly reduced, he also learned that he was assigned a new temporary home with the U.S. Army. He received official word through the State Department that he would be on secondment to United States Army Central, or ARCENT, headquartered at Shaw Air Force Base in South Carolina. In explaining this to his parents, his mother, in particular, he had to temper her expectations that this would imply a move back home. Instead, it meant a simple jaunt across town; the ARCENT military formation sustained a forward element at Camp Arifjan, Kuwait.

His mother had long hoped he would be assigned closer to home, jesting "maybe at an embassy in Columbia or even Atlanta!" He had to explain to her the foreign service didn't work that way but joked back that should South Carolina secede from the union again, perhaps he could be stationed in the foreign affairs headquarters of the new confederacy, which would certainly be closer to home than Washington, D.C.

Upon Haley's release from the hospital, he was picked up by Philson in a suburban, and they swung by his apartment to pick up a few items.

The rest of his household effects would be packed up and moved into storage until permanent orders were issued.

Though only around seventy kilometers away from the embassy, Haley felt he was on a different planet. Camp Arifjan, or *Arifjail*, as the local denizens grumblingly referred to it, had the olive drabness of all U.S. Army bases, and was matched by the even duller brownness of the dusty landscape. There was no proper green or other spirit lifting color on the base to speak of. Even the army combat uniform's camouflage scheme was dust-colored, as were the buildings, which Haley soon realized was because they were covered in, well, dust. Since Haley's arrival, he had witnessed two sandstorms which changed the scenery from light brown to bleak, desolate orange. "What have I gotten myself into," he moaned, while questioning his life choices which had led him there.

What actually led him to Arifjan was a scheme concocted by Wilson Edger. Edger, working his interagency magic, knew Haley needed a safe place to recuperate, and while recovering, Haley could be useful in developing a plan to finally go on the offensive. He asked Haley to spend time researching, drafting, and otherwise briefing and preparing Philson's team for a potential mission to counter the efforts of Ali al-Sadr and his likely backing by Muhsin Bin Laden. He also tasked Haley with exhaustively reviewing records and encounters dating back to the al-Qahtani Messianic plot and perhaps scope out trends and details that might be useful in thwarting their nemeses. Edger's scheme was clearly perceived as loony among interagency colleagues in Washington, but given Haley's history of run-ins, there was a growing consensus that he seemed adept at pulling the figurative tiger's tail. Now, however, it was time to face the tiger head-on, but to do that, they needed a strategic plan of action.

Haley himself thought this was a ridiculous notion but agreed to it because it offered him a place to rehabilitate and get in shape without jeopardizing the safety of his embassy colleagues. Plus, he had nowhere else to go.

In the mornings he rehabilitated his shoulder muscles, and during the day, and well into the evenings, he researched and otherwise provided Philson guidance in building out their yet to be determined mission plan. Haley's job was to help craft for Philson a project to pitch to his commander that would involve his team of Green Berets eliminating or capturing the targets who had made Haley's life difficult, and more strategically, were stoking undercurrents of unrest in the region.

Nimrod, Doc, and the other Green Berets tried to hypercharge Haley's rehabilitation by persuading him to join them in their "Murphs." A "Murph" he learned, was a workout that involved a one-mile run, one hundred pull-ups, two hundred push-ups, and three hundred air squats, followed by another one-mile run, all in body armor. The brutal workout regime was a favorite of and eponymously named for Michael Murphy, a Navy SEAL officer who was killed in action in Afghanistan in 2005. At Haley's most physically fit, during his enlistment in the army, he doubted he could manage half a Murph. Being a little softened by excellent dining in Kuwait, coupled with a wounded shoulder, he knew he stood no chance at all.

Though unable to compete with the Special Forces operators, over the course of the three weeks at the base, Haley began regaining strength in his muscles, improving his stamina, and reducing his pain. It would be some time before Haley could manage a respectable number of pull-ups or push-ups, but for now, he was content to get back into running and other simple workouts.

***

His days and evenings were filled with researching, compiling data, and planning. He began drafting his notes into extensive reports that covered his initial visa interviews with the younger al-Qahtani and his cousin al-Otaybi, who was still at large. He also documented his interview with and research into the elder al-Qahtani and his connection to the Iranian geneticist, Dr. Farhad Hassan. He outlined what he knew about Dr. Ibrahim Mustafa, dating back to his father's death in 1979, and his death, and that of Paula Abrams at the hands of two assailants he instinctively believed were al-Otaybi and the younger al-Qahtani.

He narrated for the first time the full details of the bomb attack of his vehicle in al-Aziziyah, Iraq, the deaths of Abdulrazzaq and Stearney, and the subsequent and brutal interrogation and torture he and Sami Yacoub faced at the hands of "Abdullah." He noted this was at the behest of Ali al-Sadr. He pulled video files of al-Qahtani's messianic reveal in Mecca before the broadcast was abruptly cut by Saudi authorities. He frequently called Khalil to check on his translation of the transcript of al-Qahtani's speech and ensured wide circulation among defense, consular, and intelligence networks of the pictures of the man in the background holding a young boy. Per al-Qahtani's remarks, the boy was key to his plan, and seemingly, the man holding him was key to the boy. He noted the need to identify this man.

Haley's notes also covered the attack on Philson and himself on the boat, adding in descriptions of physical characteristics of al-Otaybi and the method of the attack and then the later attack on the restaurant, in which he and Cooper barely escaped. He emphasized his suspicion that the second assailant, who was denied entry to the restaurant, was likely al-Otaybi.

Though not detecting any particular tie-ins, per Edger's admonishing, he also noted his ICRC work and the repatriation of Iraqi mortal remains and the mysterious map found on the corpse of a very deceased and decomposed Hussein al-Sadr. He didn't presume a connection to the other events, but noted in his findings that the boat attack ensued not long after this discovery. He also drew from his recollection and notes the commentaries of Drs. Bargouthi and al-Marri regarding palimpsests and the potential incendiary nature of material that might question the most commonly held Islamic beliefs throughout the Middle East. These beliefs, he concluded, were purveyed by the religious powers that be, who were housed conveniently in Mecca, Saudi Arabia, and under convenient social contract with the political establishment. And never far from his mind was the actual, physical role the Bin Laden barons had in building and refurbishing that establishment. This thought recalled for him his conversation with the salty French veteran Colonel Girard de Castille who participated in breaking the 1979 siege of Mecca. The colonel's account of the gruesome nature of the events—and the subsequent Saudi coverup and smuggling of the supposed Messiah, al-Qahtani, to France and his apparent ties to Ayatollah Khomeini—still haunted and mystified Haley.

Not escaping Haley was the fact that his newfound notoriety ranked well below that of another former resident of Camp Arifjan. Former U.S. Army enlisted soldier Bradley Manning also graced the base with his presence briefly while being investigated and processed for prosecution for disclosing to the public domain some 750,000 classified or otherwise sensitive military and diplomatic files. Manning seemingly directed his own personal grievances against the military, society, and nature into the betrayal of trust instilled in him and illegally transferred these files to disreputable peddlers of sensational news, reportedly on compact discs marked under Lady Gaga labels. Manning's name remained mud among patriots in the State and Defense Departments who feared how his leaking of files placed the lives of many friends of the United States in danger. His saga, in which he later identified himself as a woman, led him to a prison term, later commuted, a failed run for congress, speaking engagements, and subsequently more jail time.

Haley hoped his time in Kuwait would be less momentous. He simply sought to make sense of the last few years of his life and hopefully and presciently understand the games played by nefarious spoilers.

Philson checked in with him daily, as did Edger, who now joined him at Camp Arifjan. They spent hours each day building charts and collecting snippets of information on whom the known players were, where they were, and perhaps what they were up to. As a result of this process, they compiled more questions than they did answers.

Haley marveled at the sheer amounts of data, reports, charts, and spreadsheets he developed, all reflecting on the last two years of his life. He worked tirelessly, feeling he owed his best efforts to Paula, Dr. Ibrahim, Jordan, Philson, and others caught up in this madness, which all started with a simple visa interview. Seeing his account in writing somehow removed him into an out-of-body observer status, and he began objectively seeing linkages he had never realized. As such, he was grateful to Edger for forcing this information and intelligence reconciliation.

Several themes became apparent. They needed to find Bin Laden, al-Otaybi, al-Sadr, and the mystery minder of the young boy present at al-Qahtani's death. They needed to know if they were thwarted or if they were simply regrouping. The two attempts on Haley's life suggested the latter.

Bin Laden's whereabouts were unknown. Either the Saudis were being unhelpful, desiring to move beyond yet another embarrassing chapter, or they simply didn't know where he was. Haley was dubious about this and imagined it wouldn't be too hard to track someone of his stature down by following the money trails. Ali al-Sadr, however, they believed was in Iraq. Iraqi interior ministry officials tipped off their counterparts at the U.S. Embassy he had recently arrived in Baghdad under a fake name. Philson, Edger, and Haley agreed to start with him.

Part VII

Chapter 32

Camp Arifjan, Kuwait.

Haley perceived himself as pretty useless. He was relegated to being the "report guy" and certainly couldn't help in any real way of planning a mission to grab and bag al-Sadr. He had no idea where to find him, and even though he wanted some payback for the murder of two colleagues and his own torture in Iraq, he questioned the legality and morality of essentially kidnapping the guy. He hoped that if the operation materialized, it wouldn't take place in front of his kids, if he had any. As for other family members, based on two of the many Green Beret epithets reserved for al-Sadr, Haley was sure the villain had no parents, at least none that weren't canines.

Haley provided Edger and Philson all the details he knew regarding Ali al-Sadr: He was a large, barrel chested, hirsute, and mustachioed man. He added in the detail that he was also a bit bow-legged but knew that completed the description of just about every Iraqi man, harshly judged Haley. Predictably, this depiction helped no one on the team or anyone in his home office back in D.C. track al-Sadr down.

"There is no way of knowing where he might be, or if he's actually still in Iraq. And I'll bet he and his sugar daddy's money have bought a great deal of silence. No one in Iraq will give him up," moaned Haley during a daily planning session. "The place he held me turned out to be al-Aziziyah, down south in Wasit governorate. He could just as easily be in downtown Baghdad or at his ancestral home of Sadr City," posited Haley as he sat in an Arifjan conference room with Edger, Philson, Doc, Spook, the ever-present Nimrod, and other members of his team.

"I had a Seder meal once at a Jewish Passover celebration," interjected Nimrod. "It was when we were cross-training in Israel with their special forces *Sayeret* counterparts who were teaching us *Krav Maga* [Israeli martial arts]."

"Can't you hear the difference between 'Sadr' and 'Seder,' you Nimrod?" asked Doc rolling his eyes. "And do you even know what Passover is? You don't have to call it a Jewish Passover. That's redundant. That's like saying 'Christian Easter.' Did you flunk Sunday School? Ain't you seen the movie about Moses receiving the Ten Commandments so he could rule the planet of the apes?"

"Or maybe you prefer a Christian Christmas?" interjected Spook. "I like the movie where the Grinch stole Charlie Brown's pathetic little Christmas tree."

"I'm telling you, it was a spiritual experience for me," Nimrod continued seriously, ignoring his brothers-in-arms. "We celebrated the black sabbath by not working, and then ate macho balls with some kind of flat cracker bread. It was like boring pizza. I was still hungry, so I got up and made me a kosher ham sandwich."

Doc started rummaging through his bag threatening to give Nimrod another experimental injection, "You know, there is nothing correct whatsoever about anything you just said."

Spook circled behind Nimrod to refresh himself on some of the Krav Maga holds they had learned.

Haley found their interaction highly amusing, knowing they were a lot more intelligent than they let on.

"If we can't find al-Sadr, why not bring him out into the open?" Haley suddenly asked. "I have an idea of what would make him surface."

"Other than his man crush on you, what do you think would attract his attention?" pressed Philson.

Haley gave the slightest shrug.

"No. No way. This guy has tried to kill you on at least four occasions. No way are we dangling you on a hook," Philson snapped back. Edger nodded in agreement. Nimrod, Doc, and Spook also showed unprecedented seriousness and nodded their dissent to the idea.

"I'm not keen on being terror bait myself, but no doubt, he has a fixation on me. I don't wish to expose myself so would suggest something else . . ." Haley paused for effect. "Why don't we do some treasure hunting? Based on the map we found on the body in the desert, we have a general idea of where to look in Iraq. Given that this map was conveniently stolen in Kuwait, and just afterward, Nate and I were attacked on the boat, it's safe to assume al-Sadr is keeping an eye out for me," Haley added.

"I don't see the connection, though," quipped Edger.

"Probably not much of one. I'm only suggesting that the map on number fifty-five was valuable enough for someone to steal and risk his life in 1990 and valuable enough for someone to steal it again from the museum—after a discovery publicly attributed to me. Not long afterward, al-Sadr's goons tried to send us to Davy Jones's locker. I'm just saying we should peak into the 'Maroof' tomb and see what the fuss is about. Could be that it's already been raided. If not, it's likely important to our nemeses, as well. If our goal is to finally get ahead of these guys, and we think this might be important to them, let's take a look before they have the chance to."

Bored with weeks of planning, Philson yearned for action. So did his team. He shrugged his acquiescence toward Edger, who also nodded in the affirmative. Philson then looked to his team. "You Nimrod, please go alert Dad and the rest of the team to start getting ready to go back to Iraq. I'll work on the pitch to the colonel."

Chapter 33

Eastern Iraq. Two days later.

Much to al-Onezi's relief, the crossing from Iran into Iraq went smoothly, courtesy of a wad of U.S. dollars from al-Otaybi's pockets. The guards on both sides of the border appeared very disinterested in whom they allowed to exit or enter their countries, provided there was profit for them. Al-Onezi was glad to be outside of Iran but despised how easily his own kinsmen could be bought. "Where was their integrity," he moaned, lamenting how this and other porous border crossings led Saddam to use chemical weapons against eastern Iraqi Kurds whom he believed facilitated the incursion of Iranians into Iraq during the 1980–88 war.

Al-Otaybi continued to drive in silence. He had driven the whole trip and showed no signs of weariness or other desire to turn over the driving responsibility to al-Onezi. Their car was a small, white, otherwise nondescript, early 2000s Toyota Allion model sedan, just the car for them as they made their way to Iraq. Al-Onezi carefully crafted a lie to his Iranian religious minders in Qom saying he needed to take young Mohammed to Tehran for a medical checkup and would return the next day. He also maintained his lie to al-Otaybi that al-Sadr had summoned them back to Iraq, where Mohammed would continue his religious studies in Najaf and Kerbala. He feared for his life and that of Mohammed's should either lie be discovered.

Mohammed, for his part, slept most of the trip or engaged in long recitations of Quranic passages, often rocking back and forth in cadence to his own lilting singing of his sacred writ. The rhythmic intoning of his uttering aided him in memorizing the long and archaic passages that comprised the Quran.

During the last three hours of their journey, al-Onezi's relief grew as they passed into flatter topography and through familiar sounding names of Iraqi towns—Khanaquin, Muqdadiyah, Baaqooba, and so on. He recalled an assignment to a military hospital somewhere in the Diyala governorate, near its capital of Baaqooba, was precluded by the onset of the 2003 U.S. invasion of Iraq.

As they approached the outskirts of Sadr City, al-Otaybi suddenly picked up one of several burner phones and punched in a series of numbers. He spoke hastily as he requested directions to his destination. Al-Otaybi's eyebrows rose a bit, indicating instructions had changed. After a pause while he listened, he said a quick *"Eh, eh, fahemt [yes, yes, understood],"* and then clicked off the phone.

"I'm to continue west into Baghdad City, the al-Karkh District, on the other side of the Tigris River," al-Otaybi said. "I have been asked to arrange the recovery of some items in a shrine. What are your orders? Where am I to drop you?" he continued indifferently.

Al-Onezi steeled himself into not reacting. He had been most worried about what he would say or do when he showed up in al-Sadr City. He had the flimsiest of justifications at the ready and none he thought would satiate al-Sadr. This detour was fortunate, however, as he knew in Shia-dominated Sadr City, he would essentially be trapped. In Baghdad, on the other hand, he could blend into the background while he worked out his own plan for himself and Mohammed. He quickly contrived another lie, "I'm to continue accompanying you to Baghdad and from there, coordinate our transfer to the holy city of Najaf. Tell me where you're going, and I'll have our people on standby to pick us up for the transfer."

"You can tell your people to meet you outside the Maroof al-Karkhi shrine and mosque. Tomorrow night. I will meet some friends of Ali al-Sadr's there. Your people should avoid the mosque. There is an old train depot nearby. Have them meet you there," al-Otaybi said, continuing, "I'll be in the area scoping out the place for a couple of days and waiting for some men to help me with a project there. You need to stay out of the way."

Chapter 34

U.S. Embassy Baghdad. Baghdad, Iraq.

It was strange for Haley to be back in Baghdad and back at the embassy. It was only about seven months prior that he was asked to leave his posting, yet it seemed a lifetime. A number of colleagues that he knew from his time there had already left, given they tended to rotate after only short tours of a year or so. The local staff, of course, stayed longer. Unfortunately, though, Haley's dear friend, Sami Yacoub, had returned to Egypt. Colleagues said he was quite traumatized by the ordeal he and Haley had suffered and decided the extra money for serving in Baghdad wasn't worth it. No one blamed him. Ghada al-Jibouri was still there and in the middle of training up yet another green political officer. Haley dropped in on her to say hello.

"Clayton, it's so nice to see you. We've missed you so much here since you left. We felt cheated a bit that we didn't spend as much time with you," she kindly said.

"Ghada, I'm the one who was cheated. I learned so much from you, and there was so much more to discover. It's too bad I wasn't able to stay longer," he replied. "I was also having a nice time next door in Kuwait until some old friends showed up," he continued.

"Yes, yes, we know. We've read all about your escapades. We hope that your next assignment will be very, very quiet, and none of your troubles will follow you there. Do you have an embassy in Antarctica?"

she half-joked. She then teased, "But I hear you have your eye on someone in Kuwait?"

"I wonder what or who gave you that idea," slyly suggested Haley, knowing it must have been Khalil, as he had encouraged him to coordinate research with al-Jiboori on bilateral Iraqi-Kuwaiti relations.

"Any future for you two?" she pried.

"I doubt it. I would like to explore things further with her but am afraid that I bring a lot of unwanted attention and wouldn't want to put her in danger by association with me," he replied, looking sheepishly at the floor.

"Every relationship has its risks, Clayton." she gently chided.

"I'm kind of a special case," he retorted and then changed the uncomfortable topic to something equally sensitive. "Ghada, I need your help. My request to you is cleared through the ambassador, but please note that it's sensitive. I want you to stop me at any point, and let me know if I'm asking you to do anything you're not comfortable with, ok?"

Al-Jibouri nodded but was clearly uncertain as to the nature of Haley's proposition.

"There is a very slight chance that my friends and I will stumble across some historical items in the next day or so. I can't go into detail, but I've been sent here to ask for your help. Should we be successful, we'll need a reputable archivist, archaeologist, curator, historian, or some combination of these professions to, one, preserve our find, and two, study it and make a determination about what to do with it. We feel strongly that whatever we find may be of interest to scientists worldwide, but first and foremost, it should belong to Iraq and the Iraqi people. We're not here to steal anything, only find what might be missing and keep it out of the hands of others who would exploit it," Haley pled. "Does this make sense?"

"Not at all," al-Jibouri smiled. "But let me make some calls and line up the best and most reputable scholars to, as you say, 'have on hand.'"

"Thank you. As always, you're about two steps ahead of me," Haley smiled in relief. "I'll call you as soon as I hear anything. All we'll need from you is to have the proper experts on hand to receive whatever we find and take precautionary measures to preserve it to ensure a thorough study of it," he concluded.

"Shouldn't you just take Iraqis along with you on your project?" she asked.

"Yes, but should this effort be approached through proper channels, we fear either red tape or potentially corrupt officials may thwart it," he replied, unhappy with his own answer.

Chapter 35

Railyards, West of Maroof al-Karkhi Shrine and Tomb.
Baghdad, Iraq. 11:00 p.m.

The following night, Philson brought Haley to the team house on the secure special operations compound at the Baghdad diplomatic support center on the outskirts of Baghdad International Airport. On the outside, it appeared to be a small warehouse for ammunition storage. On the inside, however, it looked to be the ultimate man cave. It included a makeshift gym, in which Tank was powerlifting, and contained some jerry-rigged barbells made of coffee cans filled with sand epoxied to reinforcement bars, or rebar. Nimrod reclined on a weathered couch playing Call of Duty, while Doc and Spook were taking turns flicking darts at a target resembling Qassem Suleimani, the former head of Iran's Islamic Revolutionary Guard Corps.

As Haley followed Philson toward the back of the building, he noticed coolers full of Coors Light beer on ice and wondered where and how the ODA team obtained ice. Philson punched in a code on a door keypad and ushered Haley into the OPCEN [Operation Center]. Chief Reims and Dad were there analyzing maps and drinking coffee in a small three-tabled room. Phone and computer lines snaked along the floor and the walls.

"Good to see you again, Mr. Haley," Chief, or Chip, as Haley knew him, said in his thick Kentucky accent. "Are you ready for tonight?"

"We'll see," Haley replied apprehensively, suddenly cognizant of the seriousness of the mission on which he was about to embark.

"Right on. I'll grab the guys so we can start the mission brief," said Dad.

After only a few seconds, the team flowed in and took seats around a monitor. Clayton noted that for the first time since he had known the Green Berets, they appeared serious. He was in awe. Each soldier comported himself with intense focus, somberness, and fierce determination. Each team member demonstrated mastery over his role and spoke in precision over every detail of the mission plan, as laid out by the chief. He almost felt sorry for anyone these warfighters might encounter in the hours ahead.

After about an hour, the briefing came to a close and Philson asked if there were any alibis or comments. "No? Alright then. Let's get ready."

As the team filed out Haley sought a quick word with Philson about his own role, which had been clearly laid out as "observer—keep your butt in the van." Before he could make a case for something less passive, he heard the distinct sound of Led Zeppelin's "Immigrant Song" blasting through the door.

Tank motioned Haley to join him in the armory enclave next to the dartboard and gestured to equipment apparently set aside especially for him. In a cubby marked simply as "Embassy Dude," Haley found and retrieved body armor, helmet, radio, and Peltors—headphones that protected hearing while allowing transmission of communications. Haley, unable to speak over the blaring music, gestured hopefully at a nearby M4 rifle and Glock 19 sidearm.

"Sorry, dude. You're not allowed to carry," said Tank loudly, shaking his head while winking and secretly slipping the Glock under Haley's body armor.

***

Given this was a city operation, they opted for vehicles less conspicuous than tactical military vehicles or even up-armored Suburbans or Mitsubishi Pajeros. Instead, they drove old Nissan Urvans, minivan-like vehicles with five or six passenger capacity and with removable seat to accommodate cargo. These were common around the city, typically used in delivering bread, milk, or other groceries.

Four vehicles, spaced in intervals of around fifteen minutes, drove from the embassy almost due north and moved the short distance of ten kilometers. They congregated at expansive rail yards, which contained ten or eleven enormous warehouses and factories. Most of these were long dormant—since the 2003 U.S. military invasion—and they provided excellent cover for the vans as they assembled. Plus, they were conveniently located a few hundred feet away from the Maroof al-Karkhi shrine.

The shrine, per Haley's online research and study, looked like an enormous turquoise sombrero from the ground, like something one might see at the infamous and ridiculous "South of the Border" attraction on Interstate 95 between South and North Carolina.

He had perused a number of satellite photos and compared them to the photocopied map shared by ICRC. The map identified a building as roughly center point between the ancient Round City and a Tigris River oxbow, and per the overlays Haley had reviewed and the markings on the crude map, he was convinced the Maroof al-Karkhi tomb was the X that marked the spot. Per Internet articles, he was further convinced the Khans were superstitious, and if one wanted to hide treasure or material from them, the tomb of a saint would be the optimal hiding spot. If the map was accurate, Haley was confident he had identified the location intended by a survivor of the 1258 destruction of Baghdad. He wasn't sure at all if there was anything to recover, however.

Haley's adrenaline ran high as he exited the vehicle and congregated in one of the rail yard warehouses. He insisted on coming, over the objections of Edger, Philson, and the regional security officer in

Baghdad. He was allowed only under the condition that he remain with the vehicles and under the protection of the ODA team. It was highly unusual for a civilian to participate in an operation. Everything about this mission was unusual, though, so allowances were made. He had argued Iraqi Special Forces should join the team, but was overruled on this count, given coordinating such a mission would have taken a very long time and opened it up for more scrutiny and leaks. This would have defeated the purpose of potentially beating al-Sadr to the punch in finding whatever lie within the shrine's confines.

Haley moved into the back of one of the more especially equipped vans, often referred to locally as lorries, and plugged in headphones and a microphone and turned on a monitor so he could communicate with the team and watch the operation unfold. He felt pretty cool. The Green Berets were wearing camouflage with their gear, but Haley was dressed in khaki cargo pants and a black shirt, with desert motif military boots. He was fit but lacked the brawn of the team, but otherwise looked the part of the Special Forces operative, hardly the pinstriped reputation typically ascribed to State Department officers. He wondered what Cooper would say if she could see him now . . .

Philson began ordering his team to move out. Dad, Chip, Tank, Nimrod, Spook, Joseph Smith, and Doc began the trek from the rail yard to the shrine. In addition to their weapons, they carried with them rucksacks with tools they might need to excavate, including shovels, pry and crow bars, battery-operated reciprocating saws—in the event they had to saw through metal or wood— and sledge hammers—in case they were needed for stone or marble. It was only a few hundred feet, so they anticipated reaching the destination in less than ten minutes. They scurried in the shadows and across a surrounding cemetery with thousands of graves in it. Philson, and two other soldiers stayed behind with Haley to monitor from the safety of the vehicles. Only the small sliver of a moon shone on the area, meaning the team would likely not be spotted.

All seemed to be going well, according to relays coming in over the radio. Joseph Smith, the eighteen echo, or communications specialist, did most of the talking. Haley made a mental note that since their departure from the vehicles, not a single wisecrack, joke, or bit of profanity had been uttered. "These guys are all fun and games until it comes to a mission, and then they're deadly or more accurately, lethally, serious," he thought.

Joseph Smith whispered updates as they grew closer to the shrine, codenamed "casa" per the sombrero reference. The main entrance to the shrine was on a ramped walkway, which was too exposed for the group, so they opted to enter from the cemetery through a basement-level door.

"Eyes on a target," crackled Joseph Smith over the radio.

"On it," said Doc. "Moving to immobilize."

The crew in the vehicles waited and watched the green images at work, as transmitted by cameras mounted on the chests of the team.

"Target is down. Repeat. Tango is down. Nighty night," said Doc, who had just injected a tranquilizer in a night guard who had already been asleep, leaning back on his chair, next to the lower-level door. "He'll have a headache in the morning but will otherwise be okay."

"Scouting around for other guards," said Joseph Smith in his headpiece's microphone, which conducted transmissions through the skull and into the inner ear, hence the name, "bone phone." Though a tomb, the shrine to Maroof al-Karkhi also served as a functioning mosque and a national heritage site. Therefore, in planning the mission, and then reconnoitering, the team had anticipated at least a guard or two.

There apparently were no other guards at the shrine, and the team moved to the entrance. Tank and Spook extracted tools to take the door off its hinges, but Doc handed them keys he found when rifling through his "tango's" pockets.

Haley watched the screen, wishing he could be with the team. He saw them move carefully as a unit into the interior but leaving Tank behind at the door. The mosque was quite spacious, but their intended destination was easy to identify. In an alcove, of sorts, was a tall ornate, gold looking structure, built from the floor nearly to the ceiling. The shrine was a rectangle in shape, with the top half of the edifice considerably larger than its base. The apex of the shrine almost touched the nadir of a glass chandelier, which was hung from the center of a dome decorated with Arabic calligraphy. Islam, Haley knew, discouraged or forbade that characterization of nature, so Islamic art tended to display its beauty in script.

Haley marveled at the speed and fluidity of the team's movement as they crossed the expanse to the shrine in less than a few seconds. Spook and Doc immediately went to work, using their reciprocating saws with dust catchers to ensure as little evidence as possible might be left behind. They cut through existing seams on the corners so as to piece it back afterward, thus hiding their work.

They made quick time dismantling the outer structure and pulling it apart. Inside it was a rectangle box, draped in tapestry. They applied pry bars to jimmy the lid free.

The radio crackled. "Opening coffin-shaped box," came in an unidentified voice.

After an infuriating pause, "Nothing. Dust, garments, maybe. Nothing of significance."

The video feed confirmed as much. Spook's camera took primacy on the screen. As described, there didn't seem to be anything of importance in the casket. It scanned from end to end, but the tomb robbing effort appeared to be an abject failure and a waste of time.

Haley began to feel foolish and embarrassed. Though he had couched this adventure as a very low likelihood of success, he hadn't really prepared himself for coming up totally empty. He refused to imagine just how much a jaunt like this really cost. He tried to remind himself that this was his idea but not his decision. The green light for this mission was given way above his pay grade. He knew, however, that he would be a likely and convenient scapegoat. And though not at fault, this would probably end his already too short-lived State Department career. Jordan would also likely not be impressed.

As he descended into despondency, he stared at the screen, afraid to catch Philson's or Edger's eye.

"Y'all expecting guests?" suddenly crackled the radio.

"Tank? What's going on?" asked Philson.

"I'm counting upward of two zero tangos. They're coming our way. I recommend we vamoose post-haste!" he urged.

"Roger that. Everyone out. Now! Don't worry about the coffin. Just get out. I want no tussle with Iraqi police or security forces. Out!" Philson ordered.

It became even harder for Haley to follow what was going on. With mics being jostled and yelled whispers on the bone phones, it sounded like pandemonium, yet within only a few seconds, all were reported accounted for outside the building.

"Hold in place!" Dad gave a rare order. "They're coming here. To the shrine. They're going up the ramp to the main entrance. Let's see what they're up to and why it takes so many armed tangos to check on a mosque."

While the team held in place, Haley held his breath. This was very unexpected. He had feared discovery by a night watchman, not a squad of soldiers.

Joseph Smith, apparently getting silent orders from Dad, slipped back into the mosque to leave behind his camera and then slipped out again.

SMASH! The large ornate, wooden front doors burst inward.

Joseph Smith's camera was hastily inserted into the shrine and did not have sound, but still, through the greenish hue, Haley could roughly make out what was happening. A crew of armed thugs had entered the mosque by means of a police style battering ram. They certainly weren't being as careful as Philson's team.

Chapter 36

Maroof al-Karkhi Shrine. Baghdad, Iraq.

No. The new crew wasn't being careful. They ran up to the shrine and began pulling at its corners and discarding the material on the surrounding floor, leaving only the coffin, with its lid back in place. If the images transmitted to Haley's monitor had been clearer, they would have shown surprise on the faces of the intruders. Their job was surprisingly easy, but they couldn't have known the ODA team had done them this solid favor.

Like the ODA team, the new crew pried the lid from its resting place. Haley noted for the first time they moved with care but presumed this due to their concerns about dropping the heavy marble lid on toes.

As four men removed the lid, others approached the coffin and used shovels to scoop what they could out of the sepulcher and into satchels. This was clearly their goal, observed a very puzzled Haley and Philson from the vehicles.

"This has to be al-Sadr's folks. There is no other explanation for why some other group hits the same tomb as us on the same night," whispered Haley to Philson.

"No denying the odd timing. They certainly don't mind leaving a mess. I guess they didn't bring any historians or curators or archaeologists on their team either, did they?" asked Philson, staring at the melee caused by the green silhouetted characters.

"Do our guys have facial recognition ability with any of their equipment?" interjected Haley suddenly.

"Sure, but they can't see through walls. And I don't want to send them into the small confines of the mosque. No way we can get them in and out without losing someone," Philson responded.

"Of course not, but we need to get eyes on the guy who seems to be in charge. The guy standing in the background on the screen," Haley pointed. "He has the slight build and height of al-Otaybi. Either I need to get closer to try and identify him, or one of the guys can capture him in a clear photo as he leaves. Can we move someone around the front to get a shot?"

"Joseph Smith, head around the front of the building to get some photos of any squirters as they leave. We especially want to get a shot of the guy in charge. Wait till they leave. If confirmed it's al-Otaybi, be prepared to snatch and grab him. And be prepared for some resistance. Dad, make the call for action if we do indeed identify him. Remember, this guy is lethal. Rules of engagement apply. Return fire if fired upon," ordered Philson into the microphone.

"Roger. Moving," replied Joseph Smith simply.

"Tank, Spook, Doc, Nimrod, follow him. Get ready," responded Dad. "I'll cover the back entrance, in case anyone is dying to meet me."

This was painful for Haley to watch. Not only had his information resulted in a failed mission to recover historical artifacts of value, now people, including his friends, might die. And he was helpless and could only watch disaster unfold on the screen in front of him. This, he felt, was the worst moment of his life. He tried to apologize to Philson, "I'm so sorry for getting you into this." Even in the green-tinted light of the vehicle, he could see worry lines on Philson's face.

"We're good. Nobody gets us into nothing. We knew the costs of this mission and still believe in it. And don't worry about the team. Just wait till you see them in action," he smiled.

"I got a squirter coming out. Sending you a photo now. Several more filing out behind him. Two with satchels over their shoulders. Is he our boy?" crackled Joseph Smith into the live feed.

The interminable wait for the photo was excruciating. Adding more frustration was when the grainy photo came into focus, he noted the first guy was clearly not al-Otaybi. Nor was the second. Haley knew that his determination was essential to making a decision tonight that might lead to the deaths of militants on both sides of the equation.

"Negative on the first two," said Philson in response to Haley's gesture.

While waiting for photos, Haley observed the live feed from Joseph Smith's chest cam, which was aimed at the entrance. It was too far away to make positive identifications but did provide a view of what the group was up to. As they filed out of the mosque, they assembled on the ramp, which was walled in on both sides by high barricades, presumably for crowd control for faithful pilgrims intent on connecting to their spiritual heritage instead of pilfering it, as Haley cynically thought. Snapping Haley out of his reverie, he noticed one of the team peeling off and pulling his phone out of his pocket.

"Nate, tell Joseph Smith to get a close up of the guy off to the left, the one on his phone. Quick," urged Haley suddenly.

Within three seconds, a file with a photo popped up on the screen.

"That's him. That's our guy. That's al-Otaybi," Haley nearly shouted, recalling the personal visa interview he had with him, how many times he had reviewed his visa application, and of course, how he came face to face with him on the boat. Joseph Smith, Tank, Doc, and Spook, all positioned themselves at various vantage points to pin down their quarry.

"Green light. It's a go. Primary target is the guy on the phone. Appears to be wearing jeans, dark shirt, and leather jacket. Take him down," ordered Philson.

"*QIFOO. LA TATAHARAKOO. EIYAD ALA FOUQ. [STOP.
DON'T MOVE. HANDS UP]!*" shouted a voice, presumably Joseph
Smith.

The next few seconds were pandemonium. Haley could capture
very little of what was happening on his screen. He heard yelling and
shouting and the rat-tat-tat of shooting of what he presumed were the
slightly deeper tones of Kalashnikov 7.62-caliber rounds, responded to
by the higher velocity firing of the ODA's M-4s 5.56 bullets. The sounds
of live action were confused by his proximity to the calamity. He could
clearly hear the sounds of the attack from outside the van.

A loud explosion sent a shock wave through the area. Haley heard
it through his earpiece and at the same time, outside the van. He even
felt a shock wave rumble under the vehicle. He looked at Philson, who
exchanged a glance that all was okay, somehow.

"Clayton. You need to get over here now. Hurry!" said a voice
through Haley's earpiece, perhaps Dad's, after an agonizing radio silence.

After another exchanged glance with Philson and then a shrug,
the two gathered their gear, including armored vests and weapons for
Philson. They exited the van and sprinted to the shrine. Haley found
that adrenaline enabled him to keep up with Philson pace for pace. He
also wondered what he was running to and why. And he silently thanked
God for Tank's slipping a weapon under his vest giving him an extra
dose of confidence and, maybe, some invulnerability.

The two covered the distance in just under a few minutes. It shocked
Haley to see how close their stake out position was to the mosque. Until
now, Haley comprehended the distance and the actions that took place
only via maps, overlays, and computer images. Now, he found himself
running to a real location, in real time. He allowed himself to wonder
what Jordan would think of this escapade. He was sure that Glennon
would disapprove; certainly this was conduct unbecoming, or at least
out of the norm for a State Department foreign service officer.

As they approached the mosque, Dad waved them over, not to the back entrance but to the ramp, from which Haley could see the gunfight had led to considerable damage to the building. He wondered how this would be explained to the authorities.

"What happened?" Philson quickly asked. "Explain."

"I was out back so didn't see it all go down. But before we give you our brief, let me direct your attention to this gaping hole. Clayton, right this way," explained Dad, turning to Haley.

Utterly confused, Haley followed Dad. He pushed past a contingent of eight combatants with hands zip-tied behind their backs and hoods over their heads, all lined up against the wall and under the careful observation of Tank and his M-4. He then passed the remains of five militants who apparently opted to fight back against the ODA team, despite being overmatched and trapped. Beyond them, he saw the damaged mosque. And then he understood why Dad summoned him.

In a few glances, his eyes interpreted the scene. The gunfight would have only lasted seconds. Nimrod, Joseph Smith, Tank, Doc, and Spook spared those fortunate enough to not have weapons or wise enough not to fire back. Others who did met immediate lethal retribution. But closer to the mosque, one apparently opted to reach for a grenade instead of his AK-47. He had time to pull the pin on the device but not throw it. As ODA rounds sunk into his body, it pushed him back, killing him instantly and forcing him to drop his grenade, ending the lives of two remaining bandits by detonating two other grenades he carried on his belt, nearly disintegrating his body and creating the gaping hole referenced by Dad.

Haley moved past the debris and detritus of humanity left on the ramp. It was shocking, but not his first time seeing the disgusting consequence of violence. He hated it and saw it as unnecessary and unfortunate. He challenged himself as an aspiring diplomat to do all he could to prevent conflict but knew human nature and its proclivity toward violence would continue to cause misery. His thoughts did an about face, however, as he gazed into the gap.

The explosion had blown apart some of the wall on the ramp but also some of the external wall of the mosque itself. He could see into the empty space below, and at what essentially appeared to be a closed-in basement of the mosque. Haley noticed a large, ancient, crude wooden box, anachronistic to its surroundings.

"We need to grab this box and go," he said.

"Affirmative," replied Philson.

"What about our friends here?" asked Tank. "We gonna leave them to the authorities?"

"Sure. Why not? They can explain to the ministry of interior why they decided to go tomb raiding with automatic weapons and grenades," replied Philson.

"What about al-Otaybi? Did he get away?" asked Haley.

"Not exactly," said Doc. "It was more like he was blown away. When he gets to paradise, there's a piece of him for each of the seventy-two virgins awaiting him. He was the guy who reached for the grenade."

Nimrod, Joseph Smith, Spook, and Doc grabbed at the box, each holding a corner gingerly in case time had weakened its structure. The team began its move away from the mosque and to the railyards, taking a slightly more circuitous route than Haley and Philson had taken.

As they made their departure, they passed what must have been the parked convoy of the tomb raiders. Something caught Haley's eye. While glancing toward the vehicles, he noticed a man next to a white sedan and holding what appeared to be a small child in his arms. He was trying to jimmy his way into the car.

"Nate. Do you trust me?" Haley asked.

"Hardly. You've caused me nothing but grief. Do you know how much trouble I've been in since I saved your skinny butt in Iraq? What do you have in mind?" Philson shrugged and panted as they ran.

Chapter 37

"My spider sense says we need to talk to that man and boy. They must have come in with al-Otaybi and might be useful in tracking down his sugar daddy," said Haley, already setting a mental waypoint toward their new destination, only about a hundred yards away.

Philson slowly shook his head, not in the negative, but in resignation, and adjusted the course of his run toward the man. He leveled his rifle directly at the man's chest.

"Min al-ihtimal nahki ma'k [Might we speak with you]?" asked Haley breathlessly of the man as he and Philson approached after they crossed the expanse between them. The man made no effort to run away or otherwise avoid the two strangers, one of them decked out in U.S. military special forces gear, the other having the appearance of a military contractor, neither to be trifled with.

"Yes. I am happy to speak with you," said the man in accented but clear English.

"Sir, my name is Clayton Haley, and I am an American foreign service officer. We can't stay here long. There has been a disturbance over at the mosque, and we must leave this location or face unwanted interrogation by Iraqi officials. Would you be willing to accompany us to another site? I can promise you that no harm will befall you or the young boy. Might I ask if his name is Mohammed?" inquired Haley.

"Yes, Mr. Haley. I know who you are, and yes, Mohammed and I will come with you," said Dr. al-Onezi. "I hoped we might meet one day."

***

"Clayton, do you know what you're doing?" asked an incredulous Philson. "We can't take them to the embassy," he added while thoroughly frisking both the man and the boy.

"No, of course not, but we need to get them out of here. Let's find a quiet place to talk with them. Let's see what they know and might be willing to share with us," Haley responded.

"Alright," said Philson, and then speaking into his microphone, "Dad, please move the package we picked up to CJSOTF [Combined Joint Special Operations Task Force command, located in the Baghdad Diplomatic Support Center, next to the Baghdad International Airport]. I'll take Nimrod, Doc, Tank, and Clayton with me. Find a hangar or some other quiet place away from prying eyes. We'll take two vehicles, and we'll be picking up two pax, new friends of Haley's. We'll scout out a safe location in the Green Zone where we can have a nice conversation with our new friends and then join you later. I'll explain later. And Clayton asks that no one open the box until we can line up professionals to ensure that whatever is in there doesn't get contaminated."

"Clayton, can you please move your guests to the van?" Philson urged, saying, "We need to get them out of here and to some place safe immediately."

Haley gestured for the man and boy to move toward the team's vehicles, across the railyards. The sudden sound of sirens in the background added extra urgency to their haste. Haley glanced at his watch, noticing the time was now 3:00 a.m. The sun would start making an appearance in a couple of hours. There was little traffic on the road, meaning the police would likely arrive at the mosque within minutes. They needed to cover ground to the vehicles and fast.

"Sir, we can go faster if you allow me to carry the boy," said Haley to the man. "May I?"

"Yes, but do not lose my sight," urged the man without emotion.

Haley gently lifted the boy, flinching as pain from his shoulder wound stabbed at him, and started hustling toward the vehicles. The man, free of his burden, was able to keep up with him, but barely.

After less than five minutes, they crossed the railyards to the vehicles. The other ODA components had moved on to the embassy with their prize, so only two vans remained. Tank took the wheel, with Philson in the shotgun seat, as Haley directed his charges to the back of the vehicle, placing the boy in the arms of the man. Doc and Nimrod hopped in the chase vehicle. Tank, hearing that sirens had reached their destination at the nearby al-Karkhi mosque, lit out of the railyards across vacant lots and moved on to roads leading back to the Green Zone.

After a hasty discussion between Haley and Philson, they settled on moving their guests to the Royal Tulip Al-Rasheed Hotel as a convenient place to meet and chat about what Haley was up to and why he had picked up a couple of strays.

Meanwhile, Haley tried to decipher his own motives and instincts and what he hoped to accomplish. It was he who suggested the Al-Rasheed Hotel, which he recalled was famous for a number of reasons beyond its convenient location. He remembered horror stories he had heard when he served in Iraq of how Saddam Hussein's son, Uday, would exercise his unfounded and immoral right of *prima nocta* in preying on and claiming young brides married at the hotel on their wedding nights. He was told by an Iraqi one such bride was so depressed afterward that she threw herself off a balcony to end her life.

He also recalled an account much closer to home. When the U.S. military invaded Baghdad in 2003 and took over Iraqi government installations to house operations, it also claimed the Al-Rasheed Hotel as a base for American and Coalition forces. In October of that year, rockets fired by militants hit the hotel and killed Lieutenant Colonel Chad Buehring, making him the highest-ranking American KIA to date, or so Haley had heard. It also deprived his wife and children of someone known by friends and fellow church members in Fayetteville, NC as an outstanding and good man.

The drive took around twenty minutes, with Tank skirting the mosque and whatever investigation and discovery might be taking place in the aftermath of the skirmish.

They reached the hotel barricades at around 3:30 a.m. Security passed them through after seeing identification cards. They pulled over to a parking place and turned off the engine.

Haley started the conversation. "Sir, may I know your name and that of the boy, whom I presume is your son?"

"My name is Dr. Abdulaziz al-Onezi. I am from Baghdad but lived in Amman, Jordan for a few years after you invaded my country. I specialize in *in vitro* fertilization. Between Saddam and Americans, you killed my wife and my older son. This boy, my son Mohammed, is all I have left," he said in clear but thickly accented English.

Mohammed remained asleep.

"Dr. al-Onezi, I am very sorry for your losses. I hope later you and I have time to discuss the politics that got us to this point, but for now, I want you to know that I understand how the last hundred years or so have been very unfair and unkind to your people. And that you have indeed suffered at the hands of Saddam Hussein, Iran, true, the United States, and so on, and that your regional neighbors have not been helpful . . . and neither have many of the corrupt officials who have found their way into leadership here. You deserve better. I believe the fabric of people here now is the same that built multiple empires and offered the world many of the advances in science, medicine, education, mathematics, and even diplomacy. You have the potential to be great again, and most Americans believe we came to your country to open up the possibilities for you to regain your potential. That said, it's the present that concerns you and me now. May I be blunt?" asked Haley.

"I think you will be," al-Onezi actually smiled.

"Do you have any affiliation with Abdullah al-Otaybi, Ali al-Qahtani, or Mohammed al-Qahtani, recently deceased?" asked Haley.

"Yes. I know them all. I also know that you killed Ali al-Qahtani in Kuwait, and I suspect Abdullah al-Otaybi died tonight, as you are with me now and he is not. And might I suspect that you were behind the elder al-Qahtani's death in Mecca last year?" al-Onezi replied.

"To be clear, I didn't kill al-Qahtani in Kuwait, but I ensured he would never kill anyone else again. And yes, it appears that Mr. al-Otaybi brought grenades to a tomb raiding. When he and his friends fired on my friends, they did what they do better than anyone else in the world. They ended him. And for that, I won't apologize. These were violent young men who had outlived their carbon dioxide production," responded Haley forcibly.

"Were you the one who injured them on a boat?" asked al-Onezi, this time more out of curiosity than discovery.

"Yes. My pal Nate here and I were boat-jacked by these two and they found out we didn't like our fishing trip being interrupted. They were lucky Nate was feeling merciful that day," shot back Haley.

"What about the Messiah, Mr. al-Qahtani?" queried al-Onezi.

"No. I didn't kill him, but my information about what he was up to was fed to the right people, who took action before he could evoke an *Ikhwan [tribal militants]* uprising," summarized Haley.

Al-Onezi cocked his head just a little, studying Haley.

"Were you and young Mohammed with al-Qahtani when he was shot?" directed Haley.

"Yes," al-Onezi replied simply.

"I saw transcripts of the al-Qahtani speech before the Saudis cut his broadcast. Is the boy indeed the clone of your prophet Mohammed? Were you successful?" pursued Haley.

"No, of course not," al-Onezi brusquely said. "I tried. Many times and to my shame. I caused significant damage to a number of girls brought in for our great experiment. I will never forgive myself. I tried to use genetic material from the prophet, but the notes provided by the Persian, Farhad Hassan, were useless. He was a fool and a puppet of others driven by greed and power," he added, showing no desire to hold back.

"So, who is the real father of the boy? It's you, isn't it?" questioned Haley.

"You're very perceptive," al-Onezi smiled. "I had to deliver something to my taskmasters."

"I suppose you're familiar with Ali al-Sadr, correct?" said Haley, suddenly changing the subject.

"Of course. He has been my primary taskmaster for nearly ten years," replied al-Onezi simply.

"We want to find him and end his forty years of stirring up violence in the region. And I owe him some personal payback," threw in Haley, rubbing his left arm. "Will you help us?"

"Ali al-Sadr is a very dangerous man," snapped al-Onezi. "I will not cross him, and I will not jeopardize Mohammed's safety for your 'payback.'"

"Yes, of course. No one wants you or the child hurt," assured Haley. "Have you met Muhsin Bin Laden?"

"I have never had or sought out the pleasure of meeting any Bin Ladens," al-Onezi quipped.

Chapter 38

Al-Rasheed Hotel, Baghdad.

"Sidi, I need your instructions. I am in Baghdad and don't know where to go next or what to do. Why did you order me here?" al-Onezi pressed al-Sadr, in Arabic, on a burner phone he kept handy.

"Why are you in Baghdad? I never ordered you there. You shouldn't even be in Iraq. We don't have the signal to launch our little Messiah. We are not yet ready. Where is the boy?" roared al-Sadr.

"I'm sorry to upset you. I'm only following what I thought were your orders. Your man Abdullah al-Otaybi ordered me to pack up in Qom and travel with him to Baghdad. We arrived yesterday. He told me to leave the boy with his minders and trainers in Qom," al-Onezi replied defensively.

"I told him nothing of the sorts. Where is he now and why is he not answering my calls?" demanded al-Sadr.

"I don't know. He keeps me in the dark on his plans. I just know that we're in Baghdad, not far from the Maroof al-Karkhi tomb. He joined a crew of armed militants, grabbed some excavating equipment, and moved out of sight. He ordered me to stay with the vehicle we drove from Qom," al-Onezi reported.

"Oh. I heard one other thing," al-Onezi said carefully and methodically. "He called me after an hour and told me to call you and inform you he 'found it,' whatever that means and ask that you bring in your expert 'to verify its authenticity,'" he relayed as if reading from his notes. "He hoped you might suggest to us a meeting place where he could deliver what he recovered."

"I'm sorry," he added, as if an afterthought, "he also mentioned '*Beit al-Hikma*' and 'rallying the *Ikhwan.*' Do you know why he might have mentioned this?"

The line disconnected.

***

As the entire conversation was in Iraqi dialect, Haley couldn't discern exactly what was said but followed the gist of the conversation well enough to believe al-Onezi was sincere and had opted to rid himself of Ali al-Sadr. Haley imagined this change of heart likely reflected more of a desire for a better future for the boy than a newfound affinity for the United States.

He gestured the okay sign with his fingers to al-Onezi, signaling that his performance was good. "So what do you think?" Haley asked him. "Do you think he bought it?"

"I don't know. He's very clever. And he's very careful. You should never underestimate him. My advice is that we wait. Let him call us with a location to meet him and his expert," al-Onezi advised, then continued, "And you, of course, will let Mohammed and me go once we're free of Ali al-Sadr?"

"Yes. We have no issue with you. You need to reconcile with yourself about what you did to the young ladies in trying to clone Mohammed, but that's between you, God, the government of Iraq, and the families and girls you victimized. Let's just focus for now on al-Sadr," responded Haley.

***

There was very little they could do but wait. To be extra careful, Philson used his personal credit card to book a room at the hotel for al-Onezi and the boy to stay in. Haley almost volunteered his own but then checked himself, believing that al-Sadr had extensive resources and would be very suspicious if it came to be known that Haley was in Baghdad and had checked into the most famous hotel in Iraq.

By the time al-Onezi and the boy were settled into their room, it was nearly 6:00 a.m. Al-Onezi now had Haley's number and promised to call him as soon as he heard from al-Sadr.

Philson asked Tank to hang out at the hotel, just to have a physical presence nearby if needed, while he and Haley headed back to the embassy compound.

It was too early to call al-Jibouri, so Haley sent her a WhatsApp message asking her to contact the experts and notify them of the potential delivery of important artifacts. In his message, he explained it was urgent and to do everything possible to connect with them today.

"There's nothing more we can do now but wait," concluded Philson.

Chapter 38

Philson and Haley reached the CJSOTF about forty-five minutes later, most of which was spent clearing at the main security checkpoint. They headed straight for a hangar on the compound secured by Dad. As they pulled up, they saw Dad with the Urvans they had used earlier in the night. He lounged in a fabric lawn chair he must have pilfered somewhere, clearly asleep. They were all tired, as none had slept through the night. Haley hoped to get a little shuteye himself before he connected with al-Jibouri's experts and of course, whatever plans developed from al-Onezi's next interaction with al-Sadr.

First, though, Haley wanted to see his prize and what it was they had secured from the Maroof al-Karkhi tomb. He hoped and prayed it wasn't al-Karkhi's bones. He had no way of explaining that away should he be questioned as to why he dug up a ninth century mystic. As Nimrod parked the vehicle, he and Philson, joined by Doc and the others, approached the van, which had in its cargo space a large object covered in blankets. Haley removed the blankets to take a look for the first time at what they had recovered from the tomb. In the van lay a large and simple crate-like chest, the corners of which were reinforced, fortunately, with iron slats, thus maintaining the integrity of the box. It was about one and a half meters wide, nearly two meters long, and about one meter in height. It was large and unwieldy but as demonstrated by the overnight operation, could be carried by a couple of strong men. The dimensions seemed bigger than that of a coffin, relieving Haley of some of his feelings of foolhardiness. They had indeed found something.

It looked old. Very old. He ran his fingers along the grain of the wood of the box, caked in dust. Haley had no expertise in artifacts or archeology, but having worked construction during the summers to put himself through college, he knew the difference between lumber cut with power saws and that hewn by more crude hand tools. The box was clearly the latter. He desperately wanted to open the box himself, but hoping it was approximately eight hundred years, did not want to be responsible for allowing fresh air to damage the contents. Besides, it was locked, and the lock itself would need some attention to open it. It looked medieval to him, but again, knew he needed to defer to expertise on such estimations and in deciding how to open the item.

He bit his lip subconsciously, showing his tiredness coupled with impatience. He desperately wanted either to drink coffee or to sleep. His tiredness suddenly hit him. He felt the periphery of his vision blurring his mind's sight, adding numbness and cobwebs he knew would dull his senses. He needed his senses right now and lamented he couldn't yet sleep.

He pulled out his cell phone and called Wilson Edger. While punching in the numbers, he noticed that Philson, Nimrod, Doc, and Spook had all found space to either stretch out or curl up and take catnaps—some in the vehicles, some on lounge chairs, and Spook, next to the box recovered only hours before. He envied their ability to turn on and off so quickly and their common sense in taking care of the immediate need at hand, which for them, was recuperating from the night's action.

After three rings, Edger connected. Haley had no idea where he was but thought this needn't be a social call and instead, he opted to get right to the crux of the matter, speaking in code he believed Edger would break, lest prying ears learn of the U.S. role in the night's escapades. "Wilson. We had an eventful night. Not only did we eliminate Captain Hook, we recovered a very old prize under the sombrero. In fact, if the good captain hadn't caused such a scene, we wouldn't have found it. We'll be delivering it sometime today to our hosts."

"We should look at it first. Why move it over to the Iraqis?" asked Edger, ignoring the code.

"One, this box could have been sitting under the 'casa' for centuries. From what I gather from the team that pulled it out of the rubble, the container was placed in a much older monument and then hastily sealed in. They noticed different styles of bricks and rocks were used in closing up the building. The team snapped photos of the site, which we'll share with you shortly so that this makes more sense. Our best guess is that the actual sombrero as it exists now was finally completed in subsequent centuries, perhaps as late as the Ottomon era," said Haley, cognizant that he was rambling but determined to get as much information across as possible.

"Okay. This sounds promising. I can't wait to hear what's in the box, but again, why would we hand this over to the Iraqis?" responded Edger.

"Mainly because we don't have the facilities or expertise to look into this ourselves. We don't have a lab and curators. Who knows what fresh air could do to whatever is in the box? But more importantly, and the second reason we need to hand it over to the Iraqis, is that this belongs to the Iraqi people. Let them be responsible for this," lectured Haley, becoming more energized by the conversation. "I suppose if Smithsonian expert *Jason Johnson* were around, we could arrange for *his* participation in the big reveal of the contents. Are you around?" he continued snidely.

"I'm back in Amman, so the earliest I could be there is noon. Let me see if I can get Jason over there. Try to delay the delivery of the goods until noon?" Edger implored.

"I'll do what I can but believe strongly that whatever we found needs to get to the Iraqis. We've done a good job keeping it out of the now disembodied hands of Captain Hook, but it's not our property to deliberate on," said Haley.

Changing course, Haley then added, "But I need you here for another reason. We have a new development." He then told Edger of the other prize they recovered during the night's excitement, that of a doctor and his "specimen."

"I'll get on the first flight over," said Edger.

Chapter 39

Haley startled. He was completely disoriented. He felt a buzz on the outside of his thigh but couldn't comprehend what this meant or how he should interpret this new sensory information. He swatted at it, his mental faculties dully resisting arrival into awareness. In half of a split second, however, cognizance drew his mind back into his body, and he realized with intense grogginess his new surroundings. After his call with Edger, he had crawled into the van's cab to close his eyes. For just a few minutes.

Some fifteen minutes later, though, now awakening from a deep sleep, the buzz on his thigh snapped him back to clarity. He reached into the outside pocket of his cargo pants and dug out his phone. He noticed that al-Jibouri had responded to his WhatsApp messages. Her overtures were successful, and she had lined up two or three scientists to receive and study the crate and its contents. They were to meet at the Iraqi Museum at 1:00 p.m. Haley messaged back his gratitude but politely asked that she not join the meeting. He promised to explain why once he saw her. He closed his eyes again, wondering if and where he might get a bite to eat.

***

En route to the Iraqi Museum. Approximately 1:00 p.m.

Haley didn't want to take any chances, so he asked that Philson and his team accompany him to the Iraqi Museum. Their scheduled appointment was for 1:00 p.m., but given the museum's location just across town, Haley thought no need to leave the confines of the hangar before 12:00 p.m. He planned to pick up Edger from the airport and catch him up on details on their way to the museum.

The Iraqi Museum coincidentally was about equidistant between the Al-Rasheed Hotel and the al-Karkhi tomb. Haley marveled at how conveniently located these landmarks were. It sure made his life easier and drove home to him how central Baghdad was to numerous historical and otherwise important landmarks only a stone's throw away. He also mused that one could spend a lifetime exploring the history of Baghdad and other cities around Mesopotamia. Perhaps if invaders continued to try to raze the city to its very foundations as so many empires had, one might see the origins of all civilization, Haley reflected.

Doc dove the truck with Haley navigating using borrowed ODA Global Positioning System equipment. They stopped by Baghdad International Airport's arrival terminal to pick up Edger, who tried to squeeze in the front seat between Haley and Doc. Doc, seeing Edger outfitted in a suit and tie, deemed him too conspicuous to sit in front and relegated him with a gesture to the cargo space next to their prize. Edger, with his Ivy League education, seemed less comfortable in dealing with the ruffian mannerisms of Doc so reluctantly but obediently obliged and, hastened by Doc's withering glare, moved quickly to the back and scrunched up next to the crate. Just behind, in the chase vehicle, Spook drove, accompanied by a watchful Philson, Nimrod, and Joseph Smith.

Haley shrugged an apology toward Edger and directed Doc east across town and in the direction of the corners of Nasser and Allawi streets, around to the back of the large museum compound, and toward the loading dock. He knew from press accounts and his prior military service in Iraq that the Iraqi Museum had endured quite a bit of trauma and controversy. In the past, the museum had contained seven-thousand-year-old artifacts and one of the world's greatest collections of historical treasures but had been ransacked and looted over the last hundred years. Especially grievous was the damage done to the building in the aftermath of the 2003 U.S.-led liberation, or invasion, as many Iraqis perceived it. Iraqis themselves, unleashed from decades of Saddam Hussein's oppression, stole some 15,000 items of their own heritage, resulting in losses of untold treasures and knowledge of the world's collective past. It took some fifteen years for the museum to recover and open to the public again. Museum objects now on display represented Sumerian, Assyrian, Akkadian, Babylonian, and Islamic legacies, teaching the world about the history of law, war, science, script, and Mesopotamian contributions to civilization.

Much of the credit for the establishment of the modern Iraqi Museum goes to British politician, writer, and archaeologist, Gertrude Bell, quite often considered the unsung but equally impactful counterpart to T. E. Lawrence, AKA Lawrence of Arabia. Lawrence's exploits a thousand kilometers west along the Ottoman-controlled Levant and into the Arabian Peninsula propelled him into the history books. Bell was, however, quite unforgivably overlooked in the history books. Hollywood has made a couple ineffective efforts to acknowledge her imprint on the Middle East, most recently in a 2015 flick entitled *Queen of the Desert* starring Nicole Kidman, but the movie to many viewers seemed "inert" and fell short in paying adequate tribute to the woman who so shaped the country. She reportedly even sketched some of Iraq's modern day borders. Sadly, she died of an overdose of sleeping pills in 1926 at age fifty-eight, less than a month after opening the forebear of the Iraqi Museum.

Baghdadi historians have long cherished her devotion to the people of Iraq, and to this day, she lies interred in a British cemetery in the capital city. Haley hoped her memory would be honored by the turning over of the al-Karkhi crate to the museum. She would be pleased, he thought, wondering if there were items from the *Beit al-Hikma* in it. He thought it more likely that it contained some old tools used in the actual building of the mosque. No matter. This diversion sure beat drafting reports on Kuwaiti parliamentary debates, he mused, while thinking fondly of Nasser Khalil and hoping he might once again get to employ his green eyes in partnership with the gentleman.

He also hoped Jordan was doing okay. He worried about how his sudden departure and reduced interaction may have spelled an end to their relationship, with her likely thinking dating him was a very dangerous business. He missed his conversations with her and felt cheated their time together was so short.

***

Philson riding in the chase vehicle, continued his efforts to make arrangements for dealing with Ali al-Sadr, should their scheme to capture him succeed. As he traveled en route to the museum, he made a number of calls, including to his headquarters at Fort Campbell, Kentucky, his commanding officer—currently at Al-Udeid Airbase in Doha, Qatar— and most importantly, one Colonel Al Saud in Riyadh, Saudi Arabia. Al Saud and associates had assisted in thwarting the "return from absence" of the self-purported Messianic Mohammed al-Qahtani, installing himself and whom he believed to be the clone of the Islamic prophet Mohammed, Dr. al-Onezi's charge, the young boy named Mohammed. Philson, Haley, and Edger all agreed that the services of Colonel Al Saud and those under his command in Riyadh might be needed again, and soon.

Philson pinged Haley a few times via WhatsApp to update him on his requests for his leadership to coordinate with Iraqi defense and interior officials to allow Colonel Al Saud to enter Baghdad. The United States often had to facilitate talks between the two rivals, Haley understood. Ties between Saudi Arabia and Iraq had never been warm, the three knew, so getting needed cooperation was essential. The Saudis were fine with Saddam Hussein leading Iraq into a senseless 1980–88 war with their chief regional rival Iran. The Saudis were also eager to sign up to the 1990–91 U.S.-led campaign to oust him from his ill-fated invasion of Kuwait. When he was finally removed from power in 2003, lingering Saudi mistrust of Iraq only increased, however, when the Iraqi Shia majority came to power, given wide-held suspicions of the new government's ties and perhaps fealty to Iran.

Simply put, as Haley saw it, all this distrust between Iraq and Saudi Arabia boiled down to religious sway the two countries had over the region and beyond. All Shia adherents believed their religious duty was to take pilgrimages to Mecca but looked to Najaf and Karbala as their sources of inspiration and guidance—their Vatican equivalent, so to speak. Sunnis of the world, under the spiritual guidance of Mecca, perceived Shia allegiance as misguided toward traitors of the faith, prophets Hussain and Ali, both martyred and buried in Iraq. The House of Saud had only carried the mantle of the Sunni faith in recent years, however, and were predated by the Shia faithful in Najaf and Karbala for centuries.

Haley recalled trying to understand and explain this to family and friends back home in Walhalla, comparing the Sunni-Shia divide to that of the Protestant-Catholic break after the calls to reform by Martin Luther. These partitions resulted in senseless savage wars with losses of untold millions of souls. Regrettably, but predictably, Haley's explanations often resulted in glazed expressions and the occasional and overly twanged and slow response, *"Dang, boy. What do they teach you down yonder in Columbiddy [Columbia]? Why come you ain't gone up heres to Clempson [sic]. They wudda learned you right."*

Haley took these responses as indications interpretations of modern Middle Eastern turmoil didn't often impact the lives of his kinsmen more focused on college football and hunting season, "bless their hearts." Since leaving Walhalla, Haley had wondered many times how much easier his life would have been if he had just stayed home and simply followed many of his high school buddies, graduating high school and working at The Home Depot or Lowes, or dairy or pig farming, like their fathers. Instead, he was now trying to get Middle Eastern archenemies to work together to thwart the plans of other archenemies. Yes. Walhalla seemed far off in terms of distance and time, he sighed.

***

Just minutes away from the museum, a call from Philson interrupted Haley's thoughts. Tank had just informed Philson that al-Onezi received his instructions from al-Sadr. They were to meet at a site and time yet to be determined and that al-Sadr would bring with him an outside expert to discuss *Beit al-Hikma* artifacts, as referenced by al-Onezi in his previous call. Al-Onezi truthfully told al-Sadr that he was staying at the Al-Rasheed Hotel and would await further instructions. He also truthfully noted that he had not heard from al-Otaybi since their arrival near the al-Karkhi shrine in the early hours of the morning. He omitted, however, that he knew why and that he knew al-Otaybi would not contact anyone ever again. No matter, as al-Sadr likely already suspected the operation a bust. The man was too careful and too well informed not to have already heard about al-Otaybi's demise.

"We should anticipate that al-Sadr will look to clean up things here. He'll either wish to recapture the boy and his father or ensure their silence," said Philson. "We should prepare for the worst."

"Got it," noted Haley, not sure what he just acknowledged. He closed out the call just as they pulled up to the loading dock at the museum.

Chapter 40
Iraqi Museum, Baghdad, Iraq.

Awaiting their arrival at the museum were three Iraqi officials—one woman, sharply dressed but in a dated outfit and wearing an unattractive white- and peach-colored, floral print hijab, and two men, both paunchy and mustachioed and attired in dark suits. Haley quickly referenced his WhatsApp message from al-Jibouri, exited the van, and then introduced himself, saying "Good afternoon. I presume you're doctors Haddad, al-Amri, and Dagestani," not knowing which names belonged to whom. "My name is Clayton Haley, and this is my colleague Jason Johnson," he said, referencing Edger who joined him on the loading dock. "I understand that my colleague Ghada al-Jibouri contacted you regarding a delivery we have for you?"

"Yes, Mr. Haley. We were expecting you, but I admit to being very confused by this," said the apparent lead in the assembly, one of the men. His English was thickly accented but clear. "What is it that you have for us, and what do you require from us in exchange?" he asked, suspiciously.

Edger allowed Haley to do the talking, while he continued to make calls on his iPhone.

"Nothing at this point, but I hope you'll be willing to share your eventual findings with us. We have reason to believe that the crate in this van is part of Iraqi historical heritage, perhaps dating back to the thirteenth century or before. I don't have time to go into this in great detail but can inform you we were in an operation overnight to recover this crate and keep it out of the hands of those less interested in its historical value and more inclined to exploit it politically to stir unrest," said Haley, adding, "Something Iraq does not need."

"I am Badia Dagestani," introduced the sole woman in the group, stepping forward with body language that indicated her disapproval over the mysterious nature of the delivery. "You should have consulted with us. It was not your heritage to protect or recover. What is it and where did you get it?" she asked in excellent English laced in heavily exaggerated and rolled *r* sounds typical among native Arabic speakers.

"Understood, but if we hadn't have taken it, it would likely be in the hands of private collectors or Iranian revolutionaries," retorted Haley taken aback, his fatigue surfacing again and mixing with indignation. He didn't feel like being lectured for doing what he knew to be right when others on his team more readily espoused the "finders keepers" mindset. He opted not to enter into an argument or otherwise say something to increase tensions and jumped directly at the truth. "This crate was found buried under the Maroof al-Karkhi shrine, where it might be supposed to have been since 1258," he continued.

Dr. Dagestani stared at him. "Did you say 1258?" she pried after a pause, mentally translating the numbers into Arabic.

"Yes. I have reason to believe this crate and its unknown contents may have been stashed there to keep it out of the hands of the Mongol invaders," he commented. "If you'll excuse me, I'd like to show you something recovered on the body of one of the Iraqis who likely took part in the theft of the Kuwaiti national archives," he said absentmindedly while scrolling through saved photos on his cell phone. "Let me show you the image of a map found on the body of Hussein al-Sadr, who was recently found in a shallow grave along with other Iraqis along the infamous highway of Death in northern Kuwait. This map was confirmed by a senior Kuwaiti museum curator as part of the archives stolen during the 1990 invasion of Kuwait," said Haley. He noticed their tense body language, suggesting a likely move to the defensive in discussing the Iraqi invasion.

He didn't want to engage on that topic so quickly moved the conversation along. "Look at this map," he showed them the image on his phone, pinching the round city with his thumb and forefinger and then spreading them. They each looked at his phone, studying the circle on the map and then the Arabic script, both legible and illegible, and the proximity to a large river.

"Yes. I see how you drew the conclusion that this points to Maroof al-Karkhi shrine, but I wish to understand how you came to possess the crate," Dr. Dagestani pressed again.

"Our time for explanations is limited," Haley noted. "If you wish for a report on how this came into our possession, I urge you to speak to your Ministry of Interior counterparts. Perhaps their account of how they found tomb robbers at the remains of the nearly destroyed mosque will satisfy your curiosity," he insisted, worked up but still maintaining his wherewithal while intentionally leaving out salient details on how he and the ODA team found themselves at the shrine.

The museum officials were clearly not satisfied with his explanation, but their attention diverted to an object being lifted onto the loading dock under the direction of Philson and his men. Six museum laborers moved in to help transfer the crate from the ODA's care onto a large cart. Despite a great deal of cooks in the kitchen, giving conflicting directions in both English and Arabic, the laborers successfully loaded the large trunk. Edger stepped up and removed the cheap, colorful, synthetic blankets placed over it by Philson's men.

Discussion about how the trunk came into U.S. government's control ceased as the three museum officials focused their entire attention on the artifact. In fact, they stopped speaking altogether. Haley too, though he had already seen the crate, became mesmerized, as now, with covers removed, the item now enjoyed the light of day for the first time in perhaps eight hundred years. He still couldn't begin to imagine what treasures lay inside and felt his confidence growing that his efforts may have led to something significant. Edger also appeared transfixed, as despite riding in the same van, he had not yet been afforded the opportunity to study the item. Philson, too, showed interest but through eye contact, instructed Doc, Nimrod, and Joseph Smith to maintain a wary eye. Haley noticed that they allowed their hands to often drift toward bulges on their hips when the laborers got too close to him and Edger.

Haley checked himself now on his doubts about simply turning the find over to the Iraqis. Doing so may mean that it could be lost again for another eight hundred years, or maybe forever. Still, though, this piece of history didn't belong to him, and he had no right to determine its destiny, he reminded himself.

Now in daylight, Haley could study the crate more closely. The dust covering the trunk deeply ingrained itself into the wood and iron clasps, giving it an appearance gray in hue. Haley couldn't guess as to the type of material that framed the box but assumed it to be a hardwood, heavily lacquered to preserve it for a long time. It was a marvel that it still held up, he thought, but conceded that his estimates could be way off and the box no more than a hundred years old and emplaced in the shrine by Turkish renovators.

The iron strips holding the trunk together also yielded no hint as to the interior trove of secrets. The lack of ornateness suggested that its craftsman intended the receptacle for practical, not ceremonial purposes, again, stumping and frustrating both Haley and Edger on their guesses as to what, if anything, lay within its confines.

The laborers moved the cart up the ramp and into the museum proper, following Drs. Dagestani, Haddad, and al-Amri, all chatting furiously among themselves. Haley and Edger/Johnson followed them, not asking for permission. Philson came along as well, but again, through eye-directed military telepathy, ordered his team to guard the vehicles, doors, and to remain ready to respond to even the smallest urgencies.

The three scholar scientists followed signs that led them toward the museum laboratory, refurbished and upgraded after the devastation caused by looters subsequent to the 2003 invasion of Iraq. Since then, thanks largely to global interest in preserving and discovering Iraqi, Sumerian, Mesopotamian, and Babylonian heritage, the museum hosted a modern laboratory filled with dedicated conservationists. Haley hoped and prayed that political, sectarian, or tribal fealties held by restorationists would preserve the integrity of the find and, as appropriate, ensure its discovery shared with the world. Alas, given rampant corruption in Iraq or fear of how even a little provocation could incite violence should the crate's contents prove religious in nature, Haley knew there to be a strong possibility that findings might never see the light of day.

"You don't have a key?" Dr. Dagestani suddenly turned and asked Haley. Throughout the transport of the crate to the laboratory, she had been engaged in intense discussion with her colleagues.

"I'm sorry, but no. A key was found on the body of Hussein al-Sadr, but it seemed to have disappeared along with the map. Of course, when his remains were recovered, there was no way of knowing our search would lead us to the al-Karkhi shrine. It may be that you can reach out to Kuwait National Archives Director Dr. Hamad al-Marri, who might help track down both the key and the original map, which I believe also warrants forensic study," Haley added helpfully, leaving out his own suspicions that al-Marri may have been part of the reason the map and key were somehow misplaced.

"That's unfortunate," she said, adding, "and delays our study of what you have turned over to us." She paused. "There are circumstances about this discovery that you are not telling me. And given that your 'cowboys' outside helped you recover it, I think it likely that you are 'trodding'—as you say—all over our sovereignty again. Still, though, you thought to contact an Iraqi patriot, your friend Ghada al-Jibouri, who wisely called us at the museum to ensure this material was turned over the Iraqi people. And you did so without opening the box yourself, even though I imagine this pains you. I thank you, Mr. Haley."

Haley had a tired sense of vindication and assuredness that he had done the right thing. And was pleased that whatever came about as a result of the study of the contents of the crate would come about at the hands of the Iraqis, not the "American occupiers." It had indeed "pained" him that he may never know the contents of the box, as suggested by Dr. Dagestani's statement that combined both her gratitude, seemingly sincere, and her farewell, also seemingly sincere.

"What happens next?" Haley asked.

"We will need to carefully catalogue this discovery. We will send a team to the mosque to see if there are other items that need to be studied. We will contact your Dr. al-Marri friend in Kuwait, but don't suspect our Kuwaiti friends are too inclined to work with us yet. We will then carefully open the crate and see what its contents reveal, and if you are correct, we will fastidiously study each item to determine if it has any historical significance and value. If and as appropriate, we will invite relevant scholars from around the world and share with them our discovery. Please be aware, however, this task may take months, possibly years, if we find ourselves preserving antiquities or scrolls, especially if subject to damage by exposure to the elements. And be aware that we receive potential antiquities on nearly a weekly basis. We are in Iraq; if you lift a rock, you uncover a civilization. You should also note that this box could be empty or full of tools used to build or renovate the mosque. Please dispel yourself of the notion of easy treasure hunts summed up in a two-hour American movie with Johnny Depp," she smiled for the first time, gesturing to Haley, Edger, and Philson the exit from the laboratory.

As they were directed toward the exit, Haley noticed Drs. Haddad and al-Amri intensely studying the crate and ordering the laborers to hang up sheets of plastic in preparation for sealing the room to make it airtight.

Chapter 41

Sadr City. 4:30 p.m.

"We will retrieve Dr. al-Onezi and the boy at 10:00 p.m. at the construction site of the National Grand Mosque. It's a convenient location, as it's close to the Al-Rasheed Hotel. And if you care about good omens, we will take al-Thawra [Revolution] Street from Sadr City directly into the heart of Baghdad, almost right up to the mosque itself. Very fitting for our plans," said Ali al-Sadr on the phone to Muhsin Bin Laden, still in Comoros.

"Good. I am very disturbed that al-Onezi and the boy 'just showed up' in Baghdad. I find his account dubious that he was ordered by al-Otaybi to accompany him to Iraq. He should have never left Qom," replied Bin Laden.

"I agree. And my people in the interior ministry tell me that American soldiers were at the al-Karkhi mosque last night and killed most of my crew. Including al-Otaybi. They report that American civilians were present and removed an item from the mosque," commented al-Sadr.

"Yes. I've heard from my contacts well placed in the ministry as well. This is unacceptable and must be rectified. And to be clear, I will not tolerate it if *Glaiton Heeley* was involved. I ordered you to kill him," said Bin Laden ominously.

"Yes, sidi, I know. I will deal with him, and I will recover what was taken from the shrine. I have a new team assembled, which will not so easily be cowed by the Americans. I must implore you to let me grab al-Onezi and the boy first to remove them as distractions and return them to Qom to finish the boy's studies. And I must ask for latitude in how I wish to determine their future. If al-Onezi is compromised, he must be removed. The boy no longer needs him, and I think it is a mistake to keep him involved. I don't trust him," responded al-Sadr quickly changing the topic of conversation.

"I agree and also believe he has outlived his usefulness. Keep the boy safe, as he is still key to our plans. Do what you wish with the doctor. I don't care," Bin Laden said conciliatorily. He then added, "You won't fail me again."

***

Baghdad. 6:00 p.m.

"Clayton, Wilson. Tank informed me that al-Sadr made the call to al-Onezi and instructed him to meet at the National Grand Mosque in an hour. He agreed to go there and take the boy but now wants to hear from us what we have in mind. What do you know about this place?" asked Philson of Haley who was picking at the contents of an MRE, or Meal Ready to Eat, ubiquitous at military bases around the world. Edger stood by looking at Haley's gastronomical adventure with disgust. Having survived on these high-caloric forms of military sustenance during his tours of duty in Iraq, Haley had vowed not to eat these again now that he was a civilian. He found that though passable in terms of taste, they wreaked havoc on one's digestive system. He shuddered while thinking about how he once subsisted on omelet MREs for three days in a row, smiling at his battle buddies' referencing of them as "vomeletes." The meal he was picking at now was a concoction of chicken and rice with crumbled crackers and a vial of Tabasco sauce. It wasn't what he would describe as edible but did turn him off food for long enough to reflect on the museum encounter and focus on what lay ahead.

Having the afternoon to plan had also afforded him a few moments to call home and check on his mom and dad. All was well, and it was nice to know that time stood still in Walhalla as it fled by in Iraq. He also called Jordan, but she didn't pick up.

"I don't know much about it. It was a massive construction project begun some decades ago but never finished. Likely one of many of Saddam Hussein's megalomaniac inspirations to return Iraq to its glory days. If you go to Google Maps, you'll see it's exactly, to my reckoning, the site of the center of the Round City of old. I think it's safe to say that the middle of the fabled metropolis would have also had a mosque. Nowadays, the National Grand Mosque is just full of tall pillars and construction cranes. A perfect place to plan an ambush, if you ask me," Haley responded.

"Yep. That's what I was afraid of," said Philson, looking at the location via Internet pictures on his cellular phone. He didn't like this scenario at all.

"You know. We might be able to engineer this so that al-Onezi doesn't have to show up at the site. Our only goal here is to scoop up al-Sadr, right? There is no need to dangle the doctor or the boy," posited Haley.

"Correct. And from what you've told me, al-Sadr might be more interested in eliminating loose ends than concerned about the doctor's well-being," said Edger. "Might I ask that Tank hold the doctor and his son in place a few minutes longer? He should have him inform al-Sadr that he's on his way, however. I think we can quickly concoct a plan at retrieving him without exposing the child to any risks and that keeps your men out of harm's way as well."

"For planning purposes, you should also consider how easy one could get from the mosque to Revolution Street, which is a straight shot to Sadr City. If we don't grab him at the site, perhaps on the way to Sadr City?" offered Haley.

"How do you know he'll head to Sadr City?" asked Philson.

"I don't, but think it likely he would seek to hole up with Shia communities, and Najaf and Karbala are too far away for the trip tonight. Plus, in addition to the family connection, I can see him sharing political and ideological affinity with his distant cousin Muqtada al-Sadr," Haley noted, adding, "But to be clear, we're all making this up as we go along."

"Maybe we can make a few calls to see if we can steer him toward Sadr City? If he's anywhere in the vicinity of the construction site, I'm sure we can ask interior ministry officials to position some vehicles at other points of egress. I'll make some calls. Maybe we can snatch him up at some convenient location . . . say . . . right . . . here," jabbed Edger his finger on his cellular screen, marking a spot on the eastern side of the Ahrar Bridge over the Tigris River.

***

Dr. Hamad al-Marri arrived at Baghdad International Airport in the early evening. He was very unhappy. He didn't like Baghdad, the whole of Iraq, or the Iraqi people. He didn't like Ali al-Sadr. Muhsin Bin Laden terrified him. Nothing about his new arrangement appealed to him. He only engaged with these new "partners" out of his desire to quietly and discreetly track down items stolen from the Kuwaiti archives, some of which could be potentially embarrassing to his small Gulf nation. He knew the archives included some real estate arrangements that could damage certain members of the ruling family. Plus, the archives detailed some dealing among international partners that would reflect negatively on the country, including some arrangements that might seem favorable to Hezbollah. In fact, it was his family that made some of those arrangements, and he would rather not have it out in the public that

Sunnis from his tribe were on close financial terms with the Iranian-backed Shia terrorist group.

Al-Sadr's car picked them up at the airport. Al-Marri moved to the back seat. Waiting for him was al-Sadr. He also seemed unhappy. He waved for the driver to get moving and gestured to al-Marri, saying, "Come join me on an errand. Then we will see about using your expertise to determine what has been recovered in the al-Karkhi mosque."

"You have recovered the item? This is wonderful news! I have the key with me and can't wait to begin reviewing what's inside. You haven't opened it yet, have you? The contents may perhaps be hundreds of years old. It's imperative that it be moved to a proper laboratory so that we might preserve the material for proper study," al-Marri replied excitedly.

"Not exactly. Not yet. I have access to it, though. The daft Americans did our work for us and moved it to the Iraqi Museum. We can simply collect it there and move it to any location we desire. Once we decide if it has value, we hope to use it to motivate tribal unrest against uncooperative governments in the region. Certainly the Americans believe it has some intrinsic worth. Otherwise, they wouldn't have risked so much to retrieve it," replied al-Sadr.

Al-Sadr's response deeply disturbed and dissatisfied al-Marri. "If there are no artifacts to study, why did you bring me here?" he asked. "I have explained numerous times that I do not wish to come to Iraq. You and your countrymen devastated Kuwait in 1990. Even your own cousin robbed us of our heritage and carried the map you had me steal to his grave. I want nothing to do with your plots and schemes, which sow violence in the region. I only care about returning to my country that which your country stole. I demand you return me to the airport at once," al-Marri demanded.

"As I mentioned, I have an errand to run. You will join me. We will then have you look at what our inquisitive American diplomat, Mr. *Heeley* found," al-Sadr responded quietly. Ominously.

Not catching the import of al-Sadr's tone, al-Marri continued, "You didn't mention that Clayton Haley was the one who found it. He was the one who started all of this in Kuwait by recovering the body of your cousin in the first place. I don't want to get involved in an American plot here. Return me to the airport at once," al-Marri repeated.

Al-Sadr ignored him and took out his phone and began making calls. The doors clicked lock. Al-Marri now realized the extent of his dilemma and pulled out notes from his briefcase to distract himself.

Chapter 42

Al-Sadr's driver pulled up to the Islamic Dawa political party office. Shia adherents of the Dawa party, meaning call or invitation in Arabic, maintained close ties with Iran, even siding with Tehran during the 1980–88 war with Iran. They strongly opposed Saddam Hussein, but their support for Iran enabled the Ayatollahs to export their influence and occasional violence to Iraq, Lebanon, Kuwait, and elsewhere. In fact, it was largely suspected that Dawa leaders in Najaf and Kerbala helped prepare the ascendancy and return to Iran of now deceased Ayatollah Ruhallah Khomeini. Iraqi Grand Ayatollah Mohammed Baqir, father-in-law of infamous Moqtada al-Sadr, served as one of the leaders and guiding voices for political and religious inspiration for the group until Saddam Hussein ordered his assassination in 1980.

Ali al-Sadr was a lifelong member of Dawa and found its office in downtown Baghdad convenient for reconnecting with Dr. al-Onezi. The office was less than three hundred meters from the building project for the National Grand Mosque. Al-Sadr, with al-Marri in tow, exited the car, binoculars in hand, and walked to the edge of the parking lot of the office in the direction of the mosque. He surveyed the site, then withdrew his phone from his suit pocket.

"My orders are to eliminate the doctor if he doesn't readily come with you," al-Sadr spoke into his cellular phone, adding further to al-

Marri's discomfort. He sat quietly and fumed. "Save the boy at all costs," al-Sadr continued.

Al-Sadr then called another number in his contacts. Al-Marri could hear the ringing from his phone. "Abdulaziz, where are you? I'm here, ready to retrieve you. We need to move you back to Qom," al-Sadr nudged calmly.

Al-Marri couldn't make out the conversation, but al-Sadr's body language suggested he wasn't happy. "*Hadher [Fine]*, I'll give you fifteen more minutes, but you need to hurry."

Al-Sadr then called another number, which al-Marri presumed to be that of the first contact. "This is a trap. Get your men out of there. Send a car over to the hotel and kill the doctor and grab the boy. Bring him to me in Sadr City." Al-Sadr returned hastily to the car, again with al-Marri in tow. He gestured for the driver to move out.

Al-Marri became exasperated. "Sir. You are talking about murder. I won't have anything to do with this. I demand you take me back to the airport immediately. Our partnership is over," he implored.

Al-Sadr, who had been ignoring him, raised his eyes from his phone and cocked his eyebrow. "No one concludes partnership with our benefactor," he uttered tiredly.

"Be that as it may, I wish to return to Kuwait on the first available flight out of this accursed country. I'll wait at the airport. I'll catch a taxi from here," he pled again.

"No. You won't. Surely you must understand the situation you find yourself in. You're in the parking lot of the Dawa party office. My colleagues inside would not be as hospitable to you and your Sunni brethren as I have been. No," he repeated. "I am responsible for your safety, and I promised you a chance to study artifacts. You must be patient a little longer," he continued, gesturing for the driver to leave the parking lot.

Al-Marri resumed his fuming, too angry for rebuttal, but obediently sat in the car, looking back at the tall pillars and cranes set to rebuild the large mosque, long dormant. He so wished to be in Kuwait.

The driver moved south to Damascus Street, but then turned east toward July 14 Street. Al-Marri protested, "The airport is to the west. Why are we going east? Turn the car around immediately!" he ordered the driver.

The driver simply replied, "Streets are blocked. There must be an accident or more protests," pointing toward a police SUV blocking egress to the west.

Al-Marri began consulting the traffic navigation application Waze and replied, "Fine then. Take me north along July 14 Street, away from the Green Zone, and then we'll circle back to the airport."

"July 14 Street is closed too. See?" The driver pointed to more police SUVs blocking access to the road. Even al-Sadr paused his texting on his phone and looked up and down the street with concern. He turned back to his phone and made an urgent call, presumably to one of his men, to check on roadblocks.

Al-Marri, ever the historian, recalled that the designation of "July 14 Street" commemorated the 1958 coup d'état which overthrew the British mandated Hashemite monarchy, established after World War I. The revolution, as it was called, saw the killing of the then Iraqi king and his prime minister, both victims of fervent Arab nationalism. Al-Marri chided himself for his mental distraction and began issuing instructions to the driver, who, despite his protestations, kept moving east. He drove past Allawi Street and then right onto Nasser Street, named for former Egyptian President Gamal Abdelnasser, celebrated in Iraq for overthrowing his ruler, Egyptian King Farooq, in 1952. These upheavals served as sparks for regional unrest and as precursors for the 2011 Arab Spring.

Al-Marri had reached his limit. He wanted out of Iraq. He became frantic, and once the car intersected the King Faisal I roundabout, still headed decidedly east, he began yelling, "Stop the car! Stop the car! I'll simply take a taxi."

"You know, when the Mongols sacked Baghdad, they threw so many scrolls and writings into the Tigris, reports said the river turned black from ink in the papers," al-Sadr suddenly interjected calmly, instantly settling al-Marri down. "I promised you artifacts to review, correct?"

"Yes, but I—" said al-Marri.

"Go look for them yourself," muttered al-Sadr, pulling a gun out from under his left arm and firing it twice, point blank, into al-Marri's torso.

The driver instinctively pulled over on the side of Ahrar bridge, exited the car, and moved to the back seat to extricate the body of al-Marri. He then dragged him to the edge of the bridge and pushed him over it, returning to the car nonchalantly before even hearing the subsequent splash. His blood would now mingle with that of *Beit al-Hikma* scholars of old and the manuscripts tossed into the river by the Mongols, the driver thought justly. He nodded at the driver in a chase vehicle who had just joined him, likely one of al-Sadr's men dispatched to the National Grand Mosque site to retrieve Dr. al-Onezi and the boy. He then got into his car and continued driving on Ahrar Bridge in the direction of Sadr City.

Chapter 43

Ahrar Bridge, Baghdad, Iraq.

On the other side of the bridge, only a couple of hundred meters away, hovered a Blackhawk helicopter, just out of eyesight.

"That's him. Overhead surveillance confirms Tango in the back seat. The driver of the car dropped a package into the river on the other side of the bridge but confirms our tango never left the vehicle. Once the vehicle gets about twenty-five meters out, fire into the engine block to disable the car. Let's end this," ordered Philson.

Dad took the shot from the helicopter, sending three 50-caliber rounds just under the hood of the late model, tinted-windowed Mercedes. The car stopped instantly. Doc, Spook, Nimrod, and Joseph Smith all popped up from behind trees that lined the right side of the road. They approached the vehicle carefully but quickly, ordering the driver and passenger out of the car.

"Alert. New targets are approaching the disabled victor [vehicle] at a rapid clip. Be prepared to react," a tinny transmission crackled over the radio and into the team's bone phones. Nimrod and Spook turned to face the new threat. Joseph Smith kept his M-4 rifle trained on the driver in the first car, ordering him in impolite terms to exit the vehicle. No movement from the backseat yet.

"Targets are picking up speed. Prepare to return fire," the voice said again. Nimrod and Spook needed no further encouragement, both discharging their weapons in the direction of the second vehicle in its approach to join the lead car. The vehicle crashed violently into the rails of the bridge.

Meanwhile, Joseph Smith yanked the reluctant driver from the first car and quickly zip tied him. Nimrod had circled the car and using the butt of his weapon, smashed the backseat passenger window open, saying, "You. Yes, you, the big knucklehead sitting high and mighty. Out. We're going for a ride."

Al-Sadr, typically on the bullying end of circumstances, did not like what was happening. He weighed his options, including using his gun to shoot his way out of trouble, but decided against it when he saw how quickly the American assailants dispatched his men in the second car. He opted instead to surrender, knowing that these Americans had nothing on him and using his pull, or that of Muhsin Bin Laden's, he could extricate himself from any potential scrape.

He allowed himself to be zip tied and moved to the helicopter. He lost his bravado, however, when he saw Clayton Haley awaiting him in the helicopter. He lost what remained of his courage and fortitude when he saw next to Haley an Arab gentleman in military uniform. The man, whose insignia indicated his rank as a colonel and his nametag as Al Saud, yelled over the sound of the propellers with no hospitality in his tone, "I've been waiting to meet you for forty years."

Epilogue

Al-Deera Square, Riyadh Saudi Arabia. Two weeks later.
Friday afternoon. 1:35 p.m.

Al-Sadr felt terror for the first time in his life. He had found himself in Riyadh under the close watch of the Saudi royal family, the very ones he conspired against for forty years to unseat, along with Muhsin Bin Laden and Mohammed al-Qahtani. Bin Laden had communicated to him surreptitiously not to panic and that he would ensure his succor, provided he didn't divulge details of their plots, both in the past and their current activities. Al-Sadr, accustomed to dealing with powerful people, stayed quiet, but his anxiety grew with each passing day and with the dearth of communication with Bin Laden or the army of people he commanded throughout the region. He had provided no statement, despite hours of interrogation. That he had not been tortured like so many of his cellmates assured him that relief was imminent, but why was it taking so long?

Now, he found himself attired, not by choice, in a simple white tunic and driven in a nondescript white van. He didn't know Riyadh, so couldn't know that his minders were transporting him to the center of the city, near an old market. They stopped the van on a plaza of brown hued concrete surrounded by one- and two-story buildings of the same color. They directed him out toward the center of the square. His minder secured his arms behind his back and led him toward a grate on the ground the size of a pizza box.

Al-Sadr was confused. He found this to be odd treatment for one about to be released. The intense Saudi sun beating down on him disoriented him. Though not accustomed to wearing the *ghutra* and *egal* head covering which adorned men on the Arabian Peninsula, he desired the practicality of such accoutrements. The temperature reached well over a hundred and twenty degrees Fahrenheit. He wanted something to drink.

For the first time in his blurred focus, he noticed a tall man garbed in the *ghutra* and *egal* and customary *dishdasha,* similar to the long tunic he was wearing, but certainly nicer. "What was going on? And where was Bin Laden or his men?" his mind screamed. He felt outrage at the uncertainty of his circumstances and the silence from his master. Al-Sadr was no great man, but having lived and worked with powerful actors, he had become accustomed to high standards of treatment.

Another glance at his tall companion revealed that he held in his hand a sword. Al-Sadr suddenly realized his betrayal. It wasn't freedom and a return to opulence that awaited him. It was four feet of bright steel, curved aerodynamically so that its sole purpose would be accomplished with precision, haste, and finality.

Al-Sadr suddenly became aware of his own mortality and that of the lives he had ruined. He reflected on his first murder, that of a Palestinian gentleman in Medina some forty years ago, killed to protect his theft of the mortal remains of Mohammed. The sun beat heavily on him as he experienced the epiphany of having to recompense for the choices he had made in pursuing four decades of violence and plunder.

The minder yanked al-Sadr's tunic down his back, entrapping his arms and exposing his neck. With his sandaled foot, the executioner gently nudged the backs of al-Sadr's knees, forcing him in a kneeling position, just over the grate. Al-Sadr looked around, noticing a number of soldiers nearby, including that of Colonel Al Saud. Off to his right, he saw a lowly janitor with a water hose in hand, apparently at the ready to administer his task. Bystanders and rubberneckers also assembled. He somehow felt disappointment in not seeing Clayton Haley in the group. Cold steel lightly touched the top of his spine. Looking to his left, he saw the shadow of his would-be executioner, standing over him, lifting high his instrument of justice.

***

Al-Rasheed Hotel. Baghdad, Iraq. 4:00 p.m.

"Dr. al-Onezi, I just learned from my colleagues in Riyadh that the Saudi authorities executed Ali al-Sadr in what the locals call Chop Chop Square. He cannot harm you or Mohammed," conveyed Haley in the lobby of the Al-Rasheed Hotel.

Dr. al-Onezi smiled but shrugged. "That doesn't mean we're safe. It only means we have one less enemy." He held the boy closely. "And aren't you bound by rules against refoulement? You Americans are always lecturing the world about human rights, and you deliver this monster over to the Saudis?"

"We didn't turn him over to the Saudis. The Iraqis did. I would have preferred him to stand trial, but our Saudi and Iraqi partners preferred a swifter dispensation of justice," said Haley. "I'm afraid our not being able to interview him means we lost out on information vital to the projects he was working on."

Dr. al-Onezi studied Haley then conceded, "You seem to believe what you say. Maybe you're sincere. I'm sorry, but here in the Middle East, especially Iraq, we have become inured to the good intentions of people like you. The reality is that monarchs and dictators will continue to control us and make determinations on our lives. You swoop in to distribute democracy and rule of law like candy, or perhaps as a cult would do, but you don't have the staying power or attention levels to see your little projects through."

"No, we don't. But I would argue it's not up to us to see 'our little projects' through. We genuinely believe it's not the monarch or dictator that makes a nation powerful. It's the collective principles of the people that represent power. Real power. Not just power built on fear, or that of sectarian or tribal standing. Sadly, building and enforcing principles often requires sacrifice. No country knows this better than mine, having endured military, political, and cultural revolutions, civil war, and later struggles for civil rights, and we readily admit we have a long way to go. I wonder sometimes if the current generations have the fortitude of the previous men and women who fought for these principles. You'll need to determine in Iraq what you want for the future. I would suggest you start by learning from our mistakes and our successes. And speak out as a voice of common sense. You've seen first-hand the readiness of influential people to use and exploit you and your faith. One day, I hope we can have a lengthy chat about our political and spiritual differences, but I will only say, as I depart today, that little Mohammed there in your arms deserves a better country than the one he was born into. It's up to the Iraqi people, not the Americans, to determine what that means."

Dr. Al-Onezi shrugged and woke Mohammed up, left the lobby, and departed into the intense heat of summer in Baghdad.

***

D.C. Taco Restaurant. Downtown Washington, D.C. Two days later.

"Wilson, I know you're still sore at me, but I still believe we did the right thing by turning over the crate to the Iraqis. And I get the sense that Dr. Dagestani, and possibly those other two doctors, understand the importance of what was in the crate," proffered Haley to Wilson Edger over seafood tacos at a popular eatery in D.C.

"No. I actually agreed with you and appreciate your idealism and your trust in the Iraqis. There are a lot of good ones. There are some bad ones, too, and not just the ones you've had run-ins with," responded Edger, tripling up on napkins to help manage the savory but messy repast.

"It was hard giving it up without taking a look, though," admitted Haley.

"Yeah, I know. But I have a gift for you. It's a key. This key was found in the late Mr. al-Sadr's car, and it goes to the lock on the crate," Edger smiled, sliding the key across the table. "It's a nice memento recovered by your Green Beret pals. I had some of my friends run it by the museum. Confirmed. It goes to the crate, and it actually worked. We all agree that you should have it," Edger said.

"Thanks, I guess. It's pretty cool, but it sure would be nice to know what was in the mystery box," griped Haley.

"I guess you didn't hear me. This key opened the box," said Edger. "We have an idea of what's in it. Not a full reckoning, mind you, but more than a sneak preview."

"What? How? How did you get a look?" asked Haley incredulously.

"You really have to ask?" smiled Edger.

"Stop the suspense! What was in it?" asked Haley.

"Again, we don't have a full accounting, and studying the material will take years. The Iraqis are doing a good job of preserving it, though. We'll try to have real Smithsonian experts take a look, too, but you found a treasure trove of scrolls dating back well before the 1258 fall of Baghdad. I think it is proof that *Beit al-Hikma* existed. One scroll noted in Arabic that the Mongol siege was imminent, and an unknown member of the court took efforts to preserve what he could. The note was incomplete and hard to decipher, but you get the gist of it. The casket contained writings in Greek, Latin, Arabic, Aramaic, Hebrew, Nabatean, and other languages. It also had what appears to be original

Qurans. Dr. Dagestani thinks these could be among the oldest in existence, pre-dating those found in Yemen," explained Edger.

"If even a suggestion got out that these pre-date Islam this could create all kinds of reaction across the Middle East. I hope this wasn't actually Pandora's Box we opened," worried Haley.

"It might be. We're going to keep a close eye on this box and what was in it. I'll keep you posted," said Edger, wiping the last of the grease from his mouth and chin. "Gotta run!" he said, moving away from the table.

"Yeah. Me too," replied Haley. "But first, I want to check in on Jordan Cooper."

Edger smiled, while lifting his left eyebrow inquisitively.

***

Same Restaurant. Washington, D.C. Thirty minutes later.

"Hey Jordan. It sure is good to hear your voice again. How are you?" asked a concerned Haley. He didn't quite know where he stood with her.

"Things are good here but miserably hot. A sandstorm is expected in a day or two. That should cool things off and swap our humidity misery with dust misery. How are you? We're hearing some wild stories about you and some goings-on in Baghdad. Any truth to that?" Cooper asked earnestly.

"You can't believe everything you read in the papers. Lots of fake news out there," Haley deflected. He wanted to talk about what he hoped was his relationship with her, not the recent turn of events in Baghdad. "It has been a busy couple of months since I left Kuwait, though," he added, hoping to score a couple of hero points with her.

"Yeah, I know. Remember, I have my sources, and I've been checking up on you. When we reconnect, I would like to hear about what happened up there. I'll bet you can't talk over open lines anyway.

I definitely want to hear about you storming a sombrero in Baghdad," her voice smiled.

"Of course. I'll give you the full lowdown when I see you. I hope it will be soon," he said wistfully. "I'm gonna be stuck here in D.C. doing some back briefs and reports. I don't know yet when I'll be cut loose, or when I can get back to Kuwait. But it would be good to see you again," he said hopefully and nervously.

"Yeah, yeah. I miss you too," she retorted bluntly. "Hurry back. Nasser Khalil keeps asking for your green eyes."

***

Bosphorus Strait. Istanbul, Turkey.

Muhsin Bin Laden stared blankly at the water from the veranda of his palace on the Bosphorus Strait, which connected the Black Sea to the Sea of Marmara, then to the Straits of the Dardanelles and then the Mediterranean. Arguably one of the most important waterways in history, he knew, but he didn't care. He only maintained one of his residences there because it was expensive. Castles along the waterway cost tens of millions of dollars. He, of course, had to have one of the most expensive so had purchased his palace for over ninety million dollars. His spectacular estate was built in the 1800s as a tribute to a great, but now unknown, field marshal in the Ottoman army. Given the sullied Bin Laden name, however, he had it purchased under the pseudonym of al-Qureshi, the tribe from which Mohammed hailed.

He looked across the strait at the other side of Istanbul but also essentially at the beginning of Europe. He assayed his losses. Al-Sadr could be replaced. He had served his use and had proved instrumental in securing the remains of Mohammed in 1979 but failed in sending his cousin to steal relics and archives from the Kuwaitis under the cover of the Iraq invasion. And, he assessed, al-Sadr seemed to have succeeded in lining up the expertise to clone Mohammed, but Bin Laden never trusted Dr. al-Onezi and strongly suspected the experiment to have been less than billed. It was al-Sadr's utter inability to kill one pesky American diplomat that signed his death warrant, though. Bin Laden readily gave him up to his Saudi insiders. In so doing, he gave up a peace offering to the House of Saud for recent tribal stirrings and deflected growing attention on him and his operation. Yes, al-Sadr could easily be replaced. He missed the creativity and determination of the younger al-Qahtani and al-Otaybi, however.

No matter. Others could be found. In fact, Bin Laden had already activated his robust Rolodex of henchmen ready to do his bidding. He also called key members of the *Union of the Ulema* [Islamic scholars] to reconvene at his residence. He wanted to churn the organization's theological network of some fifty thousand imams, who shepherded congregations of adherents among tribal kinsmen and *Ikhwan* across the Middle East and could reach into communities in south Asia. He also thought his older brother's contacts in Al-Qaeda and the Taliban could use some new and inspired leadership and funding. They seemed ready to put up a front against what they saw was American-led western incursions into their lands, a reinvigorated Crusade, as it were. A crusade that should be countered by *mujahiddin [holy warriors]* if the right inspiration and unifying force could be found. Certainly, Western attempts to undermine the validity of the Quran would be just the rallying call. He also needed to find out what was recovered in the Maroof al-Karkhi shrine, he cajoled himself. First, though, he needed to find someone who could kill Clayton Haley.

Reference Maps

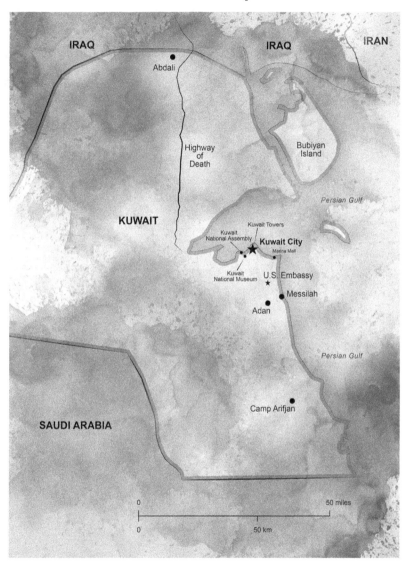

Kuwait

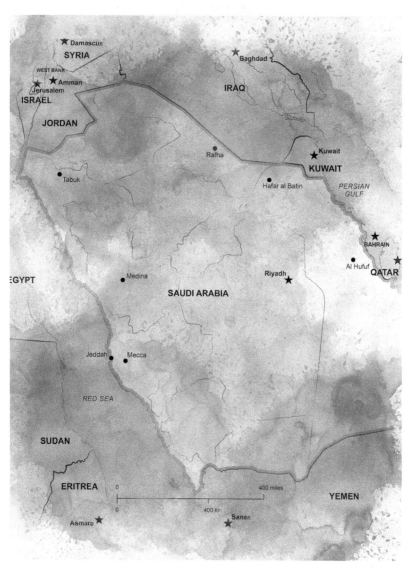

Saudi Arabia

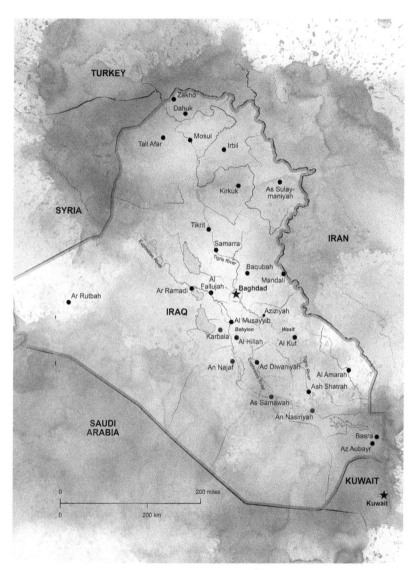

Iraq

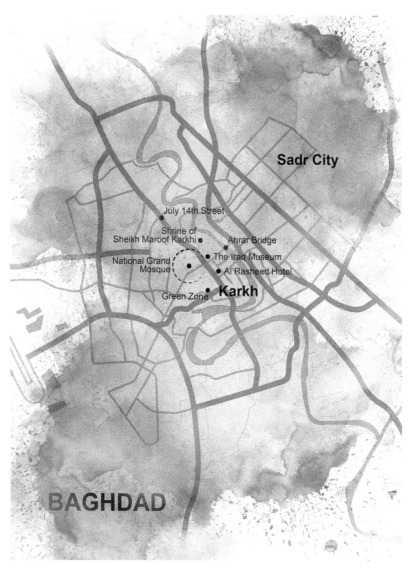

Baghdad

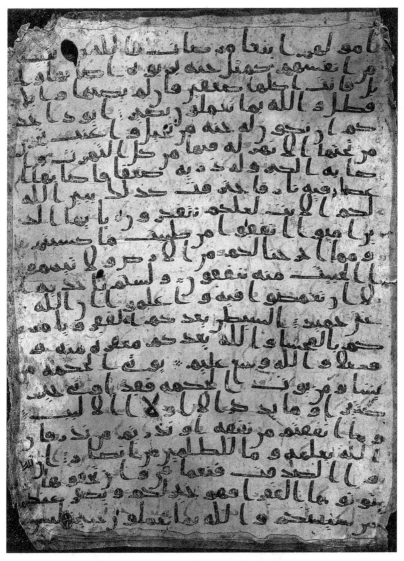

Quranic Fragment from Sana'a Palimpsest,
found in 1972 in the Grand Mosque in Sana'a Yemen.

Highway of Death—Kuwait

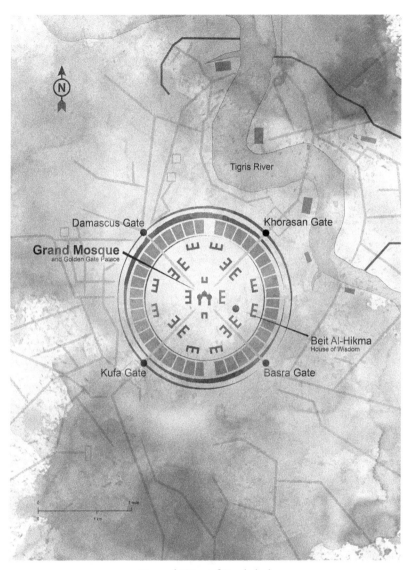

Round City of Baghdad

Shrine to Maroof Karkhi

About the Author

Ethan Burroughs has dedicated much of the last two decades to exploring the Middle East and slowly unraveling its mysteries. His encounters have taken him to Saudi Arabia, Iraq, Jordan, Kuwait, Israel, and the Palestinian Territories where he has studied the history, faith, cuisine, language, and culture of the lands which continue to grab our headlines as we search for an elusive peace. He has had the great pleasure of spending significant time with characters similar to those depicted in this account, including our unsung patriots in the Department of State and Defense. He is a U.S. Army veteran and Middle Eastern consultant.

A free ebook edition is available with the purchase of this book.

To claim your free ebook edition:

1. Visit MorganJamesBOGO.com
2. Sign your name CLEARLY in the space
3. Complete the form and submit a photo of the entire copyright page
4. You or your friend can download the ebook to your preferred device

Print & Digital Together Forever.

Snap a photo

Free ebook

Read anywhere

CPSIA information can be obtained
at www.ICGtesting.com
Printed in the USA
JSHW052318140322
23878JS00001B/21

9 781631 956799